"From the bloody, ripped-from-the-headlines opening sequence, *Silent Assassin* grabs you and doesn't let go. *Silent Assassin* has everything a thriller reader wants—nasty villains, twists and turns, and a hero—Cobra—who just plain kicks ass."

—Ben Coes

"Dan Morgan, a former black-ops agent, is called out of retirement and back into a secretive world of politics and deceit to stop a madman."

—The Stoneham Independent

Termination Orders
"Leo J. Maloney is the new voice to be reckoned with. *Termination Orders* rings with the authenticity that can only come from an insider. This is one outstanding thriller!"

—John Gilstrap

"Taut, tense, and terrifying! You'll cross your fingers it's fiction—in this high-powered, action-packed thriller, Leo Maloney proves he clearly knows his stuff."

—Hank Phillippi Ryan

"A new must-read action thriller that features a double-crossing CIA and Congress, vengeful foreign agents, a corporate drug ring, the Taliban, and narco-terrorists... a you-are-there account of torture, assassination, and double-agents, where 'nothing is as it seems.'"

—Jon Renaud

"Leo J. Maloney is a real-life Jason Bourne."

—Josh Zwylen, *Wicked Local Stoneham*

"A masterly blend of Black Ops intrigue, cleverly interwoven with imaginative sequences of fiction. The reader must guess which accounts are real and which are merely storytelling."

—Chris Treece, *The Chris Treece Show*

"A deep-ops story presented in an epic style that takes fact mixed with a bit of fiction to create a spy thriller that takes the reader deep into secret spy missions."
—**Cy Hilterman,** *Best Sellers World*

"For fans of spy thrillers seeking a bit of realism mixed into their novels, *Termination Orders* will prove to be an excellent and recommended pick."
—*Midwest Book Reviews*

Books by Leo J. Maloney

The Dan Morgan Thriller Series
TERMINATION ORDERS
SILENT ASSASSIN
BLACK SKIES
TWELVE HOURS*
ARCH ENEMY
FOR DUTY AND HONOR*
ROGUE COMMANDER
DARK TERRITORY*
THREAT LEVEL ALPHA
WAR OF SHADOWS
DEEP COVER
THE MORGAN FILES**

The Alex Morgan Thriller Series
ANGLE OF ATTACK
HARD TARGET

*e-novellas
** compilation

Angle of Attack

An Alex Morgan Thriller

Leo J. Maloney

LYRICAL UNDERGROUND
Kensington Publishing Corp.
www.kensingtonbooks.com

LYRICAL UNDERGROUND BOOKS are published by
Kensington Publishing Corp.
119 West 40th Street
New York, NY 10018

All Kensington titles, imprints, and distributed lines are available at special quantity discounts for bulk purchases for sales promotion, premiums, fund-raising, educational, or institutional use.

Special book excerpts or customized printings can also be created to fit specific needs. For details, write or phone the office of the Kensington Sales Manager: Kensington Publishing Corp., 119 West 40th Street, New York, NY 10018. Attn. Sales Department. Phone: 1-800-221-2647.

Lyrical Underground and Lyrical Underground logo Reg. US Pat. & TM Off.

First Electronic Edition: January 2021
ISBN-13: 978-1-5161-1007-0 (ebook)
ISBN-10: 1-5161-1007-2 (ebook)

First Print Edition: January 2021
ISBN-13: 978-1-5161-1008-7
ISBN-10: 1-5161-1008-0

Printed in the United States of America

This book is dedicated to all the veterans who have sacrificed so much to serve our great country, and to all the first responders and medical staff who have served so courageously during the novel coronavirus pandemic. Thank you for all you did and do.

Chapter 1

Alex Morgan pulled the long, loose gray tunic over her baggy gray slacks and shapeless gray top. She put the hijab on last, as Lily Randall did the same. They were wearing the more conservative headscarves that covered everything but their faces.

Lily examined Alex, tucking some of her wayward brown hair under the hijab. Strictly speaking, the extra care wasn't necessary. They were already dressed more traditionally than most Iranian women, who were getting increasingly more daring with their colorful hijabs that covered less and less of their hair.

Alex wished those women well, but there was no doubt that they attracted attention. The last thing she and Lily wanted to do was attract attention. Things were tense enough on the streets of Tehran as it was.

"How about me?" Lily asked.

"Perfect," Alex said. She wasn't surprised to see not a hair showing from under Lily's headscarf.

Her friend and fellow agent had dyed her usual blond locks brown, just in case anyone saw under the scarf. Even that wouldn't be catastrophic, but it would attract more attention than they wanted—which was zero attention.

Alex checked the mirror. She wasn't wearing a trace of makeup and though she usually wore very little, she felt surprisingly barefaced and vulnerable without it.

Lily, on the other hand, was wearing subtle makeup to flatten her cheekbones and create dark patches under her eyes. Even with that effort to appear less attractive, Lily was still beautiful.

"Any doubts?" Lily asked in her light London accent. Several years older than Alex herself, Lily was British and had served for years in MI6 before joining Zeta Division.

"None," Alex said. "Though I'll admit it's not what I expected. I always figured our first undercover mission together would involve an underground European nightclub."

"They're overrated," Lily said with smile. "The shoes you have to wear are ridiculous, the wigs are uncomfortable, and nobody ever tells you that those places reek."

"To be fair, these shoes aren't too bad," Alex said. They were wearing track shoes that were reasonably comfortable. She also appreciated that the loose clothing meant they'd be able to move and fight, if they had to. That clearly wasn't the intention of whoever designed this clothing for women, but it was a nice perk.

"First rule of undercover work," Lily said, "it's never what you expect."

That was true, Alex thought. Her first undercover mission had been nothing like she had expected.

"I'm sorry, Alex, that was thoughtless," Lily said.

"Not at all," Alex said. "The mission was a success."

That was true. Zeta had prevented something awful and Alex had helped. Yet there had been losses.

Losses were part of the job, Alex knew. *You never get used to them,* her father had explained. *The day you do is the day you know you've been doing this too long.*

"I want to watch it again," Alex said. Lily checked her watch and opened the laptop. She pressed a button and the video started. It was a press conference at the University of Tehran, where a woman in a green headscarf approached the podium wearing a Western-style business suit.

Maryam Nasiri was an Iranian-American professor who had emigrated from Iran as a small child and was now an American citizen. She was also one of the only two women to win the Fields Medal in mathematics for her work on an algorithm that was so far over Alex's head that her year of A.P. calculus hadn't helped her understand even the Wikipedia entry on Nasiri's work.

The mathematician had made the mistake of accepting an invitation from the University of Tehran for a reception in her honor. After that reception, her family had never heard from her again.

The university released a written public statement signed by Nasiri about her decision to stay on at the university and her excitement about finally being "home."

After a great deal of international pressure, a single public appearance at a press conference was set up and had gone viral. In the video, Nasiri appeared sedated. Standing stiffly at the podium, she spoke in a flat tone. "Thank you all for coming. I want to make it very clear how excited I am to continue my work in the country of my birth. The University of Tehran is my new home and they have given me all the resources I need to continue my work. Thank you."

Then she was ushered away. There had been no questions from the press at this "press conference."

"Let's go," Lily said. "We don't want to be late on our first day of work."

Somehow, while they were watching the video, Lily had executed a physical transformation. The more senior agent usually carried herself with the confidence of an extraordinarily beautiful woman who was also one of the most deadly agents at Zeta. She seemed to occupy a unique space between a catwalk model and an MMA fighter—and carried herself accordingly.

Now Lily's face had sunk into a dull frown. Her shoulders hunched over; her whole body loosened.

Alex did her best to imitate the stance, and the two agents walked out the apartment door. As they left, a woman a wearing a heavy, black hijab barked something at them. She was sitting behind a counter at what looked like the front desk in a small hotel.

This *was* a residence hotel of sorts, but the woman wasn't a front desk clerk. She was more like a housemother, a chaperone for the working women who lived there.

Lily replied in Persian. The rough older woman waved them on, averting her eyes.

"How did you do that?" Alex asked when they were outside.

"I added a little Kurdish accent," the agent replied.

That made sense—the Kurds were not exactly a favored minority in Iran. Plus, many were from a territory close to Iraq, which also didn't endear them to the locals. Alex had seen anti-Kurdish feelings firsthand on a recent Zeta mission in Turkey.

"I'll have to remember to do that," Alex said. "Once I learn Persian."

Alex wouldn't need to speak the local language for this mission—the rescue of one Maryam Nasiri from the mathematics department at the University of Tehran, where she and Lily were now part of the crew of cleaning women.

The university was, at best, a low-security environment. A small detail of soldiers guarded the mathematician, but after two months, reports were that they were lax in their approach to the job.

As a mission, this would be the equivalent of a "smash and grab." With any luck, Alex and Lily would have their charge out of the country before nightfall.

The streets of Tehran were bustling, and the air was warm—78 degrees, normal for spring. If it weren't for the covered women, Alex would have thought she was walking the tree-lined streets of any large European city. It was jam-packed with standstill, honking traffic—more than she would have thought even for a city of ten million people.

The cars were mostly European, Peugeot Citroëns and other smallish models with a few more expensive German vehicles. Alex didn't see a single American car on the road; no surprise really, given how the regime felt about America.

There were a fair number of motorcycles, but nothing impressive. Alex noticed smallish Hondas and Italian Benellis. She also glimpsed a few of the locally produced new Saipa electric motorbikes.

It took Alex a moment to figure out what else was missing on the streets of Tehran besides American cars. There wasn't a single sidewalk vendor. She knew that the Iranian authorities didn't approve of them and assumed the city was having one of its periodic crackdowns.

After only a few blocks, Alex was sweating under her heavy hijab.

"You okay?" Lily asked.

"I guess," Alex said. "This thing itches, and it's hot."

"Just like the wigs at the underground nightclubs," Lily said. "They're itchy as hell."

That made Alex smile and they lumbered on, eyes downcast.

And to be fair, the hijab Alex wore as part of her cleaning crew uniform was heavier than many of the ones she saw on the street, where at least half the young women were wearing nearly Western-style clothes and colorful headscarves that showed a fair amount of their hair.

They were all being watched by the green uniformed "Morality Police." This branch of law enforcement was charged with making sure that the population conformed to public morality at all times. Theoretically, men could attract the attention of the Morality Police if their beards were too long or they wore short-sleeved shirts, but as a practical matter, the police reserved their scrutiny for women whose clothing or headscarves were insufficiently "modest."

Women were taking more chances than usual today. It was Wednesday—or White Wednesday—the day that rebellious Iranian women wore white to protest the compulsory wearing of the hijab.

Alex applauded their efforts, but given the number of Morality Police on the streets, she didn't think the day would end well for the women who bent the rules too far. Already, the agents had witnessed more than one heated argument between women and these special police.

The Iranian government's official statements always referred to the mission of the Morality Police as "guidance." Of course, if that were true, Alex wondered why these *guidance officers* were armed.

The agents approached the university's main entrance, on the south side of the campus. The entryway was formed by four twisted concrete arches that were almost like modern art. The academic buildings were surprisingly modern and would not have been out of place in any major European—or even American—city.

Just to the right of the gate Alex could see a crowd forming around a woman wearing a white headscarf and shouting at two of the green-uniformed Morality Police officers. The men were flanked by two female colleagues wearing full black robes. The robed women were shouting back at the woman in white.

Alex could see the problem. The white-clad woman was wearing what would have passed for moderate makeup in the West but was very out of place in Tehran. Also, she wore her white headscarf toward the back of her head, showing fully half of her hair.

Alex supported the women's effort, but she didn't want the commotion to interfere with their mission. She heard a loud yell and watched the woman reach up to grab her white hijab. She glared at the two black-clad women, who were now screaming at her, and then she pulled off her scarf in an act of clear defiance.

There was a moment of shocked silence in the growing crowd. Then one of the men in the green uniforms hurled himself at the young woman—who Alex could now see was the age of a college student.

The girl hit the sidewalk hard, with a nearly two-hundred-pound man slamming down on top of her. Tensing, Alex prepared for action.

She felt Lily's hand on her shoulder. "We can't," the older agent said.

That wasn't true. They could. Yes, the men were armed, but there were only two of them. And the female officers in black didn't seem to have the stomach for anything other than screaming.

Alex had no doubt that she and Lily could handle the four of them before they knew what hit them and get the woman to safety, provided she wasn't badly hurt.

But that wasn't the mission.

It took every ounce of self-restraint Alex had to allow Lily to lead her away and through the university entrance.

The guards at the gate barely noticed them, too busy running outside to the commotion, which was getting louder. The two agents crossed the large campus square, which was humming with college students, about a quarter of whom were women.

At the far end of the campus stood a building that Alex recognized as housing the mathematics, statistics, and computer science departments. That was where Nasiri now "worked."

Outside the entrance was a woman Alex recognized from the mission briefing. She wore the same gray cleaning crew uniform as Alex and Lily.

Lily approached her, speaking quickly in Persian. The woman responded in kind. She then turned her attention to Alex and said in surprisingly good English, "Hello, Alex. My name is Shirin."

"There's a bit of a commotion outside," Lily said.

Shirin shrugged. "It's Wednesday," she said. "There *is* something unusual going on in here, though. They have doubled the guard around Nasiri. These men are fresh and not yet complacent."

That wasn't good, Alex thought. On paper, at least, it was an easy mission with four lazy guards. This change would make it harder.

"Do you think the regime suspects a rescue attempt?" Lily asked.

"No, but there are rumors that she will soon be moved," Shirin said.

That was new. Whatever Nasiri was working on had some sort of technological or military application. If she was moved to a secure facility, Zeta might never get another chance to get her out.

"The extra risk is within our mission parameters," Lily said. "What do you think, Alex?"

"We're prepared for this," Alex said. "Plus, we'd like to meet the woman that everyone is going to so much trouble over."

Shirin smiled approvingly. "We'll start working on the first floor," she said. "We'll reach the fourth floor by lunch, and then you can meet her."

Before they could turn to head inside, Alex heard the distinctive sound of a helicopter's rotors—and not a civilian chopper. It sounded military.

Alex was wrong about one thing, she realized, as *two* large black helicopters flew over the southern entrance. They came in fast and much lower than was normal for an urban center.

In no time the choppers made very quick and very rough landings on the campus square.

Alex and Lily stared at Shirin. "I have no idea," the woman said.

Alex heard gunfire. It sounded as if it came from the guard shack, or outside the entrance. Someone was shooting at the helicopters. The doors of the choppers opened and men wearing all black filed out. They carried rifles and returned the small arms fire with fully automatic bursts.

"I don't know what this is," Shirin said. "I was told to get you inside and provide assistance, but I can't help you with this."

"You won't have to," Lily said. "I suspect we might not be the only ones who want to get their hands on Nasiri. You've done plenty and we thank you."

Shirin pointed to the all-out firefight that was now going on across the square. In the near-constant gunfire, students were screaming and racing away from the scene. "What will you do?" Shirin asked.

"This development goes way beyond our mission parameters," Lily said, turning to Alex. "We're supposed to abort."

Alex studied the doors to the building. They were so close! A woman, an American citizen who needed their help, was only a few flights of stairs away.

"They don't look so tough. Did you *see* that landing?" she said. "Strictly amateur hour. I say we expand our *mission parameters.*"

"Agreed," Lily replied. Then she turned to Shirin and said, "Thank you again. Get somewhere safe—as far away from us as possible."

Alex and Lily turned to the building, opened the doors, and raced inside.

Chapter 2

There were two guards in the lobby holding handguns and two soldiers with their rifles in hand. By their uniforms Alex could see that the soldiers were part of the Revolutionary Guard Corps. They were a parallel service to the regular Iranian military, with their own ground forces, navy, and air force.

But unlike the regular Iranian military forces, which protected the country and people, the revolutionary forces only protected the religious regime.

They had been founded during the 1979 revolution and their allegiance was ideological. They were also better trained and had more power in Iran than the regular military forces.

That confirmed for Alex how important Nasiri was to the ayatollahs. They didn't just see her as important to the country: They saw her as important to the survival of the clerics in charge and their mission to spread their system.

The women stopped when the two soldiers' rifles were pointed at their chests. One of the men shouted at them in Persian.

Lily immediately replied, gesturing behind them. Alex couldn't understand the words, but the tone was clear. The other agent wanted the men to think they were terrified by the helicopters and gunfire.

The soldier in charge gave them only a second's glance and waved for them to go deeper inside the building.

Alex and Lily complied, pushing through double doors and entering the main hallway.

"He told us to get inside and find somewhere to hide," Lily said.

"I'm okay with the first half of that," Alex replied.

Alex saw that there was an advantage to being triply invisible here. First, they were women on an extremely male-dominated campus. Second, they were cleaning ladies. And third, they were Kurds.

They walked down the hallway and saw a number of men and a few women peek their heads out from doorways to glance at them. Alex guessed they were following a shelter-in-place protocol.

Again, another plus. Now the staff and the students had good reason to stay out of their way.

An older man, who Alex guessed was a professor, took half a step out of a doorway and shouted at them.

Lily replied meekly in Persian.

The professor sized them up, barked something short, and disappeared back into his room, slamming the door behind him.

"He suggests we hide...but do it somewhere else," Lily said.

"They really couldn't be less interested in us. Is there a level *beneath* undercover?" Alex asked.

"I think we just found it," Lily replied, a smile in her voice, if not on her face.

At the end of the hallway they came upon another man. He appeared to be a professor or an administrator, who was posted at the bottom of the stairwell. Alex assumed he was the floor's fire warden or the equivalent. He was also talking into his cell phone, frustrated.

Was the attack force in the black helicopters jamming the cell service? That suggested a level of sophistication and resources that was a notch above the physical assault—which looked like the tactical equivalent of a smash and grab.

This meant relatively high-powered and high-tech hardware and suggested a relatively high-level intelligence infrastructure.

That left them with a fairly short list of suspects.

Alex shelved that line of thinking. If everything went well, the two agents and Nasiri would get away while the guards and the soldiers duked it out with the black ops force.

They would have plenty of time to speculate about the black helicopter team from the safety of Zeta headquarters.

The man barely paid them any notice as they opened the door and headed up the stairs. Not surprisingly, the stairwell was both quiet and empty. In an emergency, people would stay where they were.

It was a smart move for civilians. Of course, Alex hadn't been a civilian for years, and the two women raced up the stairs. Alex cursed the loose robes, which slowed her down, and pushed herself harder.

When they reached the top and fourth floor, the women stopped and took a breath. Lily slowly opened the door. Alex saw two rifles pointed at them. The men holding the rifles began shouting at them in Persian.

Reacting to something one of the soldiers outside said, Lily opened the door the rest of the way, and the two agents slowly stepped outside. There were two soldiers holding rifles on them. There were also two university security guards.

Lily spoke meekly to the soldier in charge while the two guards were busy—one with his mobile phone, the other on a walkie-talkie.

Alex didn't need to speak Persian to know that neither was having much luck.

That was something. Blocking cell service was one thing. It was tricky, but you could do it by taking out or jamming a few cell towers. But a generalized jamming of radio signals was a level even higher than that.

There was noise downstairs. No gunfire, but shouting.

The lead soldier, who seemed to be in charge only of yelling at Lily, came to a decision. He barked something at the guards and then led the other soldiers down the stairs. As they walked, they didn't give the two women a second glance.

The black helicopter force hadn't entered the building yet, but they must have been getting pretty close if the soldiers guarding the floor were heading downstairs.

Alex and Lily had hoped to incapacitate a few university guards and then sneak their charge out of the building, but that was looking less and less likely. They would need weapons.

It had been too risky to bring guns with them on this mission. If they were stopped at a metal detector or frisked by security somewhere, it would be impossible for two lower-class cleaning women to explain why they were carrying pistols in a country where gun ownership for even connected civilians was practically nil.

Fortunately, the two guards in front of them were armed…at least technically. For now, their handguns were holstered while they struggled with their communications devices.

Alex could see the weapons were German-made SIG Sauer semiautomatics. The Sauer was a .45 caliber pistol, used by Swiss police and in a number of other European countries. It wasn't a bad gun, but Alex thought the weapons were wasted on these two men who seemed near panic as they shouted into a nonworking phone and walkie-talkie.

Politely, Lily interrupted and asked them something. Both guards seemed genuinely surprised that she had spoken. Alex didn't have to speak

Persian to see that Lily was asking if the women could seek shelter past the door they were guarding.

It was an interesting approach; just asking to be let inside the room where the woman they were sent to rescue was being held.

Both guards shouted something in Persian at Lily. The larger of the two gestured down the hallway, motioning them to hurry it along. Holding her ground, Lily repeated her request, putting a quiver in her voice.

The large guard in charge didn't reply. Instead, he reached out and shoved her, roughly pushing her away.

He moved more quickly than Alex had expected, but Lily was much faster. As she allowed herself to be pushed back, she reached out with her left hand to grab the wrist of his now extended right arm.

It was a fighting truism: Control the attacker's wrist, control the fight.

Alex remembered this move. It was a Krav Maga technique that Lily had taught to Alex. Lily twisted the guard's wrist clockwise while pushing his bent elbow upwards.

Done reasonably gently, the move could be used to stop a strike and make the attacker think twice about continuing.

But Lily wasn't gentle.

Alex heard the man's arm break in two places.

Immediately she turned her attention to the second guard, who, unlike Alex, was still gawking at the impossible scene playing out in front of him.

That was perfect for what Alex had planned. She used a quick palm strike to his face with her left hand. She made good contact, and the strike forced his head sharply to the side, where her raised elbow caught him on the other side of his face.

He went down and Alex was pleased to see he was unconscious.

Lily was already dragging her guard across the hallway toward an open door. Alex did the same with hers. After they pulled the men inside, the women relieved them of their guns and nightsticks, slipping the weapons into their own robes.

Alex was grateful for the loose clothing, which perfectly concealed their newly acquired weapons. Stepping back into the hallway, they closed the door behind them and quickly headed forward to Nasiri's room.

Lily knocked firmly and called out in Persian before slowly pushing the door open. Their intel had told them that there were no armed guards posted inside, but the intel hadn't predicted the assault on the campus.

Lily called into the room and said, "Maryam Nasiri," followed by a string of words in Persian.

There was a pause. A female voice replied, "I only answer to English."

Surprise registered on Lily's face. "Can we come in?"

"It's fine with me," Nasiri replied.

As Lily opened the door, Alex scanned the room. It was a medium-sized classroom with a large whiteboard and desk in the front, with about twenty student desks facing forward.

It was nearly empty, except for Nasiri herself, who was dressed in jeans and a simple cream button-top and a woman who was a few years younger in a robe and a headscarf.

"I'm Lily and this is Alex," Lily said. "We're here to help you." She turned her attention to the younger woman. "Do you speak English, too?"

The young woman, who Alex guessed was a student, nodded meekly.

"This is Kimiya," Nasiri said. "She's my translator and my assistant."

"Our records show that you speak Farsi," Lily said.

Nasiri shrugged. "Passably, but I refused to, which pissed them off."

Alex could see the woman was nervous, but there was a healthy touch of defiance in her voice. That was good. If she didn't like her captors, she'd be more likely to come with Alex and Lily.

"We're here to help you, to bring you home," Lily said.

"And where do you think my home is?" Nasiri said. "I live in New Jersey, not England."

"We know," said Alex. "I'm from Boston myself. We represent an international organization."

"We want to help you get home," said Lily, "but we're short on time."

"Are you responsible for the excitement outside?" Nasiri asked.

"No, and it complicates things," Lily replied. "Two helicopters have landed in the courtyard. We have to assume there is another group who's trying to take you."

"Who?" Nasiri asked.

"No idea," said Lily. "They appear to be European, but there's no telling who they work for."

"And we'd rather not wait to find out," Alex said, adding some urgency to her voice.

"You expect me to trust you?" Nasiri said, her voice both nervous and skeptical.

"We have two messages for you," Alex replied. "Your sister says that your dog is still afraid of luggage, and your teaching assistant says to tell you that your friends Banach and Tarski have two balls between them."

That made Nasiri smile. "Fine," she said. "How do we do this?"

"We leave immediately," Lily said. "There's no time for you to collect your things."

"I don't need anything," said Nasiri.

The mathematician's assistant spoke for the first time. "Maryam," she said in accented English, reaching out to grab Nasiri's arm. "It's not safe. You need to stay here. It's dangerous outside now, and you don't know these people. They could be the enemy."

"Kimiya, I'm leaving," Nasiri said gently. "Stay here and be quiet. You'll be fine."

Alex saw something shift in the younger woman's face. In less than a second, she stepped behind Nasiri and threw her right arm across the older woman's chest while reaching out with her left, which held a knife.

The translator now had Nasiri in a firm grip, with a knife at her throat. She kept the mathematician between the two agents and herself.

Just as quickly, Alex and Lily had their guns drawn and pointing at the translator. The problem was that she was hiding behind Nasiri, who was still processing what was going on.

"Nasiri, listen to me. This woman is not your friend, she's your handler," Lily said.

"Don't move, or she will die," Kimiya said.

"Kimiya..." Nasiri said weakly, outright fear registering on her face.

"Drop your weapons, you two," the translator said.

"We're not going to do that," Lily said. "You can still live through this. Alex, ready?" she added.

Alex knew what Lily meant. Of the two, Alex had the better angle of fire. Given that the translator was holding the blade tightly to Nasiri's throat, it would have to be a solid head shot.

Normally Alex wouldn't hesitate, but they would need Nasiri to function when Kimiya was neutralized.

"I will kill her before I let you have her," the translator said, tightening her grip. "Drop your weapons."

Nasiri yelped as the blade bit into her skin.

Whoever she was, Kimiya was well trained. Alex had to assume that she would do exactly what she said.

"You said you were my friend..." the mathematician said, her voice a whisper.

"I lied," said Kimiya. "I'm not even going to count. Drop your weapons or—"

The gunshot interrupted her, as did the small outward explosion from the right side of her skull. The translator's arms went slack. The knife dropped to the ground. For a moment, she remained standing, then she slid to the floor.

By that time, Alex had already holstered her gun and was at Nasiri's side. None of the enemy agent's blood was on Nasiri. That was good; it meant that Alex's carefully placed shot had hit the mark precisely. In a situation like this, blood on their clothes could render civilians immobile. Alex kicked away Kimiya's body as Lily grabbed the mathematician.

"Look at me," Lily said to the woman. "You're okay. Do you hear me? You're okay. But we must go."

Without waiting for a response, Lily led her to the door.

"I'm sorry if she was your friend," Alex said, following them.

"We weren't that close," Nasiri said in a shaky voice. "I never trusted her." The woman averted her eyes from the body on the floor. That was just as well; it was a mess, and the pool of blood was still spreading.

"Can you walk?" Lily asked.

"I can run if I have to," Nasisi replied. "I just want to get out of here."

Lily pulled out clean clothes and a headscarf from under her own tunic and handed them to the mathematician. The clothing matched Lily and Alex's.

"I always refused to wear one of those," Nasiri said, pointing to the scarf. "It really pissed them off."

"Good, that will help," Lily said. "They'll be looking for the person they know."

Quickly, Nasiri put on the robe, while Alex worked on the headscarf.

"What's the plan?" asked the mathematician.

"Well, it had been to just walk out of here," Lily said, "but that was before the helicopters showed up."

"The new plan is to improvise," Alex said. "But don't worry, we've done this before."

"You have? You've rescued academics being held against their will in their native country while being attacked by an unknown third party?"

Alex smiled. "Not exactly, but we have *improvised* before."

Lily opened the door and peered into the hallway. Alex could hear shouting, followed by muffled gunshots.

"We need to move," Lily said, as the three women stepped into the hallway. Keeping their pace brisk, they headed to the rear stairwell.

"Our original plan was to walk you out the back entrance and get you onto the street," Lily said. "It's still our best bet."

The trio headed through a door and into the stairwell. The stairs were silent, except for the women's breathing. Three flights later, they were on the ground floor. Lily motioned them to stop while she opened the door and scanned the area.

They could hear commotion in the distance, which Alex assumed was coming from the front of the building. However, they were now in the back, and Alex knew the rear exit to the building was not far.

"No soldiers," Lily said. "Just two university security guards. Dr. Nasiri, stay behind us and we are going to walk right out, nice and easy."

Lily stepped out first and Alex followed.

She felt the mathematician clutch the back of her robe. That was fine. It told her where the woman was at all times. Alex drew her gun, keeping it hidden in the loose folds.

Lily called out in Persian and the guards turned their attention to the women. They shouted something and waved them away distractedly.

"They are telling us to move along," Lily said, as the three women continued onward.

The guards started to shout something but were distracted by the rear door opening. When Alex saw the men reach for their guns, she half-turned and pushed Nasiri into a doorway. Lily raced across the hallway and took partial cover in a doorway across from them.

One of the guards had his gun out and actually managed to fire it once before the sound of automatic gunfire filled the corridor. Both guards fell, one of them clutching the pistol he hadn't been able to fire.

Alex and Lily waited a second, and two men in black entered the building, carrying AK-47s. They were clearly from the attack force that had landed in the helicopters.

Obviously highly trained and well armed, they easily overpowered the guards and proceeded carefully, checking the two men to make sure they were dead.

That was when Alex and Lily opened fire. The gunmen wore body armor, so Alex didn't take any chances and aimed for the head of the man closest to her. Just to be certain, she squeezed off three shots, but she knew the first one found its mark—after all, they were less than twenty feet away.

Lily did the same and both men fell.

The agents waited a few seconds to see if there were any others behind them, but none came.

That was good and made sense.

The bulk of their force was likely occupied in the assault on the front of the building.

"Let's go," Lily said.

Alex took Dr. Nasiri by the arm and led her into the hallway. They stepped around the four bodies and Alex gave a passing thought to picking up one of the AKs, but rejected the notion.

If it came to a shoot-out with a gang of mercenaries or trained soldiers out in the open, an extra pair of high-powered rifles wouldn't make much of a difference.

By the time they reached the door, Lily had already checked outside. "Clear," Lily said. Turning to Nasiri, she said, "We're close to the campus exit to the street. Our best chance is to get to the other side of the wall. Once we're on the street we'll be safe. So the new plan is to get outside and run like hell."

Nasiri agreed, and the women stepped outside.

Alex scanned the area and saw no one; no hostiles, or even any civilians. Clearly, the students and the faculty had all taken cover.

They raced along a footpath to the rear exit to the campus. It was less than two hundred yards away, which meant they would be exposed for more than half a minute.

Alex had been worried about the mathematician being able to keep up with them, but Nasiri actually edged in front of Alex as they ran. They slowed down as they approached the guard shack. Alex was surprised to see that no one was inside.

Wait, that wasn't true. There was no one *alive* inside.

Alex could see broken glass and one slumped figure in a chair.

They kept going until they were outside the gate. Not surprisingly, the street was empty. As fast as they could without drawing attention to themselves, they headed away from the university.

A few blocks over, the street looked almost normal, with people going about their business. There were a number of women out and about. Alex was relieved to see that many of them wore gray robes and headscarves similar to hers. Blending into the crowd, the trio made a left and headed north, zigzagging through the streets, blending into the crowd.

Alex felt herself relaxing by degrees.

They zigged and zagged through a few more streets and found that they had easily blended in with the flow of people.

Their clothing made them indistinguishable from the crowd of women. Even if the authorities were searching for them, they wouldn't be able to tell them from any of the women around them.

Alex put the gun back in her belt as the three women walked away from the university that had been Nasiri's home and prison for the last three months.

Chapter 3

Getting out of Iran had been tricky. Certainly it was harder than getting in. Their journey had started at the British embassy. Two weeks later they landed in Germany.

One of the mercenary helicopters had managed to escape, which had helped Zeta get Nasiri out because the Iranians believed that the gunmen had kidnapped her. If the Iranians thought she was still in-country, it would have been much more dangerous to smuggle her out through normal diplomatic channels and commercial air travel.

In Berlin, the three women boarded a Renard Tech private jet and flew back to the United States in style. They landed in Boston, and the agents escorted Nasiri to the Four Seasons Hotel, where her family was waiting.

She would spend a few days with them before her formal debriefing with the CIA. Of course, before that there would be an informal briefing at Zeta. Alex assumed that this was part of Zeta's payment for services rendered—first crack at a high-value asset that Zeta had secured.

Alex was surprised to see Lincoln Shepard and Karen O'Neal waiting for her in the lobby of Zeta headquarters. That was unusual enough, but what they were wearing was especially shocking.

Shepard, whom Alex had seen only in T-shirts, jeans, and hoodies, was wearing gray slacks with a blue button shirt—and a tie! And O'Neal had ditched her own uniform of button shirts and jeans for a silk blouse and a skirt.

Alex would have been less surprised to find them in Roman togas.

Together, the pair ran Zeta's computer and technology division in the lower levels of HQ. They rarely left their labs and computer stations and always dressed the same—until now.

O'Neal was visibly excited and the first to speak. "What was she like?" The young woman looked and sounded like someone asking what their favorite teen idol was like in person.

Still processing the unprecedented scene in front of her, Alex said, "Who?"

"Dr. Nasiri," Shepard said, a hint of impatience in his voice—another first, at least with Alex.

Alex understood. Nasiri was the winner of the Fields Medal in mathematics and Alex knew what that meant, even if she didn't understand the work that had won her the honor.

"She was…" Alex had to stop herself from offering a reflexive "nice." She thought for a moment and said, "Impressive. She didn't fold when things went sideways and adapted quickly." It was true. Alex knew they wouldn't have gotten out if Nasiri had frozen.

Shepard and O'Neal seemed not only satisfied, but pleased by that response.

"You wouldn't be surprised by that if you followed her work on the Farrell-Jones Conjecture," O'Neal said.

"We're meeting her later, just a quick meet and greet today at her hotel. We'll start the actual debriefing downstairs tomorrow," Shepard said.

That explained the clothes, Alex realized. She smiled and headed for the elevator. O'Neal caught up to her. "I just wanted to thank you," she said. Alex saw that the agent was actually choked up. "I don't want to think about what the world would've lost if you hadn't succeeded."

"That's why we're here; that's the job," Alex said, patting O'Neal on her silk sleeve and stepping into the elevator. She took it one floor down to Diana Bloch's office.

At the outer office, Diana Bloch's assistant, a twentysomething man named Peters—who had some sort of NSA background—glanced up at her and said, "The director is ready for you."

Most people at Zeta referred to Bloch as the director, although technically, she didn't have an official title. Nevertheless, Bloch was the unquestioned leader of all Zeta operations, reporting directly to Mr. Smith and the board that ran the Aegis Initiative—the shadowy international organization behind Zeta.

"Good job in Tehran," Bloch said to Alex by way of a greeting. "I've read your report and debriefed Lily. Shepard and O'Neal will be talking to Dr. Nasiri tomorrow."

"Yes, they mentioned something about that. They seemed very…excited," Alex said. "Do we have any intel on the attack force?"

"Almost certainly Russian," Bloch said. "The helicopters were common Russian Kazan Ansat light utility choppers, likely launched from the Caspian Sea."

"That means they could've come from Turkmenistan, Azerbaijan, or Kazakhstan—or even Russia proper," Alex said.

Bloch frowned. "And they could have been mercenaries hired by any number of groups. They would have had to refuel on the way in, so that suggests an intelligence network and assets on the ground."

"And whoever wanted her needed a Fields Medal–winning mathematician," Alex said.

"It's a relatively short list," Bloch said, "but the problem is that no one is quite sure what the military or technological aspects of her work might be. I'm hoping Shepard and O'Neal can help there."

"I'd like to sit in on that meeting," Alex said. "I think Dr. Nasiri would be more comfortable if I were there."

"Normally, yes," Bloch said, "but I have another mission for you and Lily, and it starts tomorrow."

Alex had been looking forward to a few days' rest and a couple of long rides on her motorcycle, but what she said was, "Of course."

"What do you know about Formula One racing?"

"A bit," said Alex.

Bloch got up and stepped out from behind her desk. "Come with me. Let's get some coffee and discuss it."

That was unprecedented. Bloch was asking her to get coffee...

First, O'Neal in a skirt and now this, Alex thought. Plus, she couldn't shake the feeling that Bloch was hiding something from her. Of course, the woman ran a spy agency, so secrets were par for the course, but Alex's spider sense was tingling. There was definitely something unusual going on.

A second before they stepped into the dining area, Alex sensed something was up. Then two things happened nearly simultaneously: She smelled a perfume she recognized as her mother's and she caught sight of her father.

Then, before she could process the strangeness of both her parents being at headquarters, she saw her mother standing next to her dad and beaming at Alex as the full room burst into applause.

Her father's partner, Peter Conley, was there with Dan Hong or Dani Guo, as well as Lily Randall; her marshal arts instructor, naval commander Alicia Schmitt; Spartan and the rest of the tactical people; ex-KGB officer and her father's former rival, Valery Dobrynin; as well as Lincoln Shepard, Karen O'Neal, and their engineering and computer people. There were also some administrative staff and other personnel—almost everyone who worked at Zeta, except for the people who were currently on assignment. The crowd formed a loose circle, at the head of which stood Diana Bloch. She was behind a table that held the final surprise, a large cake that said *Congratulations!*

Bloch raised her hand and the applause died down. Looking at Alex, she said, "Alex Morgan came to us about two years ago, first providing some informal but vital assistance and then as a full-time member of the Zeta team. Since then, she has made significant contributions to Zeta's ongoing mission, as well as US and even world security.

"We have no formal training program at Zeta," Bloch continued, "but Alex has had top-level instruction from many of you in areas ranging from combat martial arts, weaponry, technology, and some of the more subtle skills necessary for our work.

"In every area, Alex Morgan has excelled and far exceeded what would be expected from one of our counterparts at any of the US intelligence agencies. To the extent that Zeta exists as a legal entity, we are security consultants and we have no formal titles, though I know many of you refer to each other as agents and me by a number of different titles—some of which are even respectful."

That got a laugh from the room and a gulp of surprise from Alex. Bloch had made *a joke. In public.*

"And while we don't observe many of the formalities that organizations in our business do, we have no trouble recognizing accomplishment. So, Alex Morgan, I am proud to formally recognize you as a full-fledged *consultant.*

"And, of course, like any consultant in our business, Alex has taken a code name: Raven. So to Alex Morgan and to Raven, congratulations," Bloch said, raising her champagne glass. Everyone else in the room followed suit. Alex's mom embraced her, while Uncle Peter and her dad hovered nearby.

"We're so proud of you," her mom said.

"Well done, honey," her dad added.

What followed was thirty minutes of congratulations and polite conversation with the rest of the people at Zeta. It felt remarkably normal considering the work they all did, and Alex had to admit it was pleasant.

Alex was also surprised by how comfortable her mother was in the environment. She was almost friendly with Bloch and knew more than a few of O'Neal and Shepard's team pretty well.

As the event was wrapping up, Alex saw that it was almost time for her pre-mission briefing with Bloch. As her parents approached, Alex felt a flash of suspicion.

It made perfect sense for her mother and father to come by for the little ceremony in their daughter's honor. But, was it an accident that Dan Morgan just happened to be there when she was about to start an overseas mission on the international car racing circuit?

Was he thinking of coming along to keep an eye on her? Or would he be monitoring her from HQ, ready to jump on a plane if there was a hint that things might go sideways?

It had been hard enough to establish herself at Zeta as Dan Morgan's daughter. It wouldn't help to have him hovering over her on this mission, even remotely.

"Honey, we wanted to tell you something," her father said.

Here it comes, Alex thought.

"Just in case anything comes up," her mom added.

Alex took a deep breath. This was going to be tricky. She couldn't allow what she knew was coming, but her parents had been so proud during Bloch's graduation talk. But, either way, Alex knew she'd need to put her foot down.

"We'll be taking a little trip," her father said.

Jenny Morgan laughed at that. "Hardly little. We'll be touring quite a few countries, starting in India."

That wasn't *a trip.* This was *the trip.* The one her parents had been talking about for years.

Alex realized she was still unsettled, but now it was for a different reason. That trip around the world was the kind of thing parents did when they retired. And while Jenny and Dan Morgan were too young to be retiring, they certainly were in a position to do so if they wanted to.

"Your father says he's not bringing his cell phone," her mother said, "but I'll have mine. Just in case. I'm letting you know, since there might be periods when we'll be hard to reach. You can always text or email me if you need anything, and we should be able to get back to you in a few days. A week, tops."

A week, tops? Well, that was what Alex wanted, wasn't it? To be on her own, without her father looking over her shoulder?

"I have a briefing with Director Bloch now," Alex said.

"Good luck. Bloch won't tell me what she has planned for you, but I'm sure you'll do great," her dad said.

"Thanks," Alex said weakly. Then her mom hugged her and said, "We'll see you in a few weeks."

"Have fun," Alex replied as she hugged her dad and then headed for the director's office.

* * * *

Bloch was already at her desk when Alex arrived. "Come in," she said. "Take a seat."

Alex took a chair facing the director.

"Alex, I've already briefed Lily on the situation, but I'll bring you up to speed. You're aware that the Formula One season has started?"

"Of course," Alex replied. "I don't follow the sport closely, outside of some of the technical aspects, but I do know they ran the Fourth Grand Prix last week so they're about a quarter of the way through the season."

"And you're aware that Renard Tech has a team?"

"Yes, I understand that Lily sometimes travels with Scott Renard for part of the Grand Prix circuit," Alex said.

Sometimes traveled with was only part of the story. The fact was that Lily and Scott Renard had been dating for some time.

"Alex, this year I'd like you to go accompany Lily for the next few races," Bloch said. "Are you aware of the problems that have occurred around this year's events?"

"I know there was an attempted break-in at a museum in Australia, as well as a terrorist incident," said Alex. "There was a terrorist attack in Bahrain, and of course the commuter train derailment in Spain. The only countries spared any incidents during their legs of the Grand Prix were China and Azerbaijan. But, according to press reports, there is no connection between the attacks and no indication of any ties to Formula One. Can I presume there's more to the story?"

"Quite a bit. First, the 'attempted' robbery in Australia was successful. Some jewels that belonged to Queen Victoria were actually stolen from an exhibit—though that detail was not mentioned in the press reports. As far as anyone knows, there was an attempted robbery and the exhibit was safe. Replicas are on display for now while MI Six and Australian authorities try to find the originals.

"In Bahrain, at about the same time as the terrorist attack, there was a successful theft of some very valuable antiques. And our intelligence reports suggest that China had a major terrorist incident that the Chinese government, for reasons that are not clear, has refused to acknowledge. We also suspect there was a theft at one of their weapons research facilities, but there's even less information about that than about the attack. Meanwhile, in Spain, two Picassos were stolen from a private collection.

"But the most serious incident occurred in Azerbaijan. A deadly chemical plant fire on the outskirts of Baku was nothing but a cover story for the theft of plutonium from an old Soviet-era facility. At the same time there was also a theft of a significant amount of gold from a private facility nearby."

"How much plutonium?" Alex asked.

"Enough for at least one nuclear bomb, maybe two," Bloch said. "Or a series of dirty bombs."

"What are we thinking?" Alex asked. "That the thefts are meant to fund more terrorist acts? Or are they some kind of a cover?"

"We have no idea," Bloch said. "So far, Spain is the only location that doesn't fit the pattern. There was an attack in Madrid but no major theft. I need you two on the ground at the next stop," she said.

"The first time is happenstance," Alex began, "the second a coincidence..."

"The third time enemy action," Bloch finished.

"What's the fourth time?" Alex asked.

"A problem," Bloch said.

By itself, the theft of plutonium was bad. But the addition of high-level terrorist attacks and threats suggested a level of organization and sophistication that had staggering implications.

"Alex, the Renard Tech jet leaves at four tomorrow," Bloch said. "Pick up your mission file on the way out. And good luck."

"Yes, ma'am," Alex said as she headed out the door.

Chapter 4

Alex took one last look at the bike. It really was beautiful. Eight cylinders of handmade Italian engineering.

It was also older than she was and represented 25 percent of the total production run of Morbidelli 850 motorcycles.

And it needed her. Because of neglect, the engine required extensive work, but that would have to wait. The customer knew that the process would take at least months, and Alex had anticipated spending half a year with the bike.

For now, it would have to wait. She wheeled her one small suitcase out of the garage and closed the door on Morgan Exotic Motorcycle and Car Repair.

Alex felt a pang of regret leaving the shop. Just because the repair business was her cover didn't mean she didn't take it seriously—or enjoy her work.

Outside, she waited for her car. She had almost called her parents for a ride to the airport only to remember they had already left on their trip. She'd actually ordered a car to pick her up when Lily called to tell her that Scott would be sending one for both of them.

Alex heard Scott Renard's car before she saw it. The term *car* didn't do it justice.

It was a stretch limo, the biggest Alex had ever seen. It pulled up to the garage, and the driver jumped out and took her suitcase. Lily opened the limo door and greeted her.

"I thought our job was to be inconspicuous?" Alex asked.

"Our job is to maintain our cover. This is how Scott does things." Lily smiled. "Now if he had sent a town car, *that* would be suspicious."

That was true. Lily's cover was that she was the girlfriend of Scott Renard, the tech billionaire. The fact that she was his actual girlfriend made it a very easy cover to maintain.

Lily's civilian-cover business was as the owner of a corporate security firm. Alex didn't know any of the details, but she knew that Lily and Renard met a few years ago when Lily had been sent to Renard Tech undercover to investigate some corporate security threat that touched on global security.

They had been together ever since, which gave Lily the perfect cover for this mission. It also met Alex's father's criteria for a good cover—one that was as close as possible to yourself and your own life.

Dan Morgan had advised her to even use her real first name whenever possible. It reduced the chance that she would fail to answer to her cover name or, worse, respond to "Alex" when she was known to those around her as someone else.

In that respect, this cover was perfect. She was Alex Morgan, the owner of a high-end exotic motorcycle repair shop. And she was accompanying her friend Lily and Lily's boyfriend on the Formula 1 circuit.

So much of that was true, it was barely a cover.

At the airport they headed to the hangar for the Renard Tech planes. Alex had been there before. The Renard Tech logo was splashed on three small private jets—and one 727, which was the size of a passenger jet.

There was a cluster of people assembled near the bottom of the stairs leading up to the jet, but all conversation stopped when Scott Renard stepped out.

Alex had flown on his jets, and his tech and enormous computer resources had helped save her life (and the lives of a number of Zeta agents) more than once, but Alex had never seen him in person.

On the surface, the pictures she had seen in the numerous profiles and tech articles were accurate. He was handsome man in his early thirties, with sandy brown hair, who always seemed to have a day or two's stubble on his face. He was wearing his trademark hoodie and T-shirt. Of course, it wasn't just *his* trademark, she realized. It was the uniform of Lincoln Shepard, who helped run the tech division at Zeta. Alex wondered if that was just the wardrobe of that kind of tech person, or if Shepard was emulating one of his heroes.

Renard wore no jewelry other than a smart watch and on his feet were ordinary, inexpensive basketball shoes. If he weren't so good-looking, he could have been any software engineer in Silicon Valley.

What the photos Alex had seen didn't capture was his presence. When he lifted his hand the entire cluster of businesspeople went silent, waiting for his next instruction.

"One minute," Renard said pleasantly as he turned his eyes toward Lily. His entire face lit up and he broke into a broad smile. Striding over, he greeted her enthusiastically.

Even the normally reserved Lily smiled when he swept her up in his arms. They kissed. "It is *very* nice to see you," he said when he put her down.

"You too, Mr. Renard," Lily said through her smile.

Renard turned to Alex. "And you must be Alex Morgan," he said. "Nice to meet you, finally."

Alex extended her hand and said, "You as well."

"Lily speaks very highly of you and, of course, I know your father. In fact, I owe him a favor or two."

That should have surprised Alex, given how much Zeta had depended on Renard Tech resources lately, from their computer labs to their small fleet of private jets. However, Alex had learned long ago that there were a surprisingly large number of people who owed her dad favors.

"I know you are both on an assignment, but I hope you'll enjoy the time you spend with us. Have you ever seen a Formula One race in person?"

"No," Alex said.

"I suspect you'll like it. I understand you know something about high-end motorcycles, so I think you'll find the cars interesting. The sport pushes the envelope every year, and this year our car has a few tricks that I hope will surprise everyone."

Alex knew that the top Formula 1 teams, including Renard's, had budgets of as much as half a billion dollars a year.

A lot of that went into the engineering R and D that eked out fractional improvements in the cars to give them an edge against other teams that were also pouring money into new developments. Every year, this corporate arms race gave the cars a bit more speed and kept them on the road when speeds for their circuits approached two hundred miles an hour.

"I look forward to seeing what your car can do, and to meeting the team," Alex said.

"I think you'll be pleased and I hope you'll be impressed," Renard said.

Alex had seen Renard on television, in various interviews and giving testimony on tech issues before Congress, but none of that had prepared her for how handsome he was in person—or how easygoing and friendly.

That might have been because his girlfriend was present, but Alex didn't think so. She had the feeling that this was just him.

"Come on, I'll show you the plane. It's brand new," Renard said. He gave his employees some final instructions and led the women up the stairs.

The interior of the jet was exactly what she had expected from a young tech billionaire.

It had an open plan, with glass walls separating conference rooms and offices. There were also two large computer workstations with multiple screens.

In the back was a big flat-screen with video game gear on nearby shelves, as well as half a dozen cubbies filled with virtual reality goggles.

There was also a bar and a dining room, complete with a commercial-grade popcorn machine.

"Come, I'll give you a tour," Renard said. He took them around the plane, introducing them to the two flight attendants, the pilot, and the copilot. He knew all of the crew by name.

Alex noted that he seemed to be on friendly terms with everyone. Again, that could be a show for her and Lily. But you couldn't fake the fact that his employees seemed to genuinely like him.

When they were finished the tour, he turned serious. "Alex, I've already spoken to Lily about this," Renard said, "but I wanted to say it to you face-to-face. Thank you for what you did for Maryam Nasiri. She's one of my heroes and losing her to the ayatollahs would have been a real loss for all of us."

That surprised Alex. He was the third person she had met who seemed to be in awe of Nasiri.

"You should talk to Shepard and O'Neal," Alex said. "They debriefed her personally."

"Good idea. I'll grab some time with them when we're in the air." Renard's phone beeped and he gave it a quick glance. "Your motorcycle has been loaded into cargo. There'll be some great afternoon rides where we're going."

"Do you ride, too?" Alex asked.

"Not anymore," Renard said. "The shareholders don't like it. "

Something twitched on Lily's face, and Alex realized that the shareholders weren't the only ones who didn't like him on a motorcycle. Ironic, considering the types of risks Lily took every day in her job, but there it was.

A young man in a business suit approached and said, "We'll have clearance in a few minutes."

Renard introduced the man as Luiz Carter. Luiz was only a couple of inches taller than Alex herself, compact and well groomed, with jet-black hair and bright blue eyes. He was serious, and singularly focused on Renard.

From her research, Alex knew that Luiz's title was executive assistant to the CEO, but she knew a body man when she saw one. Luiz Carter took care of everything— from watering Renard's plants, to making sure he kept his doctor's appointments, to casting proxy votes for Renard at the board meetings he missed when he was busy elsewhere. Alex was also sure Luiz had had some sort of physical training so he could act as a bodyguard in a pinch.

After Carter left, Renard asked the women to excuse him. "I have a few things to take care of before we take off. In the meantime, find yourself a seat and enjoy the plane." He sniffed the air, adding, "The popcorn is fresh."

Alex fell into one of the large, comfortable leather-covered seats by the window. One of the flight attendants stopped by to make sure her seat belt was on, and Alex watched as the small tow tractor pulled the plane out of the hangar.

When they were positioned out front, the engines started and couple of minutes later the plane was taxiing under its own power. They left the hangar behind and passed the second Renard Tech hangar.

That's when Alex first saw the smoke.

It was coming from inside the hangar. "Lily," Alex called out, "do you see this?"

"See what?" Lily was on the other side of the plane. Moving fast, she got out of her seat and peered out Alex's window.

The hangar had smoke pouring from it.

"Oh my God, Alex," Lily said.

There was a flash of light, then another. It was followed by a series of small explosions, and then the hangar was behind them and out of sight.

Alex only heard the next explosion, and the one after that. They were much bigger than the first.

And she could tell they were getting closer.

* * * *

Bloch picked up the phone on the first ring.

"Conley here," said the voice on the line.

"What's happening?" Diana Bloch asked, already suspecting what the man would say.

"Once again, nothing," Conley said. "It's almost supernaturally quiet." That was not unusual; this was Malaysia, after all. It had been remarkably free of terrorism or even any political strife for a number of years. It was one of the major success stories in Southeast Asia.

And yet for over a week, Zeta's risk-assessment system had been flagging its capital, Kuala Lumpur, for the site of a major incident.

Peter Conley and Dan Hong Guo had been on-site for seven days, but there had been nothing.

Nothing yet.

"Okay," Bloch said. "But what do you think?"

"I think the city is clear," Conley replied.

Bloch had learned to trust her agents' intuition, particularly if the agent's name was Morgan or Conley.

"Stay on-site for a few days and then pack it in if the situation is still nominal," Bloch said.

"Will do," Conley said.

When Diana Bloch looked up, Karen O'Neal was waiting outside her door. Bloch motioned her in.

"You've seen what's been happening?" Bloch asked.

"I do, and I'm concerned. None of our alerts for the last two months have flagged any actual incidents."

That was the problem. And normally it would be a good thing, but this number of false positives on their threat-assessment system was a new development. Not just new, but unprecedented.

"Yes, the system has failed multiple times now," O'Neal said. She looked embarrassed, as if the failure was hers.

"Let's say the system didn't fail," Bloch said. "What if someone figured out how it worked?"

"I designed the software and I don't know how it works, not really," said Karen. "Most systems search for patterns and keywords in electronic communications, traffic movement, etc. Once a pattern has been identified, it's modeled, and a computer checks for similar patterns elsewhere. Our system doesn't look for patterns that we can then identify. It looks at metadata related to an incident and then searches for metadata that shares similar characteristics, though not necessarily set patterns. In other words, it finds similarities or patterns without needing to understand them. The key is, we don't have to make any meaningful connections, and neither does the system."

This was the third or fourth time O'Neal had explained the Zeta threat-assessment system to Bloch, and she still didn't fully understand it. She understood that the system looked for time codes and key words that described other data, but how it turned that into threat predictions, she had no idea—and it appeared as if the woman who created the system didn't either.

"Well, someone is gaming our system and has us chasing our tails," Bloch said, "and I need you to figure out how they are doing it and stop them."

"Yes, ma'am," O'Neal said. As the young woman turned to go, the phone on Bloch's desk gave a high-pitched buzz that meant trouble. Bloch picked it up to hear Lincoln Shepard's voice on the other end.

"Director, there's been an explosion at Logan Airport, at one of the Renard Tech hangars," Shepard said, clear concern in his voice. "It's a big one."

Bloch checked her watch. It was right around the time that Lily Randall, Alex Morgan, and Scott Renard would be taking off.

There it was: a major incident, and their threat-identification software hadn't seen it coming. And three people very important to Zeta Division were right in the middle of it.

Chapter 5

Renard appeared behind the two women, peering over Lily's shoulder as an explosion collapsed the roof of the hangar, and flame and debris shot out of the front. It was big, but it could have been much worse if any of the planes in the hangar had been fully fueled.

"Oh my God," Renard said, as he put his phone to his ear. "Is everyone all right? Was anyone in hanger two?" He waited a second for the response. "Good, get everyone out of there right now." He listened for a few seconds and then said, "Leave it. I don't care; just get out. We'll have plenty of time for all that later. Right now just get as far away as you can."

Alex watched the smoking hangar disappear from view as they taxied forward.

We're still moving? Alex thought. Of course. The pilot wouldn't have seen the explosion and it would take a minute for the tower to relay any information to him.

Carter was at Renard's side. "Scott, we have to stop the plane. I need to get you off as soon as possible," he said.

"No!" Lily shouted. "If there's a bomb on this plane then we're already dead. We need to get in the air, right now, before they lock the airport down. Right now, the greatest danger is on the ground, and I need to get you as far away from it as possible."

Renard weighed the two options. "Fine," he said. "Let's get out of here."

Lily waved for Alex, and the two agents sprinted for the cockpit. Lily identified herself and the pilot buzzed her in.

"There was an explosion at hangar one," Lily said, out of breath, "and we probably have less than a minute before they close down the airport. We need to get in the air immediately. What's our status?"

"We're cleared for takeoff," said the pilot.

By now Alex could see flashing lights to their right; there was heavy police and EMT activity. They didn't have much time. The plane turned from the taxiway to the runway proper.

Alex could hear a voice crackle through the pilot's headset.

"Say again," the pilot said into the microphone. "I have clearance."

That's it, Alex thought. *They're shutting down.*

"Ignore them," Lily said. "Better yet, shut off the comm. We are much safer in the air."

The pilot hesitated, but only briefly. "Tower, please repeat," he said into his headset. "I didn't copy." He flipped a switch on the panel in front of him, and the headset went dead.

"They won't like that," the pilot said.

"We need to get to safety, we can smooth it over later," Lily said.

"Okay, get to the back and get everyone strapped in," the pilot said. "It's going to be a steep ascent to get us out of this airspace."

Lily and Alex did as instructed and half a minute later they were sitting next to Scott as the plane picked up speed on the runway. True to his word, the pilot executed a very aggressive climb. Alex felt the acceleration press her back into her seat.

In about a minute, Alex judged they were higher than the three-thousand-foot range of most shoulder-fired RPGs.

In another three minutes she gauged they were above the 12,500-foot range of the most advanced shoulder-fired Stinger missiles. At that point, Alex let herself relax, but everyone was silent until they reached cruising altitude.

Renard was instantly on the phone, checking with his staff. He hung up and said, "No one was hurt, but everything in hangar one was lost."

Lily was about to say something when the pilot approached and said, "The tower was pretty upset by our takeoff, but they suddenly became extremely reasonable and chalked it up to equipment malfunction."

Alex smiled. Diana Bloch no doubt had something to do with that.

"Looks like clear skies to Monte Carlo," the pilot said. "And sir, I presume you already know what we lost," he said, glancing at Scott.

"Nothing that can't be replaced," Renard said.

"Any idea what happened?" the pilot asked.

"We don't know anything, but local and federal law enforcement is on it," Renard said.

With that, the pilot excused himself and Lily ushered Alex and Renard into the conference room.

Lily got right down to business and said, "I think we can safely assume this was an attempt on your life."

"My only question is, Why wasn't it successful?" Alex interjected. "It was clearly a sophisticated operation. How did they get the wrong plane?"

"That part's easy," Renard said. "When I first met Lily, she was a security consultant, or at least she was MI Six and working undercover very convincingly as a private security consultant."

Lily continued, "The British government had and still has a number of important contracts with Renard Tech. When there was a security threat to the company, I was assigned to make sure the threat was addressed. And, as I recall, my team's work was first-rate."

Renard smiled in agreement. "Yes, and part of the security protocols were frequent changes of flight plans whenever I or one of the senior staff would travel on corporate jets."

"It's a simple safeguard, but obviously effective, at least in this case," Lily said. "The first place we'll look is at people close to you. Scott, is there anyone in your personal life or on staff who might want you dead?"

"You know pretty much everyone in my personal life. There's nobody I know who'd be capable of something like this. As for the staff, I keep a bowl of candy on my desk at all times, so they seem to like me."

Lily ignored that and said, "Corporate rivals?"

"I don't have that many rivals in my area of the business, so I don't think so. Even if something happened to me, everyone knows the company and its most important technology would continue. Plus, Gates is too much of a stiff and Zuckerberg is more of a prankster," he said, smiling.

"You think this is funny?" Lily wasn't smiling. "You were nearly killed."

"No, I don't think it's funny, and it wasn't *just me* who was almost killed," Renard said evenly.

There was tension between them. For a moment they didn't speak, and then Lily moved forward. "Zeta will run backgrounds on everyone at the airport, but if they check out, that leaves foreign powers."

"Well, China isn't too happy with me," Renard said. "They threw money at Renard Tech to help them develop censorship tools to limit access to the Internet for Chinese people. We politely declined." Renard shrugged. "In the end they got someone else to do it."

"Would they kill you just for turning them down?" asked Alex.

"And as I recall," said Lily, "you were pretty vocal in your criticism about the regime for even asking. And they weren't too thrilled about the Renard Tech freeware that allows Chinese citizens to circumvent that censorship."

"By that measure, how many foreign powers *have* you pissed off?" Alex asked.

Renard shrugged. "Well, Saudi Arabia isn't pleased with our online educational outreach for women," he said, "and North Korea blames Renard Tech— unreasonably, in my opinion—for certain problems with their computer systems that have set back their nuclear program. Unproven, by the way. And there's—"

"I'm going to stop you right there," said Lily, without a hint of humor in her voice. "It might save us time if you listed the bad guys you *haven't* pissed off."

Alex knew that for a technology company, Renard Tech was a fly in the ointment for some of the worst regimes on earth, and clearly Renard was deeper in the fight than she had realized. Alex understood why her dad liked the man so much.

"Anyone else who might be especially ticked off at you?" she asked. "Anything unusual happen recently?"

"No, nothing unusual...though the Chinese can't be happy about our new launch- system test."

"Why?" Alex asked. She'd read about Renard Tech's space initiative. Other billionaire-funded, private space programs were focused on space tourism, or trips to Mars. Renard Tech took a different approach—asteroid mining. Much of the technology was theoretical, but they did launch some satellites into orbit recently. Could that be it?

"Any practical mining would be ten years out at least," Renard replied, "but we've had some successes. And when the system is up and running, it will break China's near-monopoly on rare earth minerals, to say nothing of nickel."

"And those are valuable?"

"They're essential for a number of industries, particularly in the energy sector," the man said. "Solar panels, advanced batteries, fuel cells. Right now, China has a stranglehold on the supply."

"That gives them not only cash but a lot of power on the international stage," Lily said. "Okay, that's two for the Chinese."

"And there's the Tibetan—"

"Right, we get it. China is *very* angry with you." Lily's tone made it clear that China wasn't alone in that area.

The question now was what to do about it.

"Is it safe to continue with the Grand Prix schedule?" asked Alex.

Now it was Scott's turn to get serious. "Absolutely. We must continue."

"Alex is right. Perhaps we should reassess," Lily said.

"Lily, you know I can't appear to be in hiding," said Renard. "I have shareholders and a hundred thousand global employees depending on me. Plus, whoever this was, they already failed."

"They might not fail a second time," said Lily.

"You will increase security and you know I'll be safe, at least in the immediate future," Renard said, an air of finality in his voice.

To Alex's surprise, Lily held her tongue.

To her further surprise, Renard softened a bit. "Excuse me, I have some work to do," he said. "You know where to find me."

He headed to one of the computer workstations and became immediately absorbed in some task.

"What's he doing?" Alex asked. "What could be so important?"

"Could be anything, and I guarantee you it's *not* important or relevant to what is going on," Lily said.

Alex raised an eyebrow.

"For a least an hour a day," Lily said, "Scott chooses a task from one of the company's project lists. It could be anything from a firewall upgrade to a slightly better batch-processing program for an inventory-control database—the kind of job that anyone could do."

"So he makes himself program every day as some sort of test of discipline?" Alex asked.

"Just the opposite. The discipline comes from limiting himself to an hour a day. The programming is what he does, it's who he is." Lily gestured to the plane around them. "This—the CEO bit, the corporate strategy—is only to protect and promote the coding. Don't get me wrong: He's a very good strategist and CEO, but he would rather be in there all day, doing exactly what he's doing. He's also a very good businessperson, but that's nothing compared to what he is as a programmer."

"So, where does pissing off international bad guys fit in?" Alex asked.

"*That* he does for fun," Lily said.

"If nothing else, I suppose," Alex said, "the programming will keep him out of our hair."

"True," Lily said. "Let's compile a list of likely suspects and have Zeta run them down. It will take a while, so let's get started."

Chapter 6

None of this seemed right to Peter Conley.

He scanned the brightly-lit storefronts and rows of small traders—apparently *reputable* small traders—selling their goods to both tourists and locals.

And it was after ten.

"*This* is Chow Kit?" Conley asked.

"When was the last time you were here?" Dani asked.

"Five years ago," he replied.

"They've made a real effort to clean things up in the last couple of years," she said.

Apparently, the Kuala Lumpur local government had decided to give the sketchy downtown of their capital a makeover—the Malaysian equivalent of what had happened in the 1990s to Times Square in New York. When he was a teenager, Conley had seen someone get shot right on Forty-second Street. Now the place was bright, clean and full of family-friendly musicals and overpriced tourist traps.

"Don't worry, Peter, this is just the surface. The real Chow Kit is still here if you know where to look," she said, giving him that smile again.

That smile had changed everything for Conley. He'd been on a mission in the Philippines when he had met Dani as a member of the staff of the Chinese minister of finance.

After a brief romance, they had helped foil a massive terrorist attack, and that's when Conley realized that she was Chinese intelligence. After the mission was over, Dani had made it clear that she wanted to defect to the US.

Conley helped her do that, and now she was part of the Zeta team.

As part of the Chinese finance ministry as well as an intelligence operative, Dani had been a gold mine of intelligence for the US and for Zeta. And because she was now part of Zeta Division, it meant that she and Conley often worked together. He found that he liked working with her almost as much as he liked the private time they spent together.

At the moment, Dani and Conley were playing the parts of hapless tourists. Given the possibility that Zeta's threat-assessment system had just been wrong, they could end up seeing the sights for a few days and then head home.

Zeta's system was good, though not perfect. There had been an unusual number of failures lately, but counterterrorism had always been played on a shifting playing field.

And yet Dani wanted to do some more digging, and because of her time in Chinese intelligence she knew the city better than he.

Shuffling through the tight spaces with other tourists, Conley and Dani wandered through the stalls full of clothing, shoes, and small electronics. All around them, vendors barked out announcements and engaged in loud negotiations with customers.

It was noisy and aggressive, but the energy was good, and it didn't leave Conley with the ominous seedy feeling he had the last time he was there.

That was progress.

After a few minutes, they left the dry half of the market for the wet section. As they crossed the dividing line, the first thing Conley noticed was the pungent smell. The goods shifted to produce, as well as canned and bottled food of every variety.

There were many fewer tourists here, fewer still as they trekked deeper into the wet section where meats were displayed in the open air and live animals were butchered in the stalls. There were the usual chickens, goats, and pigs, as well as fish and seafood of every kind.

That summed up the city for you. There were high-rises everywhere, and the gleaming monorail they had taken there still loomed behind them, but they were now in a part of the market that was doing business the way it had for two hundred years, as if nothing had changed.

And yet somehow, the place still felt safe, and Conley was comfortable in the environment. Now that they had left the tourist-friendly section, there were no more obnoxious street children aggressively hawking overpriced flowers or pickpockets working the crowd.

A few stalls deeper into the market, things began to change even more.

There were almost no women and children among the shoppers. Soon only drug addicts and prostitutes roamed the aisles. The stalls ostensibly held many of the same goods, but their boxes were dusty and faded from the sun as the proprietors pulled the real merchandise from underneath the tables and passed it to their customers in small packets or plain brown bags.

At the end of the market they came to a street where bicycles, motorbikes, and a few cars drove by.

Dani motioned for him to stop and stood with her back to the street. "Now we wait," she said. She kept a light smile on her lips, but her eyes told Conley that she was concentrating.

That put Conley on alert.

Dani continued to smile, nodding up at him as if he was still speaking, and after less than a minute, Conley could see a motorcycle approaching them, a local young man without a helmet riding the bike.

"Keep your eyes on me," Dani said to Conley.

He did his best, but his peripheral vision told him that the motorbike was slowing down to almost walking speed.

"Don't do anything," Dani said, seeing Conley tense up.

Conley nodded as the motorbike swerved closer and the rider reached out with one hand. Conley had to force himself to be still as the next few seconds played out.

Dani planted her right foot forward as the guy grabbed the strap of her purse. Then she twisted her body until she was facing the other way and threw herself forward just as the strap pulled tight in the rider's hand.

The young man had a firm grip and didn't let go as Dani leaned down into a crouch and pushed herself further forward. The rider was leaning in to Dani, with one hand on the strap of her purse and one on the motorcycle handgrip.

He lost control of the bike and swerved sharply to the right. Letting go of the strap, he fell to the street, the bike smashing down onto his right leg.

Motorbike and rider skidded for a few feet before they came to rest.

The pedestrians barely glanced up.

Instantly, Dani was back on her feet, dragging the rider out from under the bike.

The young man had a dazed expression on his face, as he tried to process what had just happened. Conley was certain that she was the first of his purse-snatching marks to ever fight back.

As soon as Dani dragged him clear of the bike, Conley checked him for weapons and pulled a switchblade out of the man's back pocket. Leaning down, Dani pulled him to a sitting position and twisted his arm behind his back.

He spoke quickly and animatedly in Malaysian. Though Conley didn't speak the language, he assumed that the young man was protesting his innocence. Dani barked something back at him in his language and then said, "In English!"

"Okay," he said. "It was an accident…"

His English was remarkably good.

Dani twisted his arm behind his back, and he yelped. "I don't care about your clumsy, petty crime," she said. "But I have some questions I need you to answer."

The rider was maybe twenty years old and seemed genuinely confused.

Dani yanked his arm again. "Tell me you understand," she said.

"I…understand," he said, looking pleadingly at Conley as if the agent could somehow help him make sense of what was happening.

"Where can I find Al-Ma'unah?" Dani asked.

Conley knew that Al-Ma'unah was an Islamic militant group in the area who had been collaborating with ISIS.

"I have nothing to do with them," he said, the beginning of panic in his eyes.

"I didn't ask about you," Dani said, wrenching his arm. "I asked where I could find *them*."

The young man met Conley's eyes, as if asking for help, and Conley just shrugged.

"We stay away from them," the young man said at last.

She pulled on his arm hard enough for him to cry out loudly.

"Okay, okay," he said. "I can tell you where they meet."

The guy rattled off what Conley assumed were street names and directions in Malaysian. Slowly, Dani released his arm.

Wobbling, the boy got to his feet and took a step toward his motorcycle.

"No," Dani said. "It's mine now."

He looked up uncomprehendingly until Dani took a step toward him. Putting his hands up, he turned and walked away with a limp.

"That's going to be hard to explain to his buddies," Conley said.

"Yes," she said, smiling.

Conley checked his watch. "Do you think the guys at Al-Ma'unah are still at work?"

"Let's find out," she said.

* * * *

Lily approached Alex and Renard in their seats and said, "Diana Bloch has smoothed things over with the FAA. No one will be waiting for us on the ground, and nobody gets arrested when we get home."

"But what do we know about what happened?" Alex said.

"Apparently two men, airport personnel, were found dead at their homes," Lily replied. "They had some loose ties to a few radical groups, but they weren't on anyone's radar."

"No connection to Renard Tech?" Renard asked.

Lily shook her head. "They'd never have gotten through the screening protocols I set up, especially for access to the hangar and the jets."

"Any direct link to known groups?" Alex asked.

"Not yet, but Zeta will know soon enough," Lily replied, turning to Renard. "The most important thing to remember is that there is no indication that you are still in danger," she said. "Even so, we will have dramatically increased security in Monaco."

"I have responsibilities in Monaco," Renard said.

"The security will be mostly invisible, or at least it won't get in your way. Of course, I'll have to stay as close to you as possible."

"Of course," he said. "Are we expecting a second attempt?"

"Besides your personal protection, we're increasing security across the board at all Formula One venues," Lily said, "but there's no indication of an ongoing plot."

"Maybe because they expected the first attempt to be successful," Renard said.

That comment hung in the air for long seconds.

Alex broke the silence. "That kind of operation takes months to put together," she said. "That will give us and Zeta plenty of time to find every single person that had a hand in the explosion."

That lightened the mood a bit. "Scott, so you can focus on a nice, relaxing remainder of the Formula One season," said Lily.

That made Renard smile again.

"Speaking of which," said Alex, "do you have a job for me?"

"A job?" Renard said.

"While I'm here. Maybe something in the pit crew?"

There was an uncomfortable silence as Lily and Renard shared a glance.

"Given my background, I'm sure I can handle something in the pit," Alex said.

Renard smiled politely and said, "We're limited to twenty in the crew and we're full," he said. "And each of those people has an average of ten years' experience. Even if we had the time to train you and integrate you into the team, regulations require pit crew members to stay on for the season. Of course, you'll be welcome in the garage and workshop areas. I think you'll like what you find there."

"Right now, I'm undercover as his girlfriend and you're here as my friend," Lily said. "We'll keep our eyes open for trouble, but you'll see that it gets busy around here pretty quick."

Alex understood. She would keep a low profile. They were there as part of a Zeta investigation into the terrorist attacks, crimes, and general suspicious activity that had dogged the Formula 1 circuit this season. For now, that would have to be enough.

Still, she felt an itch to have an immediate job, something to tackle right now. The need for near-constant activity was part of the Morgan curse, she thought.

She would do her best to settle into her cover: nothing but a close friend of a billionaire's girlfriend while the three of them toured the world on the Formula 1 circuit. If it wasn't for the lingering worry about the explosion at the hangar and the potential threat to Renard, Alex thought she might actually enjoy this mission.

As they prepared for landing, Alex and Lily confirmed the new security protocols. It was a delicate business. There had to be additional security on the ground in Monaco and in the racing areas—and that meant coordination with private security firms, local authorities, and Zeta assets—plus additional CIA and MI6 friendlies. And it all had to be done while not alerting the press or the public that the explosion in the Boston hangar was anything other than what it said in the official report: an electrical problem that ignited some fuel and took out a billionaire's private jets.

After they landed, Renard sent his body man Carter to handle the corporate investigation into the explosion and start the process of replacing the jets. Carter wasn't happy leaving his boss, but he had no choice but to follow orders.

Alex could see that it was hard for Lily to let Renard out of her sight, but their mission required that she keep to her normal routine as much as possible and that meant heading to the hotel without him, while Renard joined the Formula 1 team at the track.

In the hangar in Monaco, Alex checked on her bike as the staff pulled it out of the cargo hold of the plane. Once it was secure, she and Lily got into the waiting limousine.

"Would it be so bad if we rode along with Renard and went to the track instead of just going to our hotel?" Alex asked.

"Yes," said Lily. "It would break our established routine. Still, I might do it, but there's one contact we have to make in person."

"An asset?" Alex asked.

"More like a network. I have to let them know I'm here so they can keep their eyes open," Lily said.

At the hotel the two women headed for the concierge. He was a good-looking man of about thirty, a local, with short dark hair and a polite smile.

"My name is Paul, Ms. Randall," he said, handing her his business card. "If there is anything you need, please call me personally." He spoke in a French accent.

That wasn't a surprise. Clearly, the hotel management knew that Lily Randall was with Scott Renard, and they would go to great lengths to keep him and, by extension, her happy.

"I will, thank you," Lily said, glancing at the concierge's lapel, her eyes lingering on two gold keys embroidered into the fabric.

"I'm a friend of Pierre's," Lily said. Then she tapped her ring on the counter and Paul eyed the ring. It appeared to be a family crest ring, with a lion and a unicorn on it. The two animals appeared on the symbol for MI6; the lion for England, the unicorn for Scotland.

"Very good," Paul said. "I will tell him you are staying at the hotel."

"How is the weather?" Lily asked.

He gave her his friendly smile again. "Normal for this time of year. Nothing out of the ordinary and very good for racing."

"Excellent," Lily said.

Alex saw Lily visibly relax. Something had just happened, but what it was, Alex had no idea. The weather outside was sunny and seventy, but Alex was certain that Lily and the concierge were not really discussing the weather.

"Your bags are already in your room," Paul said. "Enjoy your stay, Ms. Randall, Ms. Morgan."

Chapter 7

The faces of two men appeared on the big screen on the wall of the large conference room, or what the staff called the War Room. One of the men was a nondescript twentysomething white male. The other was about the same age, but dark-skinned and apparently of Middle Eastern descent. Diana Bloch had to force down a spike of anger. These two had tried to kill two of her agents, as well as a longtime friend and benefactor of Zeta Division—as well as half a dozen crew on Renard's plane. Had they hit the correct hangar, they would have killed a dozen more of Renard Tech's people.

"Brad Spellman and Mohammad Omar Anbari, both deceased," said Lincoln Shepard to the assembled group, which included all Zeta personnel who weren't on assignment. "Spellman was twenty-six. He worked on the custodial staff of the Logan Airport hangars—though he was not assigned to the Renard hangars. Similarly, Mohammad Omar Anbari was thirty years old. He was a mechanic who was employed by a private jet time-sharing firm who operated out of a nearby hangar."

"What's the connection between them?" Bloch asked.

"None," Shepard said. "Spellman was a member of a group called Citizens for Economic Justice."

"Never heard of them," said Bloch, and she knew most extremist groups at least by name.

"Few have," Shepard said. "They seem to exist only on Twitter. Apparently, they don't like billionaires."

"And the other one?"

"Anbari wasn't a member of any known extremist group, but he had visited a few ISIS-related websites. He posted a few troubling comments on regular news sites, but nothing that put him on the FBI's radar. And aside from both working in the hangars, they didn't appear to be friends or even know each other. But one month ago, they exchanged a few innocuous text messages. Then two weeks later, they each received fifty thousand dollars via overseas wire transfers. After that, they received a series of packages that we presume contained the components to make the remote-controlled incendiary device that destroyed the planes. The only other thing they shared is how they died. Three days ago, they both choked to death."

"*Really?*" Bloch said.

Shepard nodded. "They lived alone, a few blocks apart, and were eating takeout after a shift when they choked on their food. Spellman was found the next day, but Anbari wasn't found until after the explosion, so the connection between them wasn't immediately made."

"Were the deaths suspicious?"

"Not at all. No sign of forced entry. No signs of struggle. Spellman's autopsy showed nothing unusual or inconsistent with choking. Anbari's autopsy is still being conducted, but I doubt there will be anything out of the ordinary. Someone went to a lot of trouble to cover their tracks."

"Fifty thousand dollars to kill strangers," Bloch said, "and they didn't even get to spend it."

"Actually, they each managed to spend quite a bit of their money," Shepard said. He hesitated. "They spent it...frivolously."

"Who pulled the strings?" Bloch asked.

"Local PD and the FBI are both on it. We're also watching the medical examiner's office to see if anything comes up. And, we're trying to track the money. So far, nothing."

Bloch knew what that meant. If Lincoln Shepard and Karen O'Neal's people hadn't found anything, it meant there wasn't anything to find.

"Keep at it," Bloch said. "I think we can safely assume these two were patsies, chosen, I'm sure, because no one would miss them. The real question is who set up the operation and what did they hope to achieve by taking out Renard? Until we know that, we're chasing shadows."

There wasn't a lot Bloch could do. She'd make calls to her contacts at the FBI and the CIA—but she didn't expect them to reveal anything her people didn't already know. The fact was that O'Neal and Shepard had *unofficial* access to both agencies' data and communications systems.

"I'll call our friend at the NSA, see if they know anything," Bloch told the group. "In the meantime, let's follow all leads. I want you thinking about who could be behind this. I want theories, people, before there's another incident."

As everyone filed out, Bloch felt a cold burn of anger in her stomach. Behind it all was one thought: Someone had nearly killed two of her people and she wanted them to pay.

* * * *

Conley slowed the motorcycle down as they approached the building. The bike sputtered a bit, running more roughly as he brought it to a stop. It was a relatively new Honda and at least a moderately expensive model.

Of course, Dan and Alex Morgan would have known the year and model on sight. They also would have been disgusted by the state of the bike. Besides the scrapes and dings on the red finish, Conley didn't think it had been tuned or serviced since it was purchased.

That was one of the many problems with criminals. No standards.

If your only job was using your motorcycle to snatch purses on the street from ladies, the least you could do was take care of the bike. Of course, now the thief had lost his mode of transportation. Maybe he'd appreciate the next one more, or—better yet—go into a different line of work. If nothing else, Dani had made the streets a bit safer and that was something.

That was one of the things he and Morgan had learned over the years. You couldn't solve every problem you faced, and even the ones you did solve didn't stay solved forever—or even for long.

Conley had made peace with that fact—though he knew Morgan still struggled to do the same. It pissed his friend off—like poor maintenance on a good machine.

Dani released her hold on him and climbed off the bike. Conley kicked down the stand and left the bike as he and Dani approached the building.

It was a small, freestanding structure in the industrial section of Kuala Lumpur, less than half a mile from the Chow Kit shopping area. It was nighttime and relatively quiet, which in an area like this wasn't necessarily a good thing.

Reflexively, Conley hit the safety on the Glock in his shoulder holster. Even if the terrorists weren't home, it was nearly midnight and there was still plenty of potential trouble lurking in the shadows.

They needed to get in and get out of there quickly.

"It says *Machine Parts Importers*, Dani said, reading the sign.

It frustrated Conley to not know the local language. He spoke five languages fluently and could get by on a few more, but Malaysian wasn't on his list. Fortunately, it was on Dani's.

"Looks like no one's home," Conley said. There was only one small window in the front in the first floor, and that was dark. The two windows on the second floor were also dark.

As they approached, Conley heard no sounds coming from inside. More to the point, the building *felt* empty to him.

The steel front door had a doorbell. Conley glanced at Dani, who placed her hand into her purse, where she was no doubt clutching her pistol.

Conley rang the doorbell. It beeped through the door. There was no other sound, no movement, no voices.

He rang it again. He knocked. No response and no sound.

Together, he and Dani did a quick examination of the door.

"No alarm," Dani announced.

Conley pulled out the small lockpick set from his wallet. He grabbed the tension wrench, chose a pick, and went to work. The lock was relatively simple. In less than two minutes, he had it open, while Dani kept watch.

He gave one last knock and pushed the door open as he and Dani took positions on opposite sides. They entered the building, guns drawn. As Dani called out in Malaysian, Conley hit the light switch by the door. Light flooded the mostly empty space that held a few desks, two worktables, and a refrigerator.

There was no movement and no people, but there was a terrible, overpowering smell.

"Oh—what *is* that?" Conley said, pulling up his jacket over his mouth and nose.

"You know," Dani said.

He did. It was a smell you never forgot. It was the smell of death.

They found the bodies in a storage area in the back. There were nearly twenty of them and by the look of the corpses, they had been dead for three days or so. A quick examination showed they had all died the same way: a single gunshot to the back of the head.

By all appearances they hadn't put up a fight. They had just kneeled on the floor, gotten shot, and then died.

"Let's get out of here," Conley said. They left quickly and relocked the door. As soon as they were outside, Conley was on the phone. Bloch answered on the first ring.

* * * *

Lily Randall walked Alex to her room, which was next door to Lily and Renard's suite.

"What agency is the concierge with?" Alex asked when they were inside.

"He's not exactly with an agency. He belongs to Les Clefs d'Or. They are an international association of concierges."

"Concierges?" Alex asked.

Lily smiled. "The best of the best," she said. "Only an elite few can join. Years of training, multiple letters of reference from current members, extensive testing. They go back seventy-five years and are dedicated to providing the highest level of customer service."

"Les Clefs d'Or?"

"Golden flowers," Lily replied.

"That explains the symbol on Paul's lapel," said Alex. "Can I presume they also operate a covert intelligence agency?"

"It's unofficial, but yes. Because of their jobs, they're connected to most service industries in their cities, as well as law enforcement and the press. And they see a lot simply by keeping their eyes open in their hotels. I encountered them when I was in MI Six. Paul will contact me if anything turns up here."

Inside the suite, Alex found her bags unpacked and her closet full of clothes she had never seen before.

"When we pushed up the timetable, we didn't have time to shop for you before we left, so I forwarded your sizes to our concierge," Lily said. "We can do some more shopping, but this will get you started."

Paul had good and expensive taste. Some of his choices were a little bright for her, but the concierge clearly knew the Formula 1 world better than she did.

Alex chose something casual: designer slacks and a top that she knew cost more than she had made most summers in high school. Lily returned similarly dressed, and they headed downstairs.

Of course, whatever Lily wore, it was as if she were introducing it on a catwalk in Milan. And she managed this with her long blond hair in nothing more than a casual ponytail.

Alex didn't think very much about her own appearance, except how it impacted her ability to operate on missions. She had inherited her father's athleticism and was pleased at what her five-foot, six-inch frame could do.

She had also inherited her mother's cheekbones and light brown hair that allowed her to be a credible companion for someone like Lily.

When they reached the lobby, Alex called into Zeta while Lily spoke with Paul. Neither had anything to report.

"If we hurry, we can catch the end of practice," Lily said.

The limo had them there in a few minutes, the driver expertly dodging traffic and throngs of people. The city was full of ultra-modern hotels and apartment buildings, along with quite a bit of old-world European and Middle Eastern architecture.

If this mission gave them some time, she wouldn't mind exploring Monte Carlo. She knew it wasn't quite a city—the government of Monaco called it an administrative area—but it looked like a city to her. Monte Carlo took up about a third of the small nation, which itself was only two square miles. Alex thought she might be able to see quite a bit of it given even half a day.

From the outside, the entrance to the racetrack was just like an entrance to a large sports stadium. Security men ushered their limo through a gate, and soon it was behind the stands.

When they were out of the car and in a covered parking area, Alex heard a roar and felt a rumble under her feet.

"Don't worry," Lily said, seeing Alex's expression.

"Wow, that's loud, and I can feel it," Alex said.

"If you think you can feel it now," Lily said, "wait until we get outside and get a little closer."

* * * *

"Who do you think did it?" Bloch asked into her phone.

Conley's voice was calm, as usual—despite what he and Guo had just found. "Could be anyone, but it was very professional. We had a few minutes on the scene, but there were no obvious signatures of any agency I know. The terrorists were brought into a room and each was killed with a single shot to the back of the head."

Various intelligence agencies had their own styles and methods, but often changed up their modus operandi when they wanted to hide who they were or cast the blame elsewhere.

"Nothing was disturbed," he continued. "No effort was made to make this look like a robbery. Whoever did this entered and did the work as efficiently as possible. Their blood wasn't up and, besides locking the door on their way out, there was no attempt to throw off the scent. And no effort was made to send a message through a gruesome death or the desecration of the bodies. Someone just wanted them dead. How long is Al-Ma'unah's list of enemies?"

"Surprisingly short," Bloch said. "Sure, they are bloodthirsty terrorists, but they have been dormant for years. Even at their height, they never operated outside Malaysia. And they had no local competition from other totalitarian religious groups in their own country."

"Malaysian military intelligence, then," Conley said.

"They are really the only suspects, but O'Neal and Shepard have been watching them closely."

Of course, once Conley and Guo were safely back at their hotel, Bloch would have a local asset call in the murders. Then Zeta could keep an eye on the official investigation and the autopsies, but she was certain they would confirm what her agents had just told her. "Malaysian intelligence shows no messages, no orders, nothing in their computer systems," Bloch went on. "And no sign that they know we've been watching. I've asked the team to find out what every member of the service has had for lunch for the last week, but we don't expect to find anything."

Since Conley and Guo were a full day's travel away from headquarters, Bloch instructed them to stay put. If another mission came up in that part of the world, she would deploy them from Malaysia.

Bloch's next call was to Shepard and O'Neal.

"Anything?"

"Nothing," Shepard said. "And no sign that they know we've been watching."

"And no overtime reports, cash withdrawals, or fund transfers to personal accounts that might indicate use of freelance assets," O'Neal added.

"Analysis?" Bloch asked.

"We will keep digging, but it wasn't Malaysian intelligence, military or otherwise," O'Neal said.

"Keep someone on it anyway. And keep looking elsewhere," Bloch said.

Someone had done this. And there had to be a sign: online chatter, telecommunications records, banking transfers. Even agencies that prided themselves on secrecy still left trails behind their operations.

They had to find something.

Otherwise, it meant that someone was better at keeping secrets than Zeta was at uncovering them.

And that was unacceptable.

Chapter 8

Damn, that's loud, Alex thought as the first car sped past them.

Besides the sound, she could feel the engine reverberate in her chest. It took a second for her to realize that the car was red and black, the colors of the Renard Tech logo.

"Is that ours?" Alex asked Lily.

The car cleared the grandstand area and disappeared around a turn. Alex knew this Formula 1 circuit used mostly city streets, which meant that she could only see part of the track—which her quick research told her was just over two miles around.

In no time, the car was back, taking the straightaway portion of the track in front of them at what she guessed was nearly two hundred miles an hour. The crowd behind her gasped as the car flew past them, and even Alex caught her breath as she felt the roar of the engine in her chest.

And this was with just one car on the track. What must it be like with twenty cars vying for position in a winner-take-all race?

Less than a minute later Alex heard the car again, but the sound of the engine told her that it was losing speed. It peaked around the turn to their right and slowed down more before turning into the pit area in front of the team garage.

There was a smattering of applause from their grandstand, which was impressive in its own right. The stands had seats for at least twenty thousand spectators, and Alex knew it was just one of the seating areas around the track.

After the car came to a stop, it was swarmed by the twenty-man pit crew in black- and-red Renard jumpsuits. They helped the driver out of the car and he turned to shake the hands of a gray-haired man in a black-and-red team polo shirt.

The driver took off his helmet, and Alex was surprised to see that he was Scott Renard. An audible gasp from Lily next to her told Alex that she wasn't the only one surprised by that information.

As they approached, Renard nodded in their direction. The white-haired man said, "Miss Randall."

"Chief," Lily said, smiling openly.

"Alex, meet Jonathan Clarke, our team principal," Renard said. "Jonathan, this is Lily's friend Alex Morgan."

Alex extended her hand. The older man shook it. "How do you do, Miss Morgan?"

"Well, how are you?"

"That depends on how our young Master Renard likes the new gearbox," he said, looking over at Renard.

"It's amazing, feels instantaneous. And it's obviously performed very well so far," Renard said.

"The carbon fiber titanium case saves some weight," Clarke said, "and the new shape gave us a brilliant boost in aerodynamics. If it holds up for the season, we'll be fine." Clarke shifted his gaze to Alex. "Scott tells me you are primarily interested in motorcycles."

"I am. Italian mostly. I have a small repair shop in Boston," she said.

"Alex Morgan... Are you part of Morgan Exotic Motorcycle and Car Repair by any chance?" asked Clarke.

Alex couldn't hide her genuine surprise. "Yes, that's me."

"Did you just take on the restoration of a Morbidelli eight-fifty?"

"You know Italian bikes?" Alex said.

"I know that one. And I know there are only four of them, so the restoration is news. It's all Philippe in the garage talks about. He'll want to meet you. A number of the team will."

"Scott, I didn't know you drove," Alex said, turning to Renard.

"Not as much as I used to," Renard said.

"The stockholders don't like it," Clarke offered.

"I only drive on practice days and try to keep the speed down," Renard said. "But I do like to test any changes in the car. It helps me tweak the programming of the simulator for our real drivers."

Alex saw Lily twitch next to her, followed by a noticeable stiffening of the woman's posture. Alex suspected there was more to that story.

It looked like Renard sensed it, too. He turned to the chief and said, "I'm going to take our guest to the paddock."

They made their good-byes and Renard took the women behind the pit area to a cluster of modern two- and three-story professional buildings.

"I know you want to see the garage and the cars," he told Alex, "but we can do that after the team qualifies this afternoon. It'll be madness in the pit and the garage until then." Gesturing to the black-and-red building with the large Renard Tech logo on it, he said, "This is our motor home."

"Motor home?" Alex said.

"That's what they call them," Lily explained. "Each team has a temporary structure that travels with them."

"These are temporary?" Alex studied the glass and steel buildings that seemed more like modern offices.

"It all breaks down to fit into cargo containers," Renard said. "That way, we can set it up again in a new city in three days. The top floor has an excellent view of the finish line if you want to watch us practice."

Inside, there were dozens of people clustered around a bar, various large flat- screens and tables, while waitstaff weaved through the room with trays in hand.

It looked like a cross between a fancy cocktail party and a hopping sports bar. In the center of the floor was a Renard Formula 1 car, a different model than the one she'd seen on the track.

"These people are partners: sponsors, journalists, Formula One people, and various fans," Lily said.

They made their way to the center where the car sat. "This is our first car," said Renard. "Our first year we didn't place in a single Grand Prix, but we learned a lot. It's still my favorite car to drive."

There it was again—the nearly involuntary twitch on Lily's face.

"Scott Renard!" a female voice shouted from halfway across the room. It took Alex a few seconds to place the accent. Russian.

A woman in a set of white driver's coveralls approached. Alex recognized the Marussia F1 logo. They were one of the newer teams—though not as new as the Renard Tech team.

"Are you driving today, or are you wearing that to flirt with me?" the woman said to Renard.

She had long blond hair and was stunningly attractive. Even in a racing jumpsuit, she looked like a model. In that way she reminded Alex a little bit of Lily.

Her face was familiar, which was not a surprise. Formula 1 only had a couple of female drivers.

"Hello, Lily," the woman said with a smile on her face.

"Hello, Jenya," Lily said.

Jenya looked Lily over and then turned to Renard. "Scott, are you my competition today?"

Renard smiled politely. "No, you'll have tougher competition than me."

"I'm sorry to hear that, *Scott*," said Jenya, her voice lingering on his name. "Since I won't see you on the track, perhaps we can catch up later?"

"Perhaps," he said evenly. He seemed immune to her playful flirting. "And who is your friend, Lily?" Jenya asked, glancing at Alex.

"Alex Morgan," Lily said. "A friend of mine from Boston. She deals in Italian motorcycles and exotic cars. Alex, this is Jenya Orlov. She drives for Marussia."

Alex extended her hand and Jenya shook it. "Of course, I've heard of you," Alex said. "Marussia is a Russian team, isn't it?"

Jenya took a second to study Alex. Before the stare made Alex genuinely uncomfortable, Jenya smiled. "Half Russian, half British. We're based in the UK, which is where I first ran into our Lily. Motorcycles, did you say?"

"Yes," Alex said.

"A bit slow for me," said Jenya. "I prefer the power and speed of Formula One. We'll have to get you in a car before you leave us." She studied Alex again. "Unless you prefer your NASCAR cars. They go slower, which I suspect goes better with your country music."

"Not slower on a long enough straightaway," Alex said.

"You think so?" Jenya said, her face showing mild surprise.

"Of course," said Alex. "Formula One cars take turns faster, but they'd better, considering that a Formula One racer—at twenty million dollars—costs more than ten times your average NASCAR racer. And that doesn't include the half-billion-dollar budgets that fund each of the Formula One teams and their R and D. Of course, the cars are still *vastly* overpowered for the money, which, I suppose, they need to be to compensate for the insane aerodynamic downforce that keeps you on the road at those speeds. As I understand it, the force is the equivalent of the stopping power of a midsized American car with its brakes fully engaged. That's a lot to overcome, so you need that power *and* that budget. And even with all of those advantages, a NASCAR racer will leave you in the dust on a highway."

Alex realized that the three people around her had gone silent, and she wondered if she had gone too far. Jenya appeared genuinely shocked, and for a second Alex wondered if the woman would hit her. Then the Russian burst into laughter.

"In that case, we definitely have to get you behind the wheel of one of our cars," Jenya said. "See if we can change your mind."

"Good luck today," Lily said. "Perhaps this year will give you your first Grand Prix win."

"Perhaps," said Jenya, "but watch my points. I play the long game." She waved to Scott. "Good to see you again, Scott. Nice to meet you, Alex." With a tight smile, she added, "Lily."

"Jenya," Lily returned.

Jenya headed across the room to greet an older gentleman in a dark suit.

"I think you made an impression," Renard said to Alex.

"Was that all true?" Lily asked.

"I think so," Alex said. Turning to Renard she added, "No offense to your sport."

"None taken," Renard said. "It's true. The cars are overengineered, but that's much of the point for me. The team shares resources with Renard Aerospace. Wind tunnel, advanced materials, fabrication resources—that sort of thing. A surprising amount of what we do to build our cars has applications in our aircraft and satellite launch systems."

"Jenya looks very familiar," Alex asked. "Where have I seen her before?"

"There aren't a lot of female Formula One drivers," Renard said. "And fewer who have qualified at the Grand Prix level."

"She's yet to win a major race," Lily chimed in. "You probably know her from the tabloids, Alex, or one of her many ads and endorsements. Most are in Europe, but some have made it to the US."

"I'm going to the pit, I'll watch from there." Renard kissed Lily and headed for the door.

"Come on," Lily said, leading Alex to the stairs. They came out on the third floor, which opened into a large outdoor deck where a crowd was gathering.

Lily was stopped and greeted almost as many times as Renard had been. That made sense. She and Renard had been together for over three years, and this must have been a big part of Lily's life outside of Zeta.

Alex smelled hot popcorn. She spied a machine next to a row of vintage arcade games. A closer look told her they were driving games.

"That's Scott in a nutshell," Lily said, gesturing to the room.

After a quick stop at the bar to get a drink, they made their way up to the deck. Standing at the railing, they had a remarkable view of the track. One of the two Renard Tech cars was at the starting line, revving its engine.

Alex knew that these practices were important. Soon the drivers would have to qualify. The qualification rounds not only determined which drivers would be able to compete, they also determined the driver's starting position.

A moment later, the Renard car shot forward. Once again, Alex was struck by how loud the engine was and how much it reverberated in her chest.

"Who is the driver?" Alex asked.

"Terry Fuller," replied Lily. "He's the younger of the two. At twenty-one, he's the youngest on the circuit this year."

"Do you think he'll give Jenya a run for her money?"

Lily actually laughed at that, watching a monitor as the car flew past them to start another lap.

"If he keeps his time up, yes," she said.

* * * *

"Give me something," Bloch said to the agents assembled around her. Once again, the group included every available agent who was in Boston at the time. "Based on Conley and Guo's observations on the scene and the follow-up work by Malaysian intelligence, we now know that the Al-Ma'unah cell had constructed several large explosive devices and stockpiled a number of weapons. We also know that the target of their planned attack was a local military base."

Karen O'Neal was the first to speak. "We can say with almost complete certainty that the murder of the members of the terror cell in Malaysia was not the work of Malaysian intelligence. The operation also doesn't fit the modus operandi or agenda of any known intelligence agency or terror group."

"Local organized crime, maybe?" Spartan asked. "Did they run afoul of some nearby gangsters?" As a TACH team leader and perhaps the best tactical person at Zeta, Spartan didn't like the murky side of their business. She always preferred a clear target and a clear objective.

On that, Spartan and Bloch were in complete agreement.

"It's possible, but we could find no evidence to support the idea. No electronic chatter in the Kuala Lumpur criminal underground. No electronic communications or cash transfers between the Al-Ma'unah cell and any known criminal groups. None of that rules out the possibility, but there's no evidence we can find."

"Where does that leave us?" Bloch asked. "The threat-assessment system identifies a potential problem. The Al-Ma'unah terrorists are the most likely candidates to carry out that kind of operation, but they get mysteriously killed before they can do it?"

"We did find that they recently received a large infusion of outside funding. We tried to track it, but whoever provided the money is very good. They used multiple offshore accounts and shell companies. And at least two of the entities who made the transfers no longer exist," O'Neal said.

"Some mysterious outside group funded them and, for all we know, directed them, while possibly another outside group murdered them just before their attack. We may be hunting two groups with unknown motives, each of which is very good at hiding," Spartan said, visibly uncomfortable.

"That is how it appears," O'Neal said.

There was more there, something O'Neal was reluctant to say.

"Appears?" Bloch asked.

O'Neal glanced at Shepard and then said, "We have a theory, but we have no real evidence for it."

"Try me," Bloch said.

"What if it's not two different groups, but one?" Shepard interjected.

"You're saying that the same people funded them, possibly even directed them, and then murdered them before they could complete their mission? Why would anyone do that?" Spartan said.

"Because of us," O'Neal said.

"Or because of our threat-assessment system," Shepard said. "It's the most accurate system ever developed, and it's helped us stop an unprecedented number of attacks, or pass along intel to the relevant agencies to prevent or prepare for those attacks. Our working theory is that someone is trying to make us chase our tail, or doubt our system, or both," Shepard said.

"That would explain the unusual number of false positives we've been getting," Bloch said.

"Okay, that makes sense, but why?" Spartan asked.

"To make us doubt our system," Shepard said. "Or maybe to keep us and other friendly intelligence services too busy dealing with phantom threats to thwart their real agenda, whatever that is."

"And those false positives may not have been false," O'Neal said. "They could have been operations like Kuala Lumpur, which were initiated and then terminated before they could happen. We only know about this one because Conley and Guo were able to track down the group planning the attack. This may have happened before," she added, "and we didn't know it."

Bloch didn't like where this was going. Zeta and its friends had a hard enough time keeping up with the threats they knew about from the players they understood.

"Since Manila, the events in the Caucasus Mountains and a half dozen other incidents," Bloch said, "we've been suspecting the existence of another player with unknown motives, either a new group or an existing one who has somehow vastly increased its capabilities. Mr. Smith and the leaders of the Aegis Initiative have been looking into the possibility."

"We're calling them Ares," Shepard said.

"Ares?" Bloch asked.

"The Greek god of war," O'Neal said. "It also means *bane* or *curse*."

"As good a name as any," Bloch said. "Have you speculated about their motives? If Zeta stands for stability, peace, and human rights, what would Ares want?"

"The opposite," said O'Neal.

"We've thought a lot about this," Shepard said. "Who benefits from oppression, instability, and war? In their extreme form, these things cause countries to fall. They create a vacuum. And who benefits from such a vacuum?"

"In the long run, it's whoever fills the vacuum, whoever seizes power," Bloch said. "Do you have any evidence to back up your thinking?"

O'Neal and Shepard shrugged. "None whatsoever," Shepard said.

"And yet it fits the facts," said Bloch. "Everyone keep this theory in mind until something better comes along. In the meantime, beat every bush, check in with every asset, call every contact you know to see if we can learn more about the situation in Kuala Lumpur. The more we learn about it, the sooner we'll know what we're up against."

After the agents filed out, Bloch sat in the room by herself and let the weight of what was going on sink in. For some time, she and Smith had been discussing the possibility of a new player emerging in the international mayhem business. Now, of course, O'Neal and Shepard had not only vocalized their theory, they even gave this theoretical agency a name: Ares.

She didn't like the sound of it, but that, she supposed, was the point.

In many ways it was a wild notion, nothing but speculation—more of a fantasy than a theory based on evidence. And there was always the danger of seeing patterns where none existed.

Pattern-seeking was human nature. Even career intelligence people—who were trained to see only what was there and not what they expected or wanted to see—were susceptible to it.

The theory also played into their ego. Zeta was a lean and very effective organization. Was it hubris to invent a worthy adversary who threatened the world that Zeta fought every day to protect?

It probably *was* pride and of the worst kind, especially since there was no actual proof that such an organization even existed.

But Bloch couldn't shake the growing sense that this enemy did exist, exactly as Shepard and O'Neal theorized.

Diana Bloch was not Dan Morgan, who—though a surprisingly thorough and meticulous planner when it came to his missions—had made a career on hunches and wild insights that more often than not turned out to be correct. Yet Bloch had done this long enough to trust her own intuition.

Something had changed during the last two years. Groups with nothing in common were suddenly cooperating. Terrorist operations in different parts of the world, seemingly completely unrelated, somehow timed their activities perfectly to push counterintelligence resources to the limit—and beyond.

Ares was as good a name as any for this new phenomenon, and it would have to do until something better came along.

Chapter 9

Not surprisingly, the dress fit perfectly. Lily had forwarded her and Alex's measurements to Paul the concierge, and he had chosen dresses for both of them for tonight. Alex knew that Dolce & Gabbana was taking some heat for their new metallics this year, which most people saw as retro. But Alex liked the high shine of the classic A-line shimmering gold dress, right out of the Dolce & Gabbana spring collection.

She liked Paul's taste and didn't care if the fashion press didn't think it broke enough ground. When it came to clothes (whether it was tactical gear or evening wear), Alex just wanted it to work for the mission. It didn't need to make a statement.

Alex was still mildly surprised when she found that she had an opinion on fashion trends. Just a few years ago, she had been in high school, and her uniform for saving the world was jeans and T-shirts—back when saving the world meant protesting some US military action or environmental policy.

She'd learned a lot about the world—and saving it—since then. She had also seen that the uniforms worn by the people who were out there actually saving the world varied wildly.

On her last undercover mission, she had posed as a spoiled heiress, but her role there was limited to logistics and support. One of the things that assignment had taught her was that there was more than one way to serve.

She had also learned that it didn't hurt to look good while you were doing it. During that time Alex had picked up a few nice pairs of shoes, like the strappy Manolo Blahniks she was wearing now.

Just as she was finishing getting ready, there was a knock on her door. Lily and Renard were waiting outside. Dressed for the evening and made up, Lily looked beautiful, which was to be expected.

Renard in formal clothes, however, was a bit of a surprise.

He was wearing a tuxedo with a crisp white dinner jacket. He had shaved and slicked back his hair.

For the first time since Alex met him, Scott Renard looked like the billionaire industrialist he was, not the slightly awkward programmer she had come to know.

"Alex, you look lovely," Renard said.

"Thank you..." Alex said. It took her a moment to process how good he actually looked. "So do you."

A few minutes later they were in the limo on the way back to the racetrack. The hospitality village created by the various team "motor homes" was hopping. Out in the open air, people in evening wear were milling around, while techno club music thrummed from inside each structure, and searchlights lit up the night sky.

Inside the Renard paddock, a crowd of well-dressed people were drinking and enjoying themselves. In the center of the floor was a DJ booth. Alex recognized the celebrity DJ who was dating some TV actress.

She saw quite a few celebrities. Some actors she knew by name and others by sight only. She recognized more than one pop singer. The rest were American and European businesspeople and politicians.

Chief Clarke and a number of others from the garage and the pit were there. Though the chief looked uncomfortable, the rest of his team seemed to be enjoying themselves.

Renard was greeted by everyone, as he, Lily, and Alex made their way to the center, where the Renard Formula 1 car sat next to the DJ booth.

Renard approached two men standing by the car. Lily greeted the men with kisses on the cheek and Renard said, "Alex, this is Alonzo Maduro and Terry Fuller, our team drivers. Gentlemen, this is Alex Morgan, a friend of Lily's."

"Miss Morgan," Maduro said politely, shaking her hand. He was in his early thirties, and from his bio Alex knew he was from Spain. He was an experienced Formula 1 driver, with a few Grand Prix under his belt as a driver for the Mercedes and Haas teams.

Terry Fuller was no older than Alex herself. "Hi Alex," he said, shaking her hand and smiling. He was good-looking in a clean-cut and earnest way, with hazel eyes and short brown hair.

"Alex is from Boston," Renard said. "She deals in exotic motorcycles, specializing in—"

"Wait—are you from Morgan Exotic Motorcycle and Car Repair?" Fuller said to her.

"Yes," Alex said, "that's my shop."

"Wow," the young man said. "You got the restoration of the Morbidelli eight-fifty, didn't you?"

"Yes, but how did you know about that?"

"There are only a handful in the world, and one is in your shop," Fuller said enthusiastically. "The restoration is big news, at least for people who follow specialty Italian motorcycles."

"Well, I've run into two of you today," Alex said. "Chief Clarke also knew about the restoration."

"I'm not surprised," Fuller said. "There isn't a lot in the motorsports world that the chief doesn't know. I've been following his career since I was a kid. He's the reason I'm here. When I heard he'd moved to Renard, I knew the team was going places." The driver began to smile, then caught himself, shooting a nervous glance at Renard. "Well, that and the fact that the team is cutting edge, of course..."

"Don't worry about it, Terry," Renard said. "The chief is the reason I'm here, too. I wouldn't have started the team without him."

"Hey, do you have a minute to get a drink?" Fuller asked Alex.

"Sure," she said.

As Terry led her to the bar, the crowd actually parted for him, with more then one person looking at him with awe, the way that people looked at actors and other stars.

Alex also noted that quite a few women eyed her with jealousy and distrust.

He was stopped half a dozen times by people asking to take selfies with him and wishing him luck. With friendly reserve, Fuller accommodated his fans, and when they reached the bar he said to Alex, "Sorry about that."

"Not at all. You are clearly a hit here," Alex said.

"Well, I do drive very fast," he said.

Alex laughed.

"Look, Formula One is not something people in America understand," Fuller said. "It's a very European sport. In the States, we have baseball and football and basketball...and hockey. But in Europe, they have soccer and Formula One, so we have to do the job of two professional sports," he said.

Behind Fuller, Alex could see three women eyeing him openly. Nodding toward them, she said, "Your public seems very...devoted."

Then Fuller did something that surprised Alex: He blushed. "Like I said, I drive fast. And the racing jumpsuits are very flattering. But it really is a team sport; there are over two hundred people on the Renard team. The truth is, driving is only half of it. The car itself is the other half."

He disappeared for a minute and returned with her gin and tonic.

"So how did you get involved with the Europeans and their sport?" Alex asked.

"My dad had a garage in Indianapolis when I was growing up," Fuller said.

"You grew up around the Indy Five-hundred," Alex said. "Oldest auto race in the world."

"Yes." He looked impressed that she had known that. "The speedway also hosts NASCAR races, and while the cars in the Five-hundred are different from Formula One, there's a fair amount of overlap with Formula One teams and drivers."

"So why not stay in Indianapolis?" Alex asked. "Why Formula One?"

"The cars," replied Fuller. "They're works of art. Don't get me wrong, I love the Indy cars. They are amazing but use mainly stock components. As a result, the Five-hundred is more of a driver's contest. But Formula One cars are custom and handcrafted. They push every performance and engineering envelope you can imagine."

That Alex understood. It wasn't a surprise that someone who saw the appeal of a machine like the Morbidelli motorcycle would be attracted to Formula 1 cars.

She decided that Fuller might be someone worth getting to know.

"Terry, are you trying to recruit Alex to team Renard?" a Russian-accented voice said from behind Alex.

"Hello, Jenya," Fuller said politely.

Alex turned and saw Jenya Orlov wearing a very revealing halter dress. Now Alex remembered where she had seen Jenya before. She'd done some risqué racing-themed ads for a Russian vodka company.

"Fuller here was making quite a case for Formula One," Alex said.

"Please call me Terry," Fuller said, and added to Jenya, "Why aren't you back at the Marussia center?"

Jenya rolled her eyes. "I'm not as much of a team player as you are. Back there, it's nothing but oligarchs, EU ministers, and Russian gas company executives. They all get a little handsy. Plus, I prefer the ambiance here." She gestured to the DJ. "The entertainment is better and frankly, so is the company."

She punctuated the last with a meaningful glance at Terry, who seemed like he might blush again.

"Perhaps you'd like to recruit *me*," Jenya said. "Do you think I would fit in at team Renard?"

"Unfortunately, we're full up," Terry said.

"Maybe it's time for your senior driver to retire," Jenya said. "Maduro is a pro, but he's never been on the podium."

That rankled Terry. "Scott has complete faith in Alonzo; we all do." He pointed to the car in the center of the lounge. "Take a good look at team Renard rear wing. It's very distinctive, and you will be seeing a lot of it on the track."

Jenya laughed and said cheerfully, "We'll see about that, Terry."

As soon as Jenya left, the three women who had been eyeing him earlier, stepped up. He took selfies with each and autographed their forearms.

"I better go and mingle," he said to Alex. "There are a lot of sponsors here, suppliers, journalists."

"Of course, I shouldn't monopolize you," Alex said.

"Will you be around during practice tomorrow?" he asked. "I can introduce you to the guys at the garage."

That was interesting, Alex thought. Not, *You can come watch me run the course,* but *I can introduce you to the guys in the garage.*

"Definitely, I'll see you then," Alex said.

After he left her, she explored the paddock and was outside enjoying the beautifully-lit track when Lily and Renard found her.

"What happened to your new friend?" Lily asked with a smile.

"Terry was in great demand," Alex replied evenly.

"Well, I've concluded my business for the night," Renard said. "We're heading out to the casino. Would you like to join us, Alex? Or, you're welcome to stay here. The party is just starting."

"A casino in Monte Carlo?" Alex said, downing the rest of her drink. "I'm in."

* * * *

"That's odd," Shepard said, studying his screen.

His system had been set to send him alerts for any unusual reports in Monte Carlo. This one definitely qualified.

"Karen, what do you make of this?" Shepard asked.

Karen O'Neal was on the other side of the wide desk that made up the front of their workstation. She wheeled her chair over and studied his monitor for a minute.

"Within normal parameters, if a little on the high side," O'Neal said.

"True, but this isn't an area in which we want to take any chances, especially with so much loose plutonium running around," he said. "The radiation detectors have been triggered twelve times in a single day. That has happened before, but only maybe twice in the last two years."

Most major cities had radiation detectors now. In fact, they were getting more and more common in smaller cities and some larger towns. And they were getting more and more sensitive every day.

That sensitivity had created a new problem. Radioisotopes were regularly used for cancer treatment and testing. That meant that cancer patients now often set off detectors, especially where large crowds were involved.

That usually meant the identified parties had a quick interview with local police and were on their way.

"What does your threat-detection system say?" Shepard asked.

"Still identifies Monaco as a high-probability target for a major event in the next week," O'Neal said. "But we've gotten so many false positives lately…"

"Right, but with Kuala Lumpur we know that at least some of those false positives were only false because someone took out the terrorists before they could carry out their attack."

"That mean we have to assume the threat to Monaco is real," O'Neal said.

"Absolutely, especially with the plutonium out there," he said.

"And if you wanted to move plutonium into a city, you'd want to test the radiation detectors," O'Neal said. "Let me take another glance at that data."

She grabbed his keyboard and clicked away. "This is what was really unusual about the radiation-sensor hits. Each one of them has been easily explained. There hasn't been a single false positive, or even a situation where the authorities couldn't find the cancer patient who set off the alarm."

"Because in every other instance in the last two years where you've had this many hits in a single day," Shepard said, "there were at least a couple you couldn't explain."

"Exactly," O'Neal said. "Someone is testing the system but wants to make sure that the test doesn't generate any special interest."

Shepard was impressed at her ability to see deviations in a system. As a mathematician, O'Neal was brilliant, but she was also very practically minded. She solved problems logically and step-by-step, whereas Shepard himself was more intuitive. Yet, when there was a quirk in the data, she zeroed in on it until she understood it.

That was one of the reasons they were such a good team.

He studied her face as she concentrated on the screen. Yes, *one* of the reasons.

"Someone is testing the radiation sensors, and someone has been testing our threat-detection system," Shepard said. "The same people?"

"It's tempting to think that," O'Neal said, "but we have no reason to believe it."

"And we can't afford to take a radiological threat lightly with missing plutonium out there," Shepard said. "This could be another false positive for our threat analysis, or this could be the reason for all the other false positives. Let's say Ares actually exists. Maybe they wanted us to let our guard down so they could execute whatever they are planning in Monte Carlo."

"Given the stakes, we have to pursue all possible leads, but that's the case with all of the threats we've had that didn't pan out," O'Neal said.

"But no one has the resources to do that every time," said Shepard, "which is part of the game. Eventually we'll miss something, and then Ares gets what they want, whatever that is." In frustration, he pounded his head down into the desk.

"What do we do right now?" she asked.

"I think we need to have Lily and Alex talk to some cancer patients."

Chapter 10

"Which casino is this?"

"There is only one for us," Renard said as the limo pulled up to the large nineteenth-century building.

"Casino de Monte-Carlo," Lily said in perfectly accented French.

It was huge and impressive, a nineteenth-century Belle Epoque structure that seemed more like a British or French manor house—or Buckingham Palace—than any casino Alex had ever seen. Though it was in the center of a bustling city, it was set back from the road behind a large circular fountain.

Though their own limousine was a Rolls-Royce, it was far from the most impressive car out front. She saw two Ferraris, a Bentley, and a vintage Lamborghini that would have impressed even her father, who was not much of a fan of European cars.

The trio was greeted at the door by two impeccably dressed and smiling staff who welcomed them warmly, but it was clear to Alex that their hospitality was directed primarily at Renard.

That made sense. He was, after all, a billionaire. And even if you had never used a computer and somehow hadn't heard of Renard Tech, everyone in Monte Carlo knew that Renard was the owner of a Formula 1 team that was the newest of the twenty teams that competed in the race, and after only five years had made itself into a real contender.

One of the staff escorted them through the large doors. If possible, the casino was even more impressive on the inside, with large vaulted ceilings, fine art on the walls, and ornate gold leaf detailing everywhere.

"Monsieur Renard, if you can wait briefly, our manager would like a word," one of the men said.

"Of course," Renard replied.

"I'm trying not to gape," Alex whispered to Lily as she looked around her.

"It never ceases to amaze me," Lily said.

A well-dressed, white-haired man greeted the group and took Renard to the side. Alex caught only a few key words, but it was clear that the manager was offering Renard the moon.

Renard listened respectfully, asked some questions, and graciously allowed the man to do his job. A fascinated Alex realized that she was in one of—if not *the*—finest casino in the world with a billionaire.

Renard shook the man's hand and thanked him.

"Scott is good at dealing with people," Alex said.

"Yes, he's good at almost everything," Lily said.

"So, I've seen him in his hoodie, his racing jumpsuit, and now this," Alex said, pointing to the white tuxedo. "Which one is his real uniform?"

Lily thought about it. "All of them," she said.

As Renard and the manager made their way back to Lily and Alex, she heard him say, "Thank you, sir, I know my way around, and we're looking forward to exploring a bit."

"Of course, Monsieur Renard, but please take my card," the manager said. "My personal number is on it, and I hope you won't hesitate to use it if there is anything you need."

"Thank you, sir, I will," Renard said, shaking the man's hand again.

As they moved deeper into the casino, Alex was struck by how little it looked like any other casino she had ever seen.

It was more like an estate or a palace than a gambling hall. Renard took them to a small private room with a bar, where he ordered them drinks and where they sat for few minutes.

It didn't take long for Scott to get antsy.

"Would you like to get started?" Lily asked.

"Yes, if you ladies don't mind," Renard said, getting up.

He led them through a large room that actually did look like a casino, with roulette, craps, and blackjack tables surrounded by the familiar slot and video poker machines.

"Didn't Albert Einstein say that the only way to beat the casino is to grab some money when they're not looking?" Lily asked dryly.

"Yes," Renard countered, "but it was Fast Eddie who said that money won is twice as sweet as money earned."

"What do you play?" Alex asked as they entered another room. This one was full of green felt tables, where neatly dressed but normal-looking people were playing various card games.

"Only one game," he said, leading them to a blackjack table. He leaned in, whispering conspiratorially, "I'm trying out a new system."

"Do you count cards?" Alex asked.

"In a way," Renard replied.

"Doesn't the casino frown on that?"

"Not the way Scott does it," Lily said.

Renard shrugged. "I haven't won yet."

"Yes, that's one way to put it," said Lily.

"Well, as long as you can afford to lose," Alex said.

"Alex, a schoolteacher could afford to lose what Scott bets," Lily said.

At the table Renard picked, Alex saw a sign with the posted minimum bet—20 euro.

Renard was immediately defensive. "It's not about the money, it's about the challenge."

Lily smiled indulgently as Renard took a seat at the table. "Feel free to explore if this is too rich for your blood," she said to Alex, leaning in and adding, "This is not going to take long, and will be followed by a period of sulking. You don't want to stick around for that."

Just as Alex turned to go check out the rest of the casino, she heard a familiar voice behind her. "Scott, how nice to see you," the voice said in a light Russian accent.

It was Jenya. Nodding to Lily and Alex, the woman scanned the table and said, "What's the matter, Scott, were the penny slots full?"

"Slots are not for me," Renard said. "The odds are terrible."

Shifting her gaze to Alex, Jenya said, "Would you like to see another side of the casino?"

As Lily took the seat next to Renard, she said, "Go, Alex. We'll be fine."

Something about the tone in Lily's voice told Alex that her partner would be relieved to be rid of Jenya. Though Renard seemed immune to the woman's charms, Alex had no trouble understanding why Lily would be uncomfortable just the same.

Plus, Alex really was interested in seeing the *other* side of Monte Carlo. "Sure," she said to Jenya, and the two of them headed out.

As they strolled through the casino, Jenya was greeted with polite hellos and "Good evening, Mademoiselle Orlov," by a shockingly large number of the staff.

Renard may have gotten the billionaire treatment from the manager, but based on the number of people Jenya knew, it was clear to Alex that she must have spent a significant amount time in the casino.

She took Alex to another bar in the back. This one was much bigger and overlooked the city. It also had a different crowd. Alex didn't recognize most of them, but the ones she did know were at the absolute top of the finance and entertainment world.

After they bought drinks at the bar and settled into the high chairs at the counter, Jenya asked, "How did you meet Scott and Lily?"

Alex didn't have to think about her reply. She had planned and rehearsed her answer, which had the benefit of actually being true. "I met Lily through work and Scott through her."

"And how does a girl from Boston become interested in European motorcycles?" Jenya asked.

"My father deals in cars, classic American cars."

That interested Jenya. "Does that mean Italian motorcycles are a rebellion?"

For a second Alex didn't know how to respond. "I never thought about it. But maybe. I do like the bikes, though. I ride a Ducati Panigale V four S."

"I don't know much about those," Jenya said, "but I understand they have a lot of horsepower. I'm more of a car person myself."

"To be expected in your business," said Alex. "You and my dad would have a lot to talk about. How does a girl from Russia end up in Formula One?"

"My own rebellion, I suppose," Jenya said.

"Did your parents work in motorcycles?"

"No. I didn't know my father. Because he wasn't there, my mother had to work quite a bit and died a few years ago."

"Oh, I'm so sorry. I didn't mean to—"

"Don't worry about it," said Jenya. "My rebellion was against the bleak life in Russia. Even when you are comfortable, it's not like America." Jenya scanned the room. "Or anything like this." Jenya smiled, adding, "And, of course, I like to drive fast, and, as it turns out, I'm good at it."

"I looked up your ranking," Alex said. "You did well last year, and the press says you're one of the drivers to watch this season."

"Yes, I'd like to beat Mercedes and Ferrari," Jenya said. "Entitled half-wits. That's one of the things I like about your Scott. All the other Formula One teams buy their engines from the same four suppliers, and three of those suppliers have their own teams. But Scott builds his own engines, and after only five years is now in a position to challenge the oldest teams in the sport. He plays every game to win, even when it's a low-stakes game of blackjack."

"Like Scott," Alex said, "I was raised to believe that anything worth doing was worth overdoing."

"Then let me show you how we overdo things in Monte Carlo," said Jenya.

The women finished their drinks and headed out of the bar to the casino floor. "What do you play?" Jenya asked.

"I grew up playing poker."

"What kind?"

"My mother's mother was a poker encyclopedia, so all of it," Alex said. "I like Guts but my favorite is seven-card Follow the Queen. In casinos, I like roulette, but just for fun."

"Smart. That's the only way to play roulette. Do you know the Monte Carlo fallacy?"

"No," Alex said.

"It's also called the gambler's fallacy," said Jenya. "It was born in this casino. In 1913, a number of wealthy patrons noticed that at one particular roulette table, black came up again and again. Every time it came up, the players increased their next bets on red, believing that every time the ball landed on black, that increased the chances of it landing on red the next time." Jenya chuckled. "By the time the night was over, the ball had fallen on black twenty-six times in a row and some of the wealthiest people in Europe had lost millions. They failed to grasp the most fundamental rule of gambling and certainly of roulette: the law of statistical probability. The game doesn't care what happened the last time, or the ten times before that. Or a hundred times before that. Each spin is a brand-new event, and the odds of red or black are always exactly the same."

"What do you play?" Alex asked.

"Our dear Scott is right to play blackjack. The odds are good, among the best in the casino, but we are in Monte Carlo; we have to play baccarat."

They entered a plush room that contained several U-shaped tables surrounded by extremely well-dressed people from around the world. There were men and women of various ethnicities in Western dress, others in colorful Indian garb, and more than one man in Middle Eastern robes.

They were greeted by two attendants who knew Jenya by name and who asked if there was anything special that the two women needed. Jenya waved them off and led Alex to one of the curved baccarat tables. There were three other gamblers at the five-person table.

Alex said she'd be happy just to watch and learn. Jenya had a brief word with a man who, Alex assumed, was the manager. He left and quickly returned with a tray of casino chips. Alex saw with surprise that they were 1000 euros each, arranged in five stacks of five.

"I have a house account," Jenya said and proceeded to explain to Alex the rules of the game. "Two cards are dealt to the player and two to the dealer, who is called the banker. The entire table bets on the outcome of those four cards. But this is not blackjack; no one chooses to take another card. Whether or not another card is drawn is determined by the rules of the house. The only choice the bettors make is whether to bet on the banker or the player. The hand with the most points wins, though sometimes there is a tie. Nine is the highest number you can get. Tens and face cards count for zero. Numbered cards count for face value, unless that value exceeds ten. In that case, you subtract ten from the total. So, two sixes become a two, and two eights become a six. It's really quite simple. Watch."

There were two squares in front of each seat, one marked *jouer,* which Alex knew was French for "player," and one marked *banque,* which meant the house or the "bank." There was another square marked *nul,* which meant "tie."

Jenya placed a bet on the square in front of her seat marked *jouer.* Alex was amazed to see that the bet was for 5000 euros.

When the other players made their bets, the croupier dealt two cars to the spot marked *player* and two to the *banque.*

The bank's hand had a jack and a four.

"*Naturel,*" the croupier announced and slid five thousand-euro chips to Jenya.

"That's was a natural; eight or nine are automatic winners," Jenya explained.

In the next hand, the bank had a three to the player's six. Jenya had bet on the bank and won again.

They had been at the table for less than five minutes, and Jenya had won 10,000 euros.

Jenya noticed Alex's amazement. "Don't be too impressed, Alex. It's still early. And as you can see, we are far from the highest rollers in the room."

That was true. At their table, a man in a traditional white Arab robe called a *thawb* was betting with 25,000 euro chips and had lost both hands that Jenya had won.

Alex watched as the man put another 25,000 Euro chip on the *tie* square.

Leaning into Alex, Jenya said, "That is what you Americans call a sucker's bet. Pays eight-to-one and has terrible odds."

Jenya lost one hand and then won three in a row. At a table with a 500,000-euro limit, it might not have been a fortune, but to Alex, to win 25,000 euros in less than thirty minutes was unfathomable.

The man in the *thawb* was having a very bad night and what started as frustration had edged into anger. For some reason, he kept shooting bad-tempered glares at Jenya and Alex.

Alex leaned in to Jenya and asked, "Why is he angry at *us*?"

"He probably doesn't approve of the way we are dressed or that we are out unescorted," Jenya replied. "Normally, that might be forgivable, since this is the West, but we're winning and he is not. I've seen him here before. He's a sheik; his name is Nazer. He has oil money, along with profits from arms he sends to his radical friends in Afghanistan… at least that's the rumor." She waved for the manager. "Five thousand for my friend here," she said.

The chips appeared in front of Alex.

"Really, that's not necessary," Alex said.

"No, but it is fun," said Jenya. "Go ahead, play. Consider it an investment. We can split your winnings. Plus, I will enjoy immensely seeing that man's face when we *both* start winning."

Alex smiled at that and Jenya said, "Unless you don't feel confident."

"As you said, it's a simple game." Alex took the seat next to Jenya and placed her first bet on *player.*

"Excellent," Jenya said. "It's still early, and these people have much too much money."

Chapter 11

Shepard heard the chime first and was instantly alert. Karen stirred next to him as he got out of bed. "It's okay. I'll check on it," he said.

Given how many overnights they pulled because of critical situations and how frequently those critical situations had been occurring lately, he was glad that they had taken the time to make a comfortable room for themselves.

Though there were a number of small dormitory-style rooms on the upper floors of the Zeta complex, those rooms were cramped for a couple. Of course, they were the only couple that worked together at Zeta—at least the only couple that lived together.

At any other intelligence agency, people in relationships weren't allowed to serve together, especially if they were in the same department. But Zeta wasn't the CIA, MI6, or any other traditional agency.

And that showed itself in big and small ways. There was much less bureaucracy, for one, and you didn't need five levels of approvals to add resources or equipment. Diana Bloch trusted her people and said yes to most requests. When she did ask for an explanation, she actually understood what she was told—which was a bit of a shock, given the highly technical nature of the work that Shepard and Karen O'Neal did for Zeta.

Bloch hadn't batted an eye when they requested approval to build themselves a studio apartment in their basement computer and lab area. There was certainly space down there, even though the "basement" housed everything from the Zeta servers, to the fabrication area, to the auto shop.

The room had been a bit of a project. The plumbing had been the trickiest part to sort out, though sonically isolating the entire structure to make sure the sound from their movies and video games didn't bleed out into the work area was a close second.

Shepard stepped over to the small workstation next to the bed. Their full rig was just a few steps outside the door, but he wouldn't head out until he knew what they were dealing with.

As soon as he switched on the monitor, he felt Karen's hand on his shoulder. "What is it?"

"More hits on the radiological sensors in Monte Carlo," he said.

"*More* hits?" said Karen. "Yes, that's one way to put it."

There were *twenty* hits in the last six hours. Most of them seemed to have been already checked out by local police and had the same MO—cancer patients setting off the alarms.

Add that to the dozen from earlier and you had twenty-two alarms in a single twenty-four-hour period.

"That's more by a factor of five than they have had in the last—"

"Ever," Karen finished for him. "They have never had more than six in a single day since the system was introduced twelve years ago. And this is after several recalibrations to account for false positives."

That was true. Even though the sensors had gotten better, the authorities in Monaco (like most jurisdictions in the world) had raised the threshold for alarms due to the increased use of various radiation-based therapies for cancer.

"Is that the game?" Shepard said. "Is someone trying to force another recalibration to make it easier to move radioactive material?"

It was a rhetorical question and Karen didn't answer it.

If so, that idea was almost comforting. It meant that whoever was gimmicking the system had a long- or at least a medium-term plan. And that meant that Zeta had time to find and stop them.

Shepard checked the time; it was just after 6:00 a.m. It was early, but he decided not to wait. He dialed the number. Diana Bloch answered immediately, as always.

"Bloch here," she said. Her voice told Shepard that not only had she been awake when he called, but she was alert.

"We're getting another spike in radiometry in Monaco," Shepard said.

Before he could finish, the numbers on his screen increased by two and then four more.

* * * *

A small crowd had formed around their baccarat table. All eyes were on Jenya, who hesitated and then said, *"Banque."*

The croupier nodded as everyone around them seemed to hold their breath. He dealt both hands from the shoe. Two kings for the banker and a four and a three for the player.

The man in the robes grunted in satisfaction. For the last hour he had made a point of betting on the banker whenever Jenya bet on the player, and vice versa. That had been unfortunate for him because Jenya was doing very well. Her initial 25,000-euro investment had more than doubled.

Since Sheik Nazer had made a point of at least tripling the amounts that Jenya was betting, he had lost considerably more than that.

Alex, on the other hand, had remained conservative and played her hunches. She had a respectable pile of chips in front of her that was at least three times her original 5000-euro stake.

Two men in suits stood behind Sheik Nazer as he played, doing a terrible job of pretending to be personal assistants instead of the bodyguards they clearly were. Over the course of the evening they had gone from hovering in the background to peering over their boss's shoulder and listening as he provided a running and often mumbled commentary in what Alex recognized as Arabic.

Since the bank had a seven, according to the rules of the game, that hand would draw no cards. However, since the two kings gave the player a combined score of zero, the croupier pulled a single card from the shoe and slid it, facedown, to the player's square.

The croupier paused for effect and then turned over the card: nine.

A gasp went around the table. The croupier paid out on Jenya's bet, sliding another 50,000 in chips toward her. Their robed friend let out a string of loud expletives in Arabic as the dealer swept away the man's 200,000 euros' worth of chips.

The sheik shot Alex and Jenya dirty looks as he continued to talk animatedly with his bodyguards. Then he barked something at the croupier, who motioned for the baccarat room manager. When the manager arrived, Nazer stood up forcefully, while his two men backed away from the table.

"I know a little Arabic," Jenya said. "Apparently, our friend thinks women at the table are causing him bad luck."

"I certainly hope so," Alex said.

The baccarat manager kept his face impassive while the sheik growled at him. After a few more moments of the harangue, the manager leaned in to talk to his croupier, who slid a small pile of chips to Nazer. Satisfied and mollified, the sheik took his seat.

"It appears that our friend has exhausted his account with the casino and was forced to secure a loan," Jenya whispered to Alex. She slid all her remaining chips into the *player* square in front of her. The bet was nearly 100,000 euros.

Alex decided to take her chips and make the same bet.

The sheik instead slid all his chips forward and bet on the banker. The croupier dealt out the cards facedown. Quickly, he turned the two hands over.

It took Alex a moment to process the five and the four in the player box. "*Naturel*," he called out.

Sheik Nazer shouted out something Alex didn't understand and stood up so quickly he knocked over his chair. He glared at Alex and Jenya and barked something in Arabic.

The manager was immediately on the scene and two more attendants in suits appeared behind him. When they had first entered the room, Alex assumed the men were just staff. Now, watching the way they moved, she realized they were well-trained security guards in very good suits—most likely retired French army special forces.

The security men flanked Nazer's bodyguards as the manager stepped up to the sheik. The robed man backed away, his bark falling to more of an angry mutter.

Satisfied, the manager flashed his professional smile and watched as the sheik and his men left the room.

The manager turned to Alex and Lily, giving them an apparently genuine smile, and said in remarkably good English, "My apologies, mademoiselles. His losses were…significant."

Jenya had the manager add her 200,000-euro winnings to her account, but Alex took her 28,000 euros in cash and handed Jenya her half. Jenya put up a token resistance, but accepted the money to honor their agreement.

Alex could have played with her own money, even the money earned from her motorcycle repair business, but Jenya clearly enjoyed being the senior partner in their new acquaintanceship.

"Now we celebrate," Jenya said, taking Alex to an outdoor bar in the rear garden. Alex wanted to buy the drinks but found that the bartender would not accept her money. He let her know that the baccarat manager sent his regards and wanted to assure them that any food or drink they desired would be with his compliments.

"We shall take him up on that," Jenya said cheerfully.

Alex slipped her bills back into her purse. "Scott says that money won is twice as sweet as money earned."

Jenya laughed. "I have seen that man gamble. He definitely does not speak from experience. He is not a gambler. He wants to make it a science, but gambling doesn't work that way. Luck is too fickle a mistress. Scott has enough other gifts; he doesn't need that one."

"You like him," Alex said. It was a statement, not a question. "Jenya, he and Lily are—"

"Oh, I know. And only a fool would try to come between them." Jenya grinned. "I have nothing but affection for Scott, but I do enjoy keeping Lily on her toes. Scott is the only thing I've seen that can make her lose her cool."

That was true, Alex realized.

A waiter appeared out of nowhere and asked them if there was anything he could get them.

"Clearly, they want to keep you coming back," said Alex, "but I'm not sure they can afford it if you do."

"Sheik Nazer's contributions to the casino more than made up for our winnings," Jenya said.

"How well do you know him?" Alex asked.

"By reputation, mostly," Jenya replied. "Though this is the second year I've seen him on the Formula One circuit. He's a coward, of course," she added. "Rumors are that he keeps strictly to the financial end of terrorism. I've also heard that he has ties to other truly reprehensible businesses. I find *those* rumors easy to believe." As Jenya spoke, she led Alex deeper into the expansively landscaped gardens. "I love this casino," she said.

"It is beautiful," agreed Alex.

"Yes, and outrageously extravagant. But it's also the product of a very successful wager," Jenya said. "In the 1850s, the royal family was going bankrupt, and they saw this place as a way to save themselves. They were betting on a history and a way of life that others thought was dying. Today the casino and the royal family are still here, and Monaco is one of the wealthiest places on earth."

"You're saying they gambled and won," Alex said.

"Without a doubt," Jenya said. "Did you know that in 1921 these gardens were the site of the Women's Olympiad, the first international athletic event for women?"

"I didn't know that, but—" Alex was interrupted by a gruff and heavily accented male voice.

"They let Western whores go anywhere these days," the voice said.

Alex swung around and saw Sheik Nazer about ten paces away, his two bodyguards ahead of him.

Alex noted three things very quickly. First, the sheik was still angry. Second, his men's body language told her they were ready to commit violence. And third, she and Jenya were more than fifty yards from the nearest other person.

Chapter 12

Alex's experience taught her to be wary. Even if she was right and the bodyguards had little or no training, they had size on their side, and that wasn't nothing. Each man was at least six-one and had a minimum of eighty pounds on either woman.

At Zeta, Alicia Schmitt had drilled in to Alex that in a fight, size always mattered. A smaller person could compensate with more skill, but there was no question that a two-hundred-pound man could be dangerous even if he was a moron.

That said, Alex felt more than ready to compensate, and was confident that she could take either of the guards before they did any real damage to her. She was also willing to bet that the sheik himself would be not much of a threat—especially if he saw one of his men bested by a *Western whore.*

The problem was that though Jenya was a full inch taller than her own five-six, Alex didn't know if she could fight. Driving a Formula 1 car competitively was an impressive feat, as was keeping your cool in a high-stakes casino game. But violence with an immediate threat of injury or death was something else entirely.

Their best chance to avoid trouble might be to run and call for help. It wasn't a particularly attractive option, but Alex was like her father in one way. She preferred to accomplish any given mission with the least necessary amount of force.

"*Ya gazma!*" Jenya called out.

What was happening? Alex thought as the sheik's anger went up a notch. "What did you say to him?"

"I called him a shoe," Jenya replied, her voice serious but far from panicked. "It's a cultural thing." Turning back to the man, she called out again. *"Ibn al kalb."*

That threw the sheik into a full-blown rage.

"I just called him *son of a dog*," Jenya said. "Apparently he is more of a cat person."

While the sheik was furious, his bodyguards looked more confused than anything. Alex knew how they felt. She didn't know what to make of Jenya taunting the man.

Nazer shouted something to his men. That shook them out of their fog, and they started advancing. Alex glanced back and noted there was a large hedge behind them, making escape impossible.

"Stay behind me," Jenya said, taking a lunging step forward.

Alex saw that Jenya meant to fight. That took any other course of action off the table since the bodyguards were now less than three steps away.

Alex planted her right foot behind her and hoped that Jenya could handle herself at least as well as she could hurl insults at the sheik.

Jenya did not disappoint. She launched herself forward to meet the man approaching her. Alex couldn't afford to take her eyes off her own attacker to track what was happening to her companion.

Her man made an awkward two-handed rush and Alex considered just throwing him to the ground, but decided that he needed more than a blow to his pride.

Stepping to the side, she grabbed his right wrist that was in the middle of a clumsy attempt at a blow. Then she stuck out her foot in front of him, tripping him forward.

As he was falling, she held his wrist with both hands and pulled, simultaneously twisting her body. His full two-hundred-pound weight was forcing him down to the ground while she pulled back up on his arm, which was now half-twisted behind his body.

Alex felt his weight dragging her toward him, but she planted her feet and pulled up with all of her might. There was a satisfying *snap* and then she let go as the man hit the ground heavily.

A fraction of a second later, Alex saw that Jenya's guard was clutching his throat, clearly having trouble breathing. Jenya herself headed straight for Sheik Nazer, who was backing away and holding up his hands, mumbling apologetically in Arabic.

Grabbing him by the tunic, Jenya slapped him hard across the face. Then she backhanded him on the other side of his face. Finally, she pushed the shocked man backwards so that he fell flat onto his back.

She stood over him, considering what to do. "*Kus ummak*," she shouted. Though clearly scared, he reacted with disbelief and didn't try to get up. He just raised his hands to his face, palms out, to protect himself. Alex thought Jenya might take things further, but what the woman did next genuinely surprised Alex.

Jenya took out her phone and snapped half a dozen pictures of the clearly terrified sheik.

The whole encounter had taken less than a minute. And before that thought had fully registered, she saw four of the hotel staff in very good suits sprinting toward them.

By the way they moved, Alex could tell these men were real security and watched as they manhandled the sheik and his guards to their feet. Jenya's guard was profusely bleeding from what was almost certainly a broken nose. He was still holding his throat and wheezing for breath.

Alex's man was awkwardly holding his right arm, which was dislocated at the elbow, broken, or both. Both men required medical attention and Jenya's man would need it sooner rather than later.

The baccarat room manager was the first senior staff on the scene, followed by the casino manager who had greeted Renard when they arrived.

Both men were apologetic and quickly agreeable when Jenya insisted that she didn't want the police or the press involved. The casino men assured both women that the sheik would no longer be welcome at the casino or anywhere else in Monte Carlo.

"No police?" Alex asked as they headed inside.

"No," Jenya said. "I want the story of me in Monte Carlo to be about my driving. Nazer's humiliation is enough satisfaction. And if he gets any ideas about retaliation, he knows I have photos. " She dismissed any further concern with a wave. "Alex, dear, you surprised me. Where did you learn to fight like that? Surely not in your bike repair shop? I saw you using a combination of judo and Krav Maga."

Alex kept her voice casual. "My father is a big believer in self-defense. He taught me a lot, and then I studied a bit more. It's come in handy more than once."

"Didn't you say that your father bought and sold American cars?"

"He's a worrier," Alex said. That certainly was true. "What about you? Where did you learn to fight?"

"My mother was also…a worrier. Russia is more of a man's world than America. And some of those men are not very polite."

Jenya announced that she was leaving and pointed Alex in the direction of the gambling room where they'd left Renard and Lily. "Alex, I enjoyed our evening immensely," Jenya said. "I'll see you at the track."

"How was your night, Alex?" Lily asked, when Alex caught up with her.

"Interesting," Alex replied. "What about you two? How did you do?"

"Fine," Renard said flatly.

"It's not about winning or losing," Lily said, a thin smile on her face. "It's fun just to play. Right, Scott?"

Renard grunted, and the three of them headed for the exit.

* * * *

The next morning, Alex and Lily were out early. They had an errand to run for Diana Bloch, and it was better for Lily's cover if she spent the day at the racetrack. Today the drivers would have more practice time on the track, and then they would have to qualify for the race.

"Where's Scott?" asked Alex.

"He's been at the garage for over an hour," Lily said.

That was impressive. It was barely 8:30 now.

On the way out, Lily greeted the concierge with a "bonjour" as they were passing by.

"Mademoiselles!" Paul replied, waving them over to his counter. "Good morning. I thought you might want to hear about something interesting that happened yesterday afternoon…a piece of local gossip."

"Of course," Lily said.

"There was a break-in at the Hôtel de Paris," he said. "But it didn't make the news."

"Why not?" Lily asked.

"It was not successful. Two Bulgarians tried to crack open the hotel safe but were caught by security. The hotel preferred to keep it quiet, and the police were very accommodating."

That was interesting but not surprising. Hôtel de Paris was the most expensive hotel in Monaco. The management wouldn't want their guests to feel like they or their valuables weren't safe.

"Was there anything important in the safe?" asked Alex.

"As a matter of fact, there was," the concierge said. "A Greek gentleman—a shipping magnate—was transporting some antique statuaries, ancient and priceless."

"But they didn't get the statues?" Lily asked.

"It appears they were apprehended before they could complete their work."

"Thank you very much, Paul," Lily said.

"Bonjour, mademoiselles," said the concierge.

That was something, Alex thought. A lead, at last. Besides the terrorist attacks, there had been a number of high-value thefts on the circuit this season. If those two things were related, maybe the Bulgarians in custody would give them a lead to the enemy—whoever that was.

* * * *

The taxi dropped them off at a small hotel on the beach. Alex was struck once again by the Mediterranean, and the lush tropical beauty around her. This was, of course, the French Riviera.

Inside the hotel, they asked for the manager, showing their new APD identification. The Administrative Police Division was an arm of Monaco law enforcement dedicated to the movement and activities of foreign nationals within their borders.

The man scanned their dark business suits and asked in French how he could be of service.

Alex's French was good but not quite fluent. However, Lily's was flawless.

Lily asked if they could meet with an elderly British couple who was staying at the hotel, assuring the man that they needed merely to ask the guests a few routine questions.

A few minutes later, a nervous man and woman appeared. Alex guessed they were in their mid-sixties.

"Would you be more comfortable if we spoke in English?" Lily asked

"Yes, please," the man replied.

Lily made a point of checking her notebook. "Paula and Ronald Wright?"

"Yes?" the woman said nervously.

"No need to worry. We have just a few questions," Alex said, adding a light French accent of her own. "As a follow-up to your conversation with the police yesterday."

"We already explained that the radiation is because of my husband's treatment," the woman said. Her voice was steady, but carried a hint of backbone. She was being protective, which was normal, and the straightforward gaze suggested she was telling the truth.

"Right. There is no problem. We are just being thorough. Is this your first visit to the Formula One circuit?" Lily asked.

"Yes," the woman said. "It's quite expensive."

"A retirement trip?" asked Alex.

"No, Ronald won a sweepstakes," Mrs. Wright said. "It included everything: tickets, hotel, even the train here."

"Well, that is quite lucky of Mr. Wright," Alex said. "Did you enter online?"

"No, it came through *GP Racing*, the magazine," the man said. "I'm a longtime subscriber. I received a notice in the mail, and then a few days later the tickets and some paperwork arrived." He became nervous again. "It came through the magazine; you can check with them."

"Not necessary," Lily said. "But do you happen to have your tickets with you?"

Mrs. Wright pulled two tickets out of her purse. Lily photographed them and said "thank you."

They could ask to see the plane tickets and hotel confirmation, but that wouldn't accomplish anything other than scaring the poor couple more. Shepard could get anything else they needed from the airline and the hotel reservation system. And of course, they would have to check with the magazine.

"Well, that's it, I think," Lily said. "Thanks so much for your cooperation." She smiled. "Have you been fans long?"

"Yes, I've been a McLaren man my whole life," said Mr. Wright.

"Then I can offer you something for your trouble," Lily said. She reached into her jacket and pulled out an envelope, handing it to Mr. Wright. "This is a small token. Consider it our apology for inconveniencing you."

Mr. Wright opened the envelope and his eyes went wide.

"What is it?" his wife asked.

"Paddock Club," he said. "Right in front of McLaren."

Alex knew what that meant. It was the equivalent of courtside seats at a basketball game.

"There is also a pass to the McLaren paddock and some other perks," Lily said.

"Thank you, I don't know what to say," he said, getting choked up.

"Just enjoy the race," Lily said. "Thanks again for helping us. By the way, I like Renard this year. What do you think of the team?"

The man snorted with derision. "They're all right, but I'm not keen on buying your way into a sport. Formula One was built by people who devoted their careers and their sweat, not billionaires who—"

"Thank you again," Lily said quickly, and she and Alex were on their way.

By noon they had interviewed two more couples. A pattern emerged. All were retirement age, all were undergoing cancer treatment, and none had entered a contest. They all had won the trip through their subscription to *GP Racing,* and this was their first trip outside the country for Formula 1.

Shepard called as Lily was finishing up with the last couple. Alex stepped aside to take the call.

"The magazine sponsored no contests and they don't sell their subscription list," Shepard told her. "The hotels, airline reservations, and tickets were all bought online by entities that no longer exist."

That was definitely suspicious, as was the fact that all the contests were for trips to the Monte Carlo race only—and the arrival times were staggered so that some had come before the start of the racing activity on Thursday and some on Friday. It was Saturday now, and they couldn't rule out the fact that more might still be coming.

"Any chance you can track down whoever is responsible?" Alex asked.

"Not so far," Shepard said. "My grandmother could have hacked into the magazine's subscription database. We're following all the leads on the ticket purchases. I'll let you know. Whoever is running this operation is good and has left no digital trail. The fact that they used snail mail for their contact with the winners makes them almost impossible to trace. We'll keep at it, see if they got sloppy somewhere."

Alex knew Diana Bloch would not be happy with this. And Shepard and O'Neal were still investigating the explosion at the Renard hangar.

"Good luck," Alex said.

"You too, Alex," Shepard said. "Keep an eye out. We sent some special equipment to the hotel."

Lily approached as Alex hung up. "Shepard has nothing," Alex said.

"I'm not surprised," said Lily. "Whoever did this got their hands on plutonium. If this is the same party, they're able to execute long lead-time operations, *and* they know how to cover their tracks. Throw in the explosion at Logan, and we could have a real situation here. I'm starting to think there may be something to Shepard and O'Neal's theory about Ares. But you know something? I'd rather face a single organization with those capabilities than two or three small but lethal factions."

Alex didn't disagree. "So now what?"

"Now we head to the racetrack," said Lily. "We're qualifying today."

Chapter 13

Alex and Lily changed out of their dark suits and got to the track just after lunch. Terry met them in front of the paddock in his Renard jumpsuit and carrying his helmet. He'd been right about one thing: The Renard racing jumpsuit was flattering.

"Hi, Alex," Terry said, smiling.

"Have you been out driving already?" she asked.

"Of course. Practice laps before and after lunch. Qualifying later this afternoon. Do you have a few minutes for a tour?"

"Sure, do you?" she asked.

"I've got an hour. I just need a few minutes to talk to the chief before we go. Showing you around will help me relax," he said.

Alex didn't think relaxing was his primary goal for the tour. He clearly just wanted to spend time with her, and she decided that it couldn't hurt. Of course, she wasn't about to get involved with one of Renard's drivers. There wouldn't be any point, and it might actually compromise her mission on the circuit.

But there was no reason to be rude.

Terry took her to meet the pit crew and gave her a quick rundown on everyone's jobs. Once Alex saw what each of the twenty-person team did (including the two people assigned to *each* tire), she was embarrassed that she thought she'd be able to just step into a role on such a highly specialized crew.

"We're one of the few teams that regularly gets pit times under two seconds," Terry said, with obvious pride.

"Two seconds?" Alex repeated. "That's quick."

"Most of the stops are tire changes only," Terry said. "It takes a little longer if we have to change out the front wing. And every year we improve. I think Scott wants the record, but only if we can do it safely."

Alex was more in her element in the garage. She understood the car and was surprised at how many parts they had on hand and how much they could repair overnight.

After they answered her questions, two of the mechanics pumped her for information about the Morbidelli 850 in her own shop.

Alex walked with Terry up to the front where Chief Clarke waited next to a bank of monitors manned by five operators who kept an eye on every aspect of the car's performance.

Terry and the older driver, Maduro, huddled with the chief and Renard while Alex took a place next to Lily up front.

"How was Terry?" Lily asked.

"Fine," said Alex.

Then there was a long, awkward silence between them.

"It's okay, you know," said Lily, nodding toward Terry. "There's no rule against it. And even if there were, you Morgans aren't known for following the rules."

"It's not like that," Alex said.

"Really? Did you see the way he looked at you?" Lily said.

"He just wants to get a glimpse of the motorcycle in my garage," Alex said.

She realized how that sounded a fraction of a second before Lily started laughing. "Of course, the motorcycle," Lily said.

"Let's just watch this, shall we?" Alex said as the pit crew rolled the Renard cars into position.

* * * *

"Director," Shepard said on the phone to Diana Bloch, "could you come here and take a look at something?"

Not once in Bloch's time at Zeta was that ever a preamble to good news.

"On my way," Bloch said as she got up from her chair.

Less than a minute later, she was at Shepard and O'Neal's workstation, studying the monitor over Shepard's shoulder.

O'Neal pointed at the screen. "There it is, Director," she said. "We're getting a spike on hits to the radiation-sensor network."

"Over how long a period?" Bloch asked.

"The last hour," O'Neal replied, her tone maddeningly even.

"Thirty radiological hits in the last hour? Has that ever happened—"

Before Bloch could finish, the number ticked up to thirty-four, then forty-two, then there was a flash of numbers that increased too fast to follow. Finally, the numbers were replaced by a series of dashes, and then nothing.

"What was that?"

"I don't know," Shepard said, furiously tapping on his keyboard.

O'Neal jumped on her computer and did the same, leaving Bloch standing between them, feeling something she never liked to feel: *useless.*

"Was it a radiological event?" Bloch asked, hating the terrible euphemism the term represented.

There was an awful delay before one of her people spoke.

"No," said O'Neal.

"It appears that the sheer volume of positive hits crashed the system," Shepard said.

"The last number we had was ninety-two," O'Neal added.

"So someone was flooding the system to crash it?" said Bloch.

"Most likely," Shepard said.

"What does that get them?"

"A little time to move material about the city with no active sensors," Shepard said. "But not much time. A full system reboot should take no more than twenty minutes. I can tap into their network and we can watch the reboot in real time."

The screen changed and a new window popped open. It was in French, with various graphics Bloch didn't understand and some numbers that also made no sense to her. She did understand the status bar, though. It was at about 20 percent.

"Let's say they have twenty minutes to move radioactive material without any prying eyes," she said. "What would that achieve?"

"Moving it to a secure location. Twenty minutes is enough time to get the material out of the city. Of course, getting it across the border into France would be tricky, but whoever is doing this is clearly very capable."

"It would also, I presume," Bloch said, "buy enough time to move a device into position and trigger it."

"Yes," said Shepard.

They all watched the status bar make its painfully slow march. Fifty percent. Sixty-five. Ninety…

When it was finished and flashed *100%,* Bloch was relieved that no other alarms went off.

"Just one more minute," Shepard said.

The minute stretched to two.

When the status bar reappeared on the screen, both Shepard and O'Neal gasped.

"What?" Bloch leaned in, glaring at the screen and then at her two agents. "What does it mean?"

"Something went wrong with the reboot," Shepard said.

"Will it work a second time?"

"Possibly." He sighed.

"Unlikely," said O'Neal. "These are hardened software systems designed to recover completely in the unlikely event of a crash. This isn't like the operating system of a normal computer."

"What's happening now?" Bloch asked.

Shepard and O'Neal didn't reply. They worked furiously until the status bar finished and started over again.

"Most likely a virus," Shepard said. "Something that could have been lurking in the backup system but waiting until the crash to get introduced to the main system."

"How long to fix it?" Bloch asked.

"That depends on the nature of the virus," said Shepard, "but even if they had help, I'd say days. At least."

"Days!" Bloch took a deep breath and lowered her voice. "What you're telling me is we have loose plutonium that could very well be in this city and no way to track it? For *days*?"

Neither agent answered her question, but no answer was necessary.

* * * *

After three rounds of qualifying laps, both Renard drivers qualified for the race and scored high enough to get fourth and seventh starting positions. Alex didn't understand all of the intricacies of the process, but the value of a good starting position was clear. The first position was in front, on the inside. That literally put the car in the lead and in position for the shortest time on the first lap. For everyone else, the closer they were to that position, the better.

Alex noticed that Jenya had gotten third position while the other driver for Marussia was in the back.

Renard and the chief were happy with the positions and were the first to congratulate the drivers, who were swarmed by the team members.

As soon as he was able to come up for air, Terry looked around until his eyes settled on her and then he smiled.

When he approached, she said, "Well done. You weren't lying: You do drive very fast."

"Seven is pretty good for a second-year driver."

"What can we—" Alex began but stopped when Lily approached and literally pulled her away from Terry.

"Sorry, I need to borrow her," Lily said.

She led Alex to the back of the garage, which was now empty with everyone up front celebrating their showing.

"We've got a new situation," Lily said. "Bloch just called me. The radiation-sensor system in the city is down, and by that I mean completely down."

"How long before it goes back up?" Alex asked.

"Apparently days."

"But the race is tomorrow!" Alex tried to stay calm. "We have no way to track the movement of the radioactive material. And we are about to have a quarter of a million people in a very small area."

"We have a few portable sensors," Lily said. "And the local police are scrounging for Geiger counters. The best we can hope for is having police with no training on the equipment running around the city—with well over a hundred cancer patients who will show radioactive to any sensor."

This was terrible. "What do we do?"

"Let's head back to the hotel," Lily said. "We'll check out the equipment Shepard and O'Neal sent us, and hope for a break."

"That's the whole plan?" said Alex. "Wait around and hope we get lucky?"

"*Plan* is a strong word for what he have here," Lily said.

Chapter 14

When they arrived at the hotel, Paul was waiting for them. "Ms. Randall, Ms. Morgan, I have an interesting addendum to the situation at the Hôtel de Paris. I have learned that sometime yesterday, the concierge at the hotel arranged for the statuary to be moved to a new, more secure location."

"What location?" asked Lily.

"The casino. It has a cooperative arrangement with some of the better hotels. They hold special items for certain guests, if those items are of significant value. The casino has the largest and strongest vault in Monaco."

"Stronger than any of the bank vaults?" Lily asked.

"Considerably," he said.

"Thank you, Paul," said Lily. "That is interesting information. I think it may be extremely useful."

"I'm glad to be of service," he said. "Bonsoir, mademoiselles."

In the elevator, Alex turned to Lily and said, "What chance is there that the theft is unrelated to the radiation sensors being out?"

"Pretty slim," replied Lily. "What if those statues aren't really statues? And, whatever they are, someone just moved them to the most secure place in Monaco."

"Maybe we got that bit of luck we ordered," Lily said.

Back in the room, they found the equipment that Shepard had sent. The Geiger counter attachments for their phones were the most important pieces. As they examined the supplies, they conferenced with Shepard over their ear comms.

"Can the Geiger counters differentiate between different kinds of radiation and help us zero in on plutonium?" Lily asked.

"The output pulse from the sensor always has the same magnitude, so no," Shepard replied.

"Right, the output pulse..." Alex said. "That's unfortunate, because we may have a lead. There's a chance that the material was moved to a vault nearby."

"A vault?" Shepard repeated.

"Yes, apparently the Monte Carlo Casino has the strongest vault in Monaco," said Lily.

There was dead silence on the other side.

"Is that a problem, Lincoln?" Alex asked. "If it's there, at least we know it's not going anywhere."

"Yes, that will be helpful. Get there with your meters and let me know what you find," Shepard said. "Let me know as soon as you have something."

Lily took one look at Alex's face and asked her if there was a problem.

"Shepard's spider-sense is tingling," Alex said. And hers was, too.

Lily shrugged and said, "Maybe he's worried we won't be able to get in to the vault. If we can't break in, Bloch will have to sort it with the management. And if we will have a hard time getting in, so will the bad guys," Lily said.

"Yes, that's probably it," Alex replied.

* * * *

"How is it a problem if the plutonium is safely in a vault that's impossible to get into?" Bloch asked. She didn't like this, Shepard was clearly worried, and even O'Neal looked nervous—which was something that Bloch had seen only rarely.

"Because our operating assumption is that we are facing a dirty bomb scenario," Shepard said. "A traditional explosive that would spread plutonium in a defined area. And that would be pretty devastating. We'd be seeing deaths in the thousands within five years, and it would render one of the wealthiest and most densely populated places in Europe uninhabitable."

"What happens if a dirty bomb goes off in what's essentially a giant bank vault?" asked Bloch.

"It wouldn't," said Shepard. "No one would put one there. Definitely no one who was able to acquire the plutonium in the first place *and* pull off the sophisticated operations we've been investigating." He paused. "But you might put a nuclear bomb in one."

That stopped Bloch cold. "But they've just had the plutonium for less than a month. Could any terrorist organization build a bomb in such a short time?"

"Not easily," Shepard said, "but there's no reason to assume they waited until they had the plutonium. In the Manhattan Project during World War Two, the facility at Los Alamos did almost all the work on the bomb mechanisms and casings before they received the nuclear material. In fact, most of the time they were working, they weren't sure it would arrive."

"How hard would it be to build a bomb and how many people could do it?" Bloch asked, knowing she would not like the answer.

"Certainly an organization like Zeta could do it," Shepard said. "But, honestly, a decent engineer and a nuclear physics PhD could do it. At least they could build the simplest kind of weapon."

"You're telling me that a number of universities or private companies could make a nuclear bomb?" Bloch asked.

"Yes."

"Could we track the materials they would need?"

Shepard shook his head. "Not really. They are too common. There were two types of bombs used in the Second World War. The first was an implosion device. It used shaped traditional explosives to hit a bowling ball–sized amount of nuclear material from all sides to shrink it to about the size of a baseball. That set off a chain reaction that created the nuclear explosion over Nagasaki. The second type was used in Hiroshima. It was a much simpler gun-style design, in which you take a small amount of nuclear material and shoot it at a larger mass. Less of the material goes critical, as a result the explosion has a slightly lower yield in terms of both explosive power and radiation, but the results were still extremely devastating."

"What would happen if you detonated a device like that inside the vault?" Bloch asked. "Assume the worst and they use all of the plutonium they may have."

Shepard looked pale and anxious. "We're not sure because it's never been done, but it would be bad. There were two bank vaults near ground zero in Hiroshima and they were left standing. We saw the same thing in the early bomb testing in the US.

"Ordinary vaults are remarkably strong, but if you detonated a bomb inside one of them, you'd have tremendous overpressure that would magnify the force of the blast. And then there's another problem. Most of what we think of as nuclear fallout is actually vaporized bomb parts and casing. In this scenario, the vault and everything inside it would be vaporized, as well as much or all of the surrounding building. The blast would be fatal to anyone in a half-mile radius, but afterward, the amount and reach of the radioactive fallout would be enormous."

"And it would happen in the middle of Europe," Bloch said.

"Once we have the specs on the vault," O'Neal said, "I can run the numbers and give you a clearer picture of the yield and the fallout."

"Let's focus on making sure that if there is a bomb there, Alex and Lily get to it before it goes off. We must assume we're on a ticking clock. If it's going to detonate, it's most likely going to happen before the end of the race, which is now less than twenty-four hours away."

Shepard and O'Neal were already on their feet. "We'll monitor their progress and be ready with any help they need."

Before they were out the door, Bloch picked up her phone. There was a short list of people who needed to know the stakes, and only one person who could get them into the vault.

* * * *

"Let's start at Hôtel de Paris," Lily said to Alex. "We'll see if Paul can get us in to see their safe."

When they arrived at the hotel, a concierge named Raphael was waiting for them. Alex was not surprised to see the embroidered gold leafs on the lapel of his jacket.

"I'm a friend of Pierre's," Lily said, shaking his hand and showing him her ring.

"Very good. How can I help you?" Raphael asked.

He showed them the secure room the hotel used to keep important patrons' valuables. It was a reinforced storage room, with racks on each side that were stacked full of individual strongboxes of various sizes. Each box was secured with a combination lock. At the end of the room was a large antique safe, about six feet tall and three feet wide.

"The room is monitored twenty-four hours a day by a video," Raphael said. "There is also an alarm on the door and motion sensors inside. The burglars disabled both alarms."

"How did they get caught?" Lily asked.

"It was luck, really. Somehow they tapped into the video camera feed and replaced it with a loop. Judging by when the loop began, they were in there for over an hour. The statuary was locked away in the large safe, but apparently they had trouble opening it. They would have succeeded, but one of the housekeeping staff happened to be nearby, picking up cleaning supplies, and she heard them," Raphael said.

"Had they gotten the safe open?" Alex asked.

"Yes, but they didn't have time to even get out of the room before the police arrived. As I said, we were fortunate."

"So, they disabled the alarms, hacked into the video feed, got into the room and managed to open the safe, but were caught by housekeeping. That *is* lucky," Alex said.

"Did they disturb anything else?" Lily asked. "Did they open any of the other containers?"

"No, just the statuary," he said.

Alex pulled out her phone and attached Shepard's radiation meter. She scanned the room and then scanned it again.

Nothing.

Shepard had warned them that traces might be difficult to find if the plutonium was encased in lead, but there should have been something.

They both scanned every inch of the room and turned up nothing on their meters.

The concierge waited patiently for them to finish. "Is there any danger to the hotel?" he asked in a remarkably even tone.

"None at all," Alex said.

Lily thanked Raphael, and they headed outside.

As they walked out, Alex vacillated between relief and worry. On the one hand, it appeared their theory had been wrong. If the plutonium bomb hadn't been stored in the hotel safe, it was unlikely that the device was now in the casino vault.

On the other hand, in that scenario at least they knew where the bomb was. But if it wasn't here, it could be anywhere in Monte Carlo or the larger Monaco. Or anywhere in Europe.

"We should scan the casino just to be on the safe side," Lily said.

Since the casino was literally across the street, it took them less than five minutes to reach the front doors.

One of the attendants out front recognized the two women, smiled, and gave them a polite, "Bonjour."

The familiarity made Alex feel vulnerable. Quite a few of the casino staff would recognize both of them. If this turned into a real operation, their covers would be blown.

Rather than head inside the casino, Alex and Lily made a point of taking pictures of each other outside the building and studying the façade as they walked around to the back entrance.

Alex tried Bloch again. The director's assistant picked up and said she was in conference. Alex hoped it wouldn't be too long before Bloch called her back. To rule out the casino they would have to scan the vault itself.

"Alex, look at this," Lily said as she examined her phone.

Before Alex could get there, she heard the distinctive crackling sound of a Geiger counter detecting radiation.

Alex attached her own meter to her phone, and it immediately started making the same sound. The closer they got to the building, the louder the sound from the Geiger counter.

"I think that's it," Lily said. Then she put down her phone. "Bloch is not available. I'm guessing that she's still working on getting us in there."

"She'd better hurry. If there's really a bomb in there, it could go off any time in next twenty-four hours."

Of course, getting into the vault would be a mixed blessing, since it would put them in a heavily reinforced space with a thermonuclear device.

But one problem at a time.

Chapter 15

Mr. Smith's face appeared on Bloch's computer screen. Behind him was a green tent that Bloch placed as army issue. She heard what sounded like a jet overhead, followed by a hum she didn't recognize. He could have been anywhere in the world, from a desert in the Middle East to an army base in New Jersey. He was wearing his business suit and tie. At least in his middle sixties, Smith was handsome and he wore his signature calm but concerned expression.

Mr. Smith waited for the sound to pass. "I've read your report. I will try to get you access to the vault," he said.

"Sir, time is critical. We likely have less than twenty-four hours. If we have to go through channels—"

Smith held up his hand. "You don't have to explain it to me, Diana. I understand what we're facing and the potential consequences. The problem isn't getting your people into one of the most secure vaults in the world, on foreign soil, in the middle of a high-profile annual event when the local authorities have their hands full with hundreds of security threats a day, and when tourists outnumber the local population by a factor of ten to one. There's something else at work here, and the situation may be out of my hands."

That stunned Bloch. Smith could lean on heads of state and on multibillion-dollar, multinational corporations. When it came to the levers of power, there was virtually nothing that was out of his hands.

Smith paused, as if he was unsure of what to say next—another first in Bloch's experience. Then his face set and when he spoke his voice was firm. "The owner of the Casino de Monte-Carlo is a member of our board."

That took a second to sink in. That meant he or she was a member of the board of the Aegis Initiative, the mysterious organization that funded and supported Zeta Division.

Smith had explained to her that the organization was founded by a group of very wealthy and very powerful people. However, Mr. Smith was the only member of that select group whom Bloch had ever met.

"But, sir, I thought the royal family is the majority owner of the casino," Bloch said. And then she understood. "The prince," she said.

"Stay by your desk," Smith said, and the connection went dead.

Five minutes later her computer beeped and the screen showed an incoming message. A crest appeared on the monitor as a voice said, "Hold for His Royal Highness." The crest was replaced by the face of a serious man in his early sixties. Though they had never met or spoken, Bloch recognized him instantly.

"Ms. Bloch, Smith has briefed me. How can I be of help?" he said in a light French accent.

"Your Highness," she said. "We need access to the casino and its vault. I know your government has its own people, but our agents and resources—"

"I'm well aware of Zeta's resources," the prince said.

Of course he is, Bloch thought, with a twinge of embarrassment. He helped provide those resources.

"We can work discreetly," Bloch said. "We'll just need to reach the lower level and the vault."

"I don't want anything to interfere with your operation," he said, "and I don't want to risk an information leak. Tell your agents to stand by. The casino will announce a potential gas leak and we will clear it out."

That would help. It would also be expensive to close one of the biggest casinos in the world on one of its busiest days of the year.

"Your Highness, we have every confidence in our ability to neutralize this threat," she said. "However, the potential consequences are grave. You and your family might wish to take a short trip until the problem is solved."

"Impossible," said the prince. "My place and the royal family's place is here. Besides, I have complete faith in you and your people. And we have a race tomorrow. I admit I'm a Renault man, but I'm very interested in this new team, Renard. I'm counting on you to make sure that the most interesting thing to happen in Monaco tomorrow is that contest."

"Yes, Your Highness," Bloch said, and the screen went blank.

As she called Lily Randall's number, Bloch realized that a royal prince had just put the fate of his country and his family in her hands.

And yet that was the only part of this task she could wrap her head around. If Zeta failed, the consequences to Europe and to the rest of the world would be more than she could calculate.

* * * *

A man Alex didn't recognize met them at the service entrance. He was wearing a suit and clearly part of the management team for the casino. She felt a twinge of relief that he wasn't anyone she had met last night; for now at least, her cover was secure.

She berated herself for thinking about such a mundane and selfish matter when everyone in Monte Carlo was in grave danger.

Through the open lobby, she could already see patrons of the casino filing out in an orderly fashion.

"Mademoiselles, I am the assistant manager, Mr. Boucher. Are you with the gas company?" he said, with no hint of humor or irony in his voice.

"Yes, we are," Lily replied.

"I have been told to give you access to any areas of the casino that you require to make your *repairs*," he said.

"We need to get to the vault," Alex said, "and we need it opened."

"Oh, no, no. I'm afraid that is impossible," the man said. "Our casino manager is…indisposed."

"I don't think you understand," Lily said. "This is an emergency. This is possibly the biggest emergency you will see in your lifetime. We need to get in there, and we need to get in there now."

"If it were in my power, I would open if for you," Mr. Boucher said, "but only the manager can do that and he is unwell; he is in the hospital."

Alex and Lily exchanged a look. *Hospital?* Alex mouthed inaudibly.

Lily turned to the man. "The casino must still operate, must it not, even in his absence? What have you done in the past when he's been unavailable? Or on vacation? We need to execute *that procedure* immediately."

"It requires two people to open the vault," Boucher said, "the manager and our *Chef de la sécurité*. Both suffered the same ailment last night. Usually, when they are away, they provide temporary codes to their lieutenants, but as this was sudden…"

Alex felt a cold chill run down her spine.

To make it worse, as they stepped inside the building and headed down the hallway, the meter on her phone was spiking. Though she had turned the sound off to avoid panicking the staff, she could see the needle graphic jumping on her phone screen. The expression on Lily's face told Alex that hers was doing the same.

That settled it. Alex now had little doubt that she and Lily were following the trail of the missing plutonium. And that trail ended inside the vault that they had absolutely no way to open.

* * * *

Bloch tried to keep the expression on her face impassive, but she knew she was making a bad job of it. She was scared and she had little doubt that Shepard and O'Neal could see it.

They looked up from their computers as she entered their workstation. Bloch didn't waste any time. "We have a problem," she said. "We've cleared out the casino, but something has happened to the only two people who can open the vault."

They looked up at her, as if waiting for her to give them orders. The problem was that Diana Bloch had absolutely no idea what to do. The manufacturer of the vault had long gone out of business. They could try to track down the contractors who had serviced and upgraded the mechanism since, but that would take time.

Time they didn't have.

"We need to break into that vault," Bloch said, "and we need to do it fast."

Shepard and O'Neal exchanged a glance.

"I know what I'm asking is impossible," Bloch said, "but we left *impossible* behind days ago. We must do this. There is no other choice. Just tell me what you need. Tanks? An air strike?"

"Actually, I think O'Neal and I might be able to take care of it," Shepard said.

"What?" Bloch asked.

"I think we can do it. The process is tricky, and it will take some work on this end, but I think we can talk Lily and Alex through it," Shepard said.

"Just like that?" Bloch asked.

"When I was in graduate school, I belonged to a group called Friends of Feynman," said Shepard. "We would study problems—how to break into bank vaults, for example—and work out theoretical solutions. We studied a number of vaults by the same manufacturer as this unit, so barring any surprises, I think we can do it."

"Who is Feynman?" Bloch asked.

"Richard Feynman was a physicist on the Manhattan Project. One of his many hobbies was safecracking, so this is—"

"Great," Bloch said, cutting him off. "Get our agents in there stat. We still have a bomb to defuse."

Chapter 16

The manager brought them to an elevator that took them down one story to the basement of the casino. It emptied into a large corridor with a high ceiling. Mr. Boucher led them down the hallway toward double steel doors. When they reached the doors, he entered a code into a keypad and held a card up to a sensor next to the pad.

Something clicked inside the door, and it opened to a vestibule that was dominated on the far wall by a circular vault door. It was massive, reaching almost from floor to ceiling. On the front was a keypad, a large steel wheel, and a slightly oversized combination-lock dial. It looked like an ordinary bank vault, only bigger and stronger.

Much, much stronger.

Two uniformed guards sat at a table, their eyes tracking the women as they walked in. After a brief conversation with Boucher, they left the room. The assistant manager gave Alex and Lily a polite smile and said, "I will give you privacy to do your work. Don't hesitate to call if you require further assistance."

The man must have had questions, but he didn't ask them, remaining unfailingly polite. Whatever strings Bloch had pulled to get them in here must have come from very high up for him to give two strangers free access to the vault.

Once they had the room to themselves, Alex turned to Lily and said, "Do you want to call Scott?"

"I don't think he can help," Lily said. "And I don't think this is going to be primarily a programming challenge. If Zeta needs Scott's resources—"

"That's not it, Lily. Maybe he could take a short trip…leave the area," Alex offered.

Lily didn't say anything and Alex saw the smallest crack in her cool, professional demeanor.

"I thought about it," Lily said, "but I don't think he would do it. He won't leave his team and he can't pull them all out. More than likely he'd show up here and...just get in the way."

Then Alex saw it. Lily wasn't worried. She was scared. She wasn't just frightened of what would happen to them if the atomic bomb went off in the next room. Or what would happen to the city above them. She was scared for Scott.

Alex watched as Lily pushed those feelings aside, and her iron control returned. "We'll just have to make sure we get this done."

Alex put in her ear comm as Lily did the same. Shepard talked them through setting up some cameras, installing some electronic sensors, and placing a laptop on the security guards' table. There were still electronics and tools that Alex didn't recognize in their kit, but Shepard said they wouldn't need them until later.

Lily flipped the cameras on. "Shepard, are you getting this?" she asked.

"Yes," he said, "and she's a beauty."

"*She* appears to be pretty tough," Alex said. "But we have no heavy equipment. No drills. How are we going to get in there?"

"No drilling and no hacking at the walls," he said. "They are a special concrete mixture. Bank vaults use steel fiber to reinforce their mix; this one uses carbon and titanium. Plus, there's gravel in there as well, made with particularly hard stone that will tear up any drills we could use. And that's just the walls. There are layers of steel, titanium, and copper in the vault door, and all that metal is wrapped around the same concrete mix in the door's core."

"If we had to, could we blast the hinges or the walls?" Lily asked.

"The walls are rated for fourteen-thousand pounds of pressure per square inch," said Shepard, "and the door is even stronger. Even if we could get enough explosives down there, we don't want to shake the contents. The simplest nuclear bomb design is a ballistic device. It's basically a gun that uses an explosive charge to fire a plutonium bullet at a larger mass of plutonium. And like any gun, we don't want to shake it too much."

"Okay, then, good safety tip: Don't rattle the atomic bomb," Alex said. "Okay, how do we get in?"

"You go through the front door," Shepard said. "There are two issues. One is the combination. That's a simple four-digit code. Normally you need two people to open the door. For security reasons, each person is given two of the four numbers. The second problem is the time lock. It's electronic and won't allow the combination mechanism to open the door. But one thing at a time. We'll handle the combination first. Don't worry about the door; opening it is going to be easier than defusing the bomb."

Following Shepard's instructions, Alex attached three rectangular sensors to the front of the vault. They were different sizes, with various lights and switches on the front. The back of each was magnetic, and they stuck to the door of the vault.

After switching each one on, they carefully calibrated the sensors, adjusting their placement and settings until Shepard was satisfied.

"Watch out for the one on the right," Shepard said. "It uses X-rays."

"Excuse me—X-rays?" Lily asked.

"Your exposure will be no higher than what you'd get at the dentist," Shepard said.

"You're comparing this to going to the dentist as a *selling point*?" asked Alex.

"Given what's behind that door," Shepard said, "I think X-ray radiation is the least of your worries."

"Fair point," Alex said. "What now?"

"This is like an old movie," he said. "What we're doing here is basically putting our ear to the safe and spinning the dial until we hear a *click*. Because of the construction of the door, we'll be listening with a microphone, a sonar-based device, and X-rays. They will tell us when we've hit the right number. It's trial and error until we'll get there. What's supposed to happen is that once you've put in the correct combination, it will release a mechanism that allows the wheel in the front to turn, which then retracts twenty-four steel bolts that circle the door and hold it closed."

"And we're done?" Alex asked.

"No," Shepard said. "Then we'll have to deal with the time lock. It's an electronic system that keeps the mechanical system from opening the vault until a certain, preset time. We'll get to that later. For now, let's focus on the combination. That's the easy part."

"I thought getting into the vault was the easy part," Alex said. "Defusing the atomic bomb was supposed to be the tough part."

"Correct," said Shepard. "This is the *easiest* part of the easy part."

Alex did the honors for the first number, slowly turning the dial of the vault clockwise until Shepard told her to stop, go back, start again.

"Stop!" Shepard said. "Now both of you stand back."

"Why stand back?" Alex asked.

"I'm going to use the X-ray unit to confirm our results," Shepard said.

While Shepard was working, Lily handed Alex a cup of coffee and said, "There's a machine in the corner." To Alex's surprise, the coffee was pretty good.

A minute later Shepard said, "One down." There was a little too much enthusiasm in Shepard's voice for Alex's liking, and she was suddenly sure he was enjoying himself, as if breaking into a giant, impenetrable vault was something he'd always wanted to try. Of course, knowing Shepard, there was an excellent chance that was true.

Lily did the second number, which they nailed in just thirty minutes. And then Alex did the third. When Lily let go of the dial for the last time and the two women stepped back, almost two hours had passed. Alex's nerves were fried.

So much for the easy part.

"Okay, Shepard," Alex said. "How long will the hard part take?"

"That's the beauty of it," he said. "While you've been doing that, we've done all the hard work on this end. The team has written a program that's going to reset the clock in the vault and make it think it's time to open. Then you'll be able to enter the combination and just open the door."

Shepard talked the women through placing another device on the door that latched on magnetically. "This is going to get us into the system for the time lock. Normally, it can only be accessed from the inside, but we'll get around that by using a series of electromagnetic pulses…"

As he continued, Alex realized he was bragging. Fair enough—there were probably only a handful of people in the world who could pull this operation off.

"Now, pull the thumb drive out of the laptop and insert it into the equipment," Shepard said. "We'll take over from here. Why don't you two relax for a few minutes until the new software is installed.

"Getting the software right was tricky," he added. "The internal clock is synced to the atomic clock in Boulder, Colorado. The system makes adjustments of small fractions of nanoseconds a few times a year. We removed some safeguards to allow us to jump ahead several hours and trick the vault into thinking that it's time to open. Just hang on…"

Alex and Lily waited. After a few minutes Alex heard some muttering and cursing on Shepard's end.

"Everything okay, Shepard?" Lily asked.

He didn't answer right away and then said, "Switch the device on the door on and off. We're going to try that again."

Alex didn't like the sound of that, but followed the instructions. They waited a few more minutes, and then she definitely heard Shepard cursing.

"Is there a problem?"

Another pause and Shepard said, "See those two red lights on the digital keypad?"

"Yes."

"The one on the right should be green. That would tell us the time lock is disengaged. But we've altered the vault's software, so the indicator may just be wrong, and the time lock may already be open. There's a simple check; just try the combination."

Lily dialed in the numbers, taking care to hit each one precisely. As she worked, Shepard said, "When you are through, the indicator light on the left should turn green."

Alex finished the sequence. The indicator light turned green.

"Great!" Shepard said with relief. "Now both of you spin the large wheel in the front."

The stainless steel wheel was in the dead center of the vault with four large "spokes" that each radiated a foot outward. Alex grabbed two of the spokes, Lily grabbed the other two, and together they tried to turn the wheel counterclockwise.

"It won't budge," Lily said.

"Try the combination again," Shepard said. This time, his voice didn't sound relieved or hopeful. After all, they had gotten the green light on the mechanical lock system. That part of the process was working. Clearly, the problem was the digital time clock mechanism.

They tried again to budge the wheel. They failed again.

"What now, Shepard?" Lily asked.

"Give me a sec," Shepard said. The line went dead for nearly a minute. When Shepard came back, Alex heard the forced calm in his voice. "No problem. Just sit tight while we tweak the software."

Then Shepard cut the line.

This time, it was longer than a minute.

Alex and Lily shared a glance before either one of them spoke.

"Do you want another cup of coffee?" Alex asked.

"Sure," Lily said. "It's actually not bad."

Before Alex could take a sip of her new cup, the door opened. It was the assistant manager, Mr. Boucher, pushing what appeared to be a room service cart.

The man didn't even look at the equipment laid out around them or at the vault itself.

"The kitchen has prepared something for you," Boucher said.

"What about the gas leak?" Alex asked.

"We all know there is no gas leak," he said conversationally. "Nevertheless, out of an abundance of caution, I sent almost everyone home. I'm sorry to say because of that, our full menu is not available. I hope these few items I've brought you will suffice."

He proceeded to uncover the dishes, an assortment of grilled vegetables, beef tenderloin, grilled scallops, and a potato soufflé. There was also some sautéed fish.

Gesturing to the fish, Boucher said proudly, "Caught this morning on the Riviera."

They sat in front of the food and he poured them wine from a newly opened bottle he had brought. After he was finished, he took a slight bow. "I will be nearby if there is anything else you need."

The food and wine were delicious. To Alex it felt a bit like a last meal. At least it was a good one.

"If this is how they treat you in Monte Carlo when you're trying to break into their vault," Alex said, "remind me to come back as a paying customer."

Chapter 17

As the two agents walked into Bloch's office, Shepard looked sick and O'Neal looked nervous.

"Be straight with me," Bloch said. "How bad is it?"

"It's bad," Shepard said. "We have the combination for the safe, but my software fix for the time lock didn't work."

"So, try again," Bloch said, not liking where this was going.

"We did," said Shepard. "We tried again and again. All we've managed to do is trip another layer of security, and now there's a twenty-four-hour lockout."

"Meaning you've made it worse," Bloch said.

"It's my fault," said Shepard.

"I don't want to hear that! Don't accept responsibility, solve the problem!" Bloch raised her voice for the first time since this mess had started. "Tell me there's something we can do other than call for an air strike."

"An air strike is out of the question," said Shepard. "Excessive vibration can set off the bomb. The odds of nuclear detonation in that scenario would be extremely high. We'd have a better chance of the bomb not detonating because of a defect."

Bloch couldn't sit for another second and sprung from her chair. "You're telling me," she said, "that our best chance to avoid a catastrophic nuclear blast is to hope our adversary made a mistake in building what you've told me is a fairly simple device. The same adversary who got their hands on plutonium in the first place and then sneaked a bomb into a vault we can't crack? Do you understand why this is unacceptable to me?"

"Yes," said O'Neal and Shepard together.

"No more excuses," Bloch said. "I need you to fix it and fix it now. You told me the time lock is basically a computer. Hack it, reprogram it, do whatever you have to, but get us inside."

"We've tried everything we can," Shepard said. "The system won't accept any new instructions, including any changes to its operating system until the end of the lockout period. The only way to end that lockout and make changes would be to guess a twenty-four-digit entry code out of billions of combinations."

"So?" Bloch said. "Put the problem to your expensive, cutting-edge computers until you get the right answer."

"We're talking about tens of millions of hours of computing time," Shepard said. "Even if we could get access to other large systems, getting the code would take more than twenty-four hours."

"I don't know what to tell you, Shepard," Bloch said. "Do what the British did in World War Two: Make a machine that can crack the code."

"Alan Turing spent years doing the conceptual work and his teams spent years building the device," O'Neal said.

"You'll have to do better than that," Bloch said, feeling the anger drain out of her as she sank back into her chair. "We have Alex and Lily a few feet away from the bomb. Give them something to work with, something to try. That's an order."

Grimly, Shepard and O'Neal nodded and left her office.

Bloch didn't like the expressions on their faces. They seemed like people running out of time and on the verge of losing hope.

She knew the feeling.

* * * *

Lily sat at the table, waiting quietly. That was something Alex couldn't do. Right now, there was only one thing she *could* do, and that was to pace around the room. Of course, it was pointless, but given a choice, she'd rather take pointless action than do nothing. That was the Morgan curse—one of them, anyway.

And then she realized there was one other thing she could do. "Lily, maybe you could go see Scott. I'll hold down the fort here."

"What?" Lily said.

"Under the circumstances, two of us here doing nothing is no better than one of us," Alex said.

"When Shepard calls with his fix, we'll still have a nuclear bomb to defuse," Lily said.

"Two things about that," Alex said. "One, if that happens, you'll be less than fifteen minutes away. Two, we both know that Shepard is out of ideas."

Before Lily could protest, Alex said, "You know that very soon we may get a call to pull out. Bloch will do that just before the local authorities start evacuating everybody."

"Do you think Bloch and Zeta are close to giving up?" Lily asked.

"It wouldn't be giving up to save as many people as they can," said Alex. "If you're with Scott, you can help him get the team out. Of course, the bomb may be on a timer and could go off in the next ten seconds, or eight hours from now. If it happens before we evacuate, it won't matter if you're here or with Scott. Or, whoever made the device might remote detonate it when the evacuation starts. If that's the case, you'll be with Scott when it happens."

Lily looked pained. "You think Scott wouldn't be able to leave knowing what's going on, but *I* could?" she said, sounding insulted.

"Not the same," Alex said. "Of course Scott wouldn't run out on you, or me, or the team, if it left us in danger. But here, the risk for both of us is the same either way."

"If it comes to that, I couldn't face him knowing we failed to stop it," Lily said. "No. If this turns into an evacuation, we'll all go together."

Alex saw there was no convincing her.

"Besides, I'm the senior agent here," Lily added. "If anyone's going to stay behind, it'll be me. If I had made you the same offer, would *you* go?"

"In a hot second," said Alex and Lily laughed.

"Is it an American thing? A competition to make the sacrifice play?"

Now it was Alex's turn to smile. "You prefer the British way: The band keeps playing on deck as the *Titanic* goes down?"

"I don't like either of those endings," Lily said.

"Good thing it's not the end yet, then. My father has three steps for survival. First, be smarter than the enemy. Second, be faster than the enemy. And third, if all else fails, be luckier."

That got another smile from Lily. "Do you feel lucky today, Alex?"

"Sure," Alex said. "We've crashed and burned on the first two."

* * * *

Shepard had Lily and Alex rig up a wireless receiver so he could load new software directly into the time lock system. It was faster and saved Alex and Lily the time required to physically move the software from the laptop to the vault.

This was a game of seconds and every one counted. The problem was that the new equipment allowed Shepard to fail faster with each attempt. He made another tweak in the software and tried again, transmitting the new system update. It took less than a minute for his screen to flash *UPDATE REJECTED*.

He wanted to pound his head into the desk, but started over. Shepard prided himself on writing clean code that ran as simply and efficiently as possible. Not all programmers were so meticulous. He decided to try changing parameters that didn't alter the code and got there less quickly and less elegantly.

He added some redundancies. Then he eliminated his signature code groupings. After that, he tried some particularly egregious deep nesting. It pained him to do the work—which felt more like vandalism than programming. But short of any new ideas, he was forced to keep trying variations on the same approach and hoping that eventually the vault would accept the new software.

The problem was that even if his approach eventually worked, it would likely take more time than Alex and Lily could afford to wait. Of course, there were far more people involved then Alex and Lily, but the real stakes were overwhelming and difficult to comprehend. He found that concentrating on the people he knew helped him to focus.

While he worked, O'Neal was at her station trying to work a different sort of miracle by trying to write an algorithm that would somehow generate all of the possible twenty-four-digit security codes with hardware that was grossly inadequate for the task.

Shepard transmitted another version and this one was promptly rejected. Before he could begin again, O'Neal said, "What if the code isn't random?"

"What do you mean?" he asked.

"You said the programming code you've seen is built around prime numbers. What if the system generates its codes using prime numbers? Or semi-primes?"

It made sense and might work, but they had the same problem. O'Neal could do the math and, together, they could write the program to generate all possible security codes under those parameters. That would drastically reduce the processing time, but it still wouldn't be fast enough to help them.

"We're back to having to build the machine that can do the processing," Shepard said.

"What if someone else has already built it?" O'Neal replied.

"But no one has…" Shepard said, but even as he said it, he realized that it wasn't true. At least not officially.

"Even if it exists, it would take a week for you to do the math and for me to learn how to program the machine," Shepard said.

"True, but what if we had some help, an expert?"

Shepard fell in love all over again with Karen and did the only thing he could think of: He kissed her.

He called Bloch. "Director, we have an idea, but you're not going to like it."

* * * *

Shepard and O'Neal were out of breath when they appeared in Bloch's office.

"There is a machine that can do the calculations and we don't have to build it. We just need access," he said.

"Whatever it is, if I can't get it for you, I'm sure Mr. Smith can," Bloch said. "Just tell me who to call."

"There's a system called M-five," Shepard said and Bloch's face fell.

"The M-five doesn't exist," she said automatically.

"Not officially, but we all know it does," Shepard said.

Bloch sighed. She knew the M-5 was the name the internet had given to the Defense Department's next generation of computers that used quantum processors. "DARPA has denied the computer's existence to my face. I'm sure I can get you immediate access to the Google machine, or the one at IBM," Bloch said.

"The M-five is at least twice as fast as those," Shepard replied.

He was right. They didn't have time to waste. Of course, they didn't have time for the approvals that would be necessary to get access to this nonexistent machine either.

"Is there anything else you and Karen need? Would you like to take *Air Force One* on a joyride?"

"There is something. We'll need an outside expert," he said.

"I presume you have someone in mind."

"We do. Maryam Nasiri," Shepard said, smiling.

That was interesting, and there was a nice symmetry there. Alex and Lily had gotten Nasiri out of Iran, and Bloch knew she was a leading expert in quantum computing. Bloch didn't come close to understanding how quantum computers actually worked, but she knew they were the future of cryptography and defense. Currently there was a bit of a secret arms race between China, Russia, and the US to build the fastest machine.

"Is Nasiri available?" Bloch asked.

"Karen is on the phone with her now. If you give us approval, we can brief her," Shepard said.

In a way, Nasiri might make things easier for Bloch to do her part. Zeta had gotten the woman out of Iran partly as a favor to the DOD, and sooner or later Bloch suspected Nasiri would be tapped for the M-5 project.

Well, it looked like sooner.

"Get yourselves ready. Let me see what I can do," Bloch said.

As soon as Shepard darted out the door, Bloch hit a special, secure line on her phone that was dedicated to only one person.

When someone on the other side picked up, Bloch gave the operator a code. There was a brief pause and then the voice said, "Hold for the president."

Chapter 18

Something was different; Alex could hear it in Shepard's voice over her ear comm. For once, the development wasn't bad news. He was excited, and it was less than an hour since they had last heard from him.

Lily raised an eyebrow and Alex could see that her partner had heard the same thing.

"We have something we want you to try," he said. "We may have progress on the emergency lockout code, but I'd be more comfortable if you entered it manually."

"Okay," Lily said. "But I thought there were hundreds of millions of variations."

"Billions, actually, but we've narrowed it down a bit. I need one of you to input the following on the keypad."

Alex pointed to the pad and said, "You are the senior agent."

Lily stepped up and said, "Go ahead, Shepard."

Shepard called out each of the twenty-four numbers and Lily carefully entered each digit.

The British woman was remarkably cool, but as she entered the last few numbers, Alex could see that even Lily Randall was starting to sweat. They would have to pace themselves; even if there were just a few hundred of these, it would take a while.

For the last four digits Alex held her breath; she only released it when Lily entered the last number: seven.

There was barely a second before she heard a beep, and for the first time since they started this operation, the time lock indicator light turned green. Alex almost didn't believe it.

"We're green on the time lock," Lily said.

"What? The first time?" Shepard said.

"Apparently," Lily said.

"Are we a go on the combination?" Alex asked.

There was the slightest pause before Shepard said, "Yes, go ahead."

Alex was up. She approached the dial and ran through the four-digit combination, which she had memorized by now. When she reached the last number, she heard a *click* inside the vault, and the second indicator light turned green.

"Apparently it's open," Alex said. As Shepard had said earlier, now came the hard part. They had to find and identify the nuclear bomb—hoping they didn't hit a booby trap and that the bomb's timer didn't go off before they finished.

Through her ear comm Alex heard some rustling on Shepard's side of the line. Karen O'Neal's voice said, "O'Neal here."

"Hi Karen," Alex said.

There was more rustling and then, "Bloch here."

"Director," Lily said.

Alex was happy to have them all on the line, but that meant the danger was far from over.

"Turn on your body cams," Shepard said.

"We're with you," Bloch said, and Alex was touched by the image of Bloch and O'Neal huddled over Shepard's monitor.

"Whenever you're ready," Shepard said.

Alex and Lily both grabbed the wheel on the vault door and Alex—even though she knew intellectually that the lock had opened—was still surprised when the large wheel started moving.

It took only a moderate effort to turn it and thus retract the twenty-four bolts that anchored the giant circular door to the frame. When the wheel stopped, the two women pulled on it and the door swung open. It moved slowly but with less effort than Alex would have guessed, given its extreme weight. She chalked that up to good engineering.

Alex was keenly aware that this was one of the critical points in the process. If the bomb was booby-trapped, a motion sensor pointed at the door was one of the most obvious safeguards. However, that thought was purely intellectual. After the last couple of hours, Alex couldn't muster much worry. If a detonation occurred, it would happen too fast to give her any time to think about it.

When the door was fully opened, Lily peeked around it first. "Oh, my," she said as she peered inside.

"What is it?" Bloch said, a note of concern in her voice.

Alex stepped around to see for herself and said, "Wow."

Whatever she had been expecting when they opened the door, it wasn't this.

* * * *

Bloch tried to make sense of the split screen image on the large monitor in the workstation. "I'm getting your body cam feeds, but what am I seeing?" Bloch asked.

"We're not sure," Lily said.

"Both of you move so your cameras can scan the room," Shepard said.

The video images on both sides of the split screen panned the vault, showing what Bloch had expected—mostly. There were metal shelves that contained large containers of high value chips. It made sense that they would be kept in the vault.

There were other bins full of cash, in different currencies and denominations. There were also large rectangles of euros, neatly marked and wrapped in plastic. These, Bloch knew, were new, uncirculated bills.

All of it made sense, but there were two things that absolutely didn't track, given the meticulous organization inside the vault. One was what seemed to be the remains of a rock—or a statue—that had been pulverized. It was on the left side, near the vault door.

Farther down, near the center of the room, were large plastic bins that had been opened and turned over. Casino chips littered the floor.

"Before you go any further, take a reading on your radiation meter," Bloch said. A few seconds later, she could see her agents waving their phones in front of them while numbers flashed on one of the smaller monitors in the workstation.

"Okay, we're getting higher readings. Nothing dangerous, but it definitely seems like you are closer to the source. The good news is you haven't set off any motion or body-heat–based booby traps."

"All good news cheerfully accepted," said Alex.

"Let's get a peek at the debris near the front," Shepard said. "Give us a good scan and get as close as you can."

Both cameras turned to the rocks and dust on the floor. Lily's voice sounded. "I think we found the statues—or what's left of them."

Bloch gave Shepard a glance. He appeared as confused as Bloch was herself.

"Karen?" he asked. "Anything?"

"Radiation is no higher," O'Neal said. "The bomb wasn't hidden inside them."

That made sense. Bloch was far from an expert, but she knew that the statues were not big enough to house a nuclear bomb.

Yet something had smashed them to pieces.

"Step all the way inside," Shepard said. "And keep taking the readings."

"We're seeing an uptick," O'Neal said.

"Let's get a good look at the mess," Shepard said. As they approached the open bin, O'Neal said, "Still rising, but lower than we'd expect if that's the device."

They got a view of the inside of the open case. There were chips lying there, but they were dwarfed by the large metal cylinder that dominated the interior.

"I think we found the atomic bomb," Alex said.

"Readings are still lower than they should be," O'Neal said.

"Does lower mean *safe*?" Lily asked.

"Perfectly," Shepard said. "Even fully enriched radioactive material is pretty safe. You could play catch with it without a problem."

"Maybe when we get out of here," Alex said.

"Get a light on the contents," Shepard said.

Lily shined a flashlight into the case, and Bloch saw the problem. The bomb casing—assuming that's what it was—was open and a fair amount of casino chips had spilled into it.

"Somebody made a mess inside your bomb, Shepard," Alex said.

"Not just that, but it appears they took the plutonium out," he said.

Shepard had the agents poke around inside the cylinder, which made Alex nervous despite his assurances that it was perfectly safe. After a few minutes he declared that someone had gotten there before them and taken the plutonium out.

"They left behind a perfectly good bomb casing," Alex said.

"Apparently," Shepard agreed.

Alex could hear Shepard and O'Neal whispering.

"This leaves us with a few questions," Lily said.

"Karen and I have a theory," Shepard said. "If you two could turn around and walk slowly out of the vault, we can test it." As the women approached the door, Shepard asked them to stop and scan the area with their body cameras. There was more whispering on Shepard's end. "Look up and to the right."

Alex and Lily obliged.

"See that lever on the wall?"

"We do," Lily said.

Just above their heads was a lever with a red handle. Next to it a sign read *L'urgence*.

"That's the emergency release lever," Shepard said. "It keeps people who get trapped inside from suffocating in bank vaults. It's easy to use and only works if you are on that side of the door."

Attached to the lever was a black, four-legged, spindly...*something.*

It reminded Alex vaguely of a creepy robot "dog" from the Internet that she'd seen open doors and climb stairs.

"What is that thing?" Alex asked.

"See if it comes off," said Shepard.

Alex grabbed it and it came off the lever easily enough, with only suction cups on its feet to hold it to the wall. It was just over two feet long with two claws in addition to its four feet.

It definitely resembled a small dog, but there was a metal stub where the head should've been, and when Alex turned it over, there was a red light in the center of a small lens. "I get the feeling this thing is staring at me."

"It might be. Put it down," Shepard said.

"Good work Lily, Alex," said Bloch. "Now get out of there. We'll have the case and the robot picked up."

"Can anyone tell us what's going on?" Lily asked.

"This is just a guess," said Shepard, "but we think the bomb was smuggled in with the chips, and the robot was smuggled in inside the statues. When we examine them, I think we'll find the valuable statues are nothing but forgeries."

"That doesn't make any sense. If the bomb was smuggled in with the chips, why have a robot open the door?" Alex asked.

"Because the robot belongs to someone else," Shepard said. "Someone who wanted the plutonium but not the bomb."

"Someone smuggled in the bomb and then someone else smuggled in the robot to snatch the plutonium?" Alex said.

"That's our current guess," Shepard said.

"We'll know more when we examine the scene," Bloch said. "But for now, you two can take the rest of the night off."

Chapter 19

After a long, hot shower, Alex felt better. Once she got dressed, she felt better still. She made a point of overdressing a bit, certainly for what she had planned. She'd gotten that trick from her mother, who always made a point of dressing up when she was sick and encouraged Alex to do the same. Of course, Alex wasn't sick, but it had been a long day and she felt wiped. When she got to her room, she had been shocked to find it was only 8:00 in the evening. It felt like the middle of the night.

Lily called, asking if Alex wanted to join her and Renard at the paddock. Alex was only mildly surprised that Lily sounded normal—almost casual, actually—as if she hadn't spent most of the day waiting to be vaporized by a nuclear bomb.

But that was Lily Randall. Part of it, Alex knew, was the British stiff upper lip, but most was just Lily herself. Alex said she might stop by later. Lily paused. "Alex, are you all right?" she said. "Do you want me to come over? Scott has to show his face, but we could do something."

Alex was touched by the concern in her partner's voice. "I'm fine," she said. "I was just planning a low-key evening. I'll get some rest and see you tomorrow. Have fun at the paddock."

Alex gave herself one last check in the mirror, grabbed the bottle of champagne she had chilling in the ice bucket on her dresser, and headed for the door. The room she was going to was just three floors up. She was there in no time. The hallway was empty, which wasn't a surprise, since everyone was at the paddock or some other pre-race event.

Almost everyone.

Terry opened the door in a T-shirt and sweatpants. He was surprised and clearly pleased to see Alex.

"Hi," he said.

"Hi, Terry. I just wanted to say good luck tomorrow."

"Thanks," he said. "You going out?" He scanned her dress. "You look great, but I really can't go out the night before a race. I was planning to stay in..." He gestured to his clothes.

"Actually, it's been a bit of a day," said Alex. "Would you mind some company?" She raised the bottle of champagne.

"Not at all," he said. "If you don't think it would be too boring."

Alex leaned in and put her hand on his chest. "No, I don't think so," she said, reaching up to kiss him. He kissed her back enthusiastically.

As they continued to kiss, Alex pushed him back into the room, the door swinging shut behind them.

No, Alex thought, *this won't be boring at all.*

* * * *

When Bloch headed downstairs, she was playing a hunch, a hunch that turned out to be correct. The lights were off in the basement, except for the glow that came from the monitors in Shepard and O'Neal's workstation.

The couple appeared to be dressed for bed, in T-shirts and sweatpants. Bloch felt like she was intruding. Despite the fact that this was a workplace, she knew that she was.

Lately, her two agents had spent at least as many nights here as they did at home. She also knew that for the young couple, the personal and the professional were so intermingled that the distinction had become less and less meaningful.

"Director," O'Neal said.

"We were just finishing up." Shepard sounded apologetic, as if working this late might be a problem.

"I just wanted to see if anyone else was up," Bloch said, taking an empty seat.

Something of how she was feeling must have showed on her face, because Shepard said, "Everything okay?"

Bloch shrugged, too tired to pretend that she was more in control than she was. "The royal family of Monaco is very grateful. In fact, the prince has invited you both, as well as your friend, Ms. Nasiri, to be his honored guests next time you are in Europe. Our president is happy, but the EU prime minister has 'concerns' about our methods, and DARPA thinks we owe them a favor."

"I'm not sure that's true," O'Neal said. "I suspect that Maryam Nasiri put them five years ahead of where they were in their cryptography program."

That was interesting. "Good to know," Bloch said. "I'm sure they will try to recruit her when she's through with all of her debriefings."

"I don't think she'll want that. She only wants to go back to her university. However, I think she might be open to consulting for Zeta," Shepard said.

"That's *very* good to know," Bloch said. "I have my own thoughts, but what do you two make of today?"

"We're preparing a full briefing—" O'Neal started to say.

"Just tell me what you think," Bloch said.

"As I said," Shepard said, "we think someone smuggled the bomb into the vault in a container of new chips. Operationally, that required a high degree of sophistication and organization. We have no way of knowing for sure," he added, "but I'd bet it was the same group who stole the plutonium and built the bomb."

"Why assume the same group did all three?" Bloch asked.

"Because all three operations were complex and required a great deal of money and expertise in a number of areas," O'Neal said.

Shepard continued for her. "You could pay someone to acquire the plutonium, build the bomb, or beat the casino security, or do any combination of those things, but in highly sophisticated and complex operations, the greater the number of people involved, the greater the chances of a leak. Of course, when you deal with mercenaries and contractors you greatly increase you risks," he added.

"Does the attempt on Renard's life fit into this?" Bloch asked.

"We think so. The same with the aborted operation in Malaysia," Shepard said. "All of them are not only sophisticated from intelligence and technical points of view, but they are utterly ruthless. They killed more than a dozen people in the chemical fire used as a cover in Azerbaijan; they murdered an entire terror cell in Kuala Lumpur; and if their bomb had gone off, we'd be looking at hundreds of thousands dead and massive destruction."

"Ares?" Bloch asked.

"Yes, the more we see, the more we think this is a group with the resources and capabilities of Zeta," Shepard said.

"It makes sense," Bloch said. "And it fits the facts. But then who took the plutonium from the vault? I'm positive it wasn't one of our friendly intelligence agencies. Was it Ares? Was it part of some bizarre setup? Create a problem and then solve it? Something like what happened in Malaysia?"

"We thought of that, but it doesn't fit the profile of Ares we're developing," O'Neal said.

"How so?" Bloch asked.

"It wasn't ruthless enough. They didn't kill the Bulgarians who were caught in the theft at Hôtel de Paris, which, we now know, was a successful exchange of fake statues for real ones. Now we've learned that both the casino manager and the chief of security were drugged but have since recovered."

"That definitely doesn't fit the limited profile we have for Ares," Bloch said.

"Whoever did it also presumably facilitated the escape of the Bulgarians from the local jail," Shepard said.

"What?"

"Yes," said Shepard. "We thought you knew. We just got the report."

"It happened while all eyes were on the casino vault," O'Neal said.

There weren't many intelligence agencies that could mount the hotel and casino operation. The major Western powers could probably do it, as well as Israel, China, and Russia. That was it.

"That raises more questions," Shepard said. "Yes, whoever stole the plutonium prevented a catastrophe, but they still took the plutonium. And the original statues are nearly priceless and remain missing."

"Not just the statues," Bloch said. "I just heard from the prince; apparently, a fair amount of cash was stolen from the vault."

Now it was Shepard and O'Neal's turn to be surprised.

"Someone grabbed priceless artifacts and a pile of cash while averting a nuclear disaster," Shepard said. "Who would do that and what would drive them?"

"That's the question of the day—one of them, anyway," Bloch said. "It seems we have more than one new player on the scene. In addition, we still have loose plutonium out there, as well as a threat to Scott Renard and the two agents who are assigned to him."

"We'll have our full report on your desk in the morning," O'Neal said.

"I don't want to see either of you in this office until noon," Bloch said. "Get some rest and come to me fresh tomorrow."

"Yes, Director," said O'Neal.

Bloch got up and saw the two of them staring intently at their monitors. "And that rest is to start immediately."

"Yes, ma'am," the two said in unison.

Chapter 20

When Alex woke up the next morning, Terry was already dressed.

"Morning," he said.

"Good morning," she said. They were both smiling. "It's your room—you don't have to leave."

"I was just going for a walk." He looked slightly uncomfortable. "Would you like to come? It's just a silly ritual I have before a race."

Who is this man? Alex thought. "Silly rituals are where I live. Give me twenty minutes," she said.

She found him waiting in the lobby. It was still early and the hotel was just waking up. He smiled when he saw her and then kissed her.

"Thanks for this," he said.

"I figured a good-morning kiss was the least I could do," she said.

"Not that—but thanks for that, too. I mean, my walk," he said.

"You *do* know that you are one of only twenty Formula One drivers in the world, right?" said Alex. "Plenty of women would be happy to take a walk with you. I've personally witnessed half a dozen of them throwing themselves at you."

Terry shrugged. "They have no interest in me. The idea of me, sure. Formula One driver me, no question. But the actual me, not so much…"

"That sounds lonely," she said.

"I soldier on." He sounded philosophical. "On the plus side, I have tons of women throwing themselves at me."

Alex laughed. "Okay, where are you taking me?"

"I like to walk the track," Terry said.

A few minutes later, the car dropped them off at the Renard garage. The chief was there, along with a few others. They greeted Terry and then stepped back. Clearly, they knew about his ritual.

Alex and Terry began to walk along the track. "Fair warning," he said, "it's just over two miles. I keep a pretty good pace. I do it in under thirty minutes."

"I'll try to keep up," Alex said. "Do you like that it's a street circuit?"

"You've been doing your homework," he said, smiling. "Yes, I do. It's my favorite course. There are only four street circuits in Formula One today."

Alex's research had told her that most Formula 1 tracks had been built for the race. Only a few of them used actual city streets.

"I understand that it's narrow and twisty," Alex said. "They say it's the hardest."

"It is the most challenging and the one where winning is more about the driver than the car," Terry said.

They passed a church standing on a nearly 90-degree corner turn that Alex couldn't imagine taking at any real speed. "I've also heard that this circuit is the most dangerous," Alex said.

"Yeah, there's not a lot of room to move," said Terry, "and you do have twenty cars on the track. One driver said it was like racing a bicycle around in your living room."

"Do you worry?" Alex asked.

"Not really," he said. "It can be dangerous, but it's not what most people think. The movies don't get that part right. We don't struggle with whether or not we're going to die every time we get into the cockpit."

"Of course, I don't want to make you nervous," she said.

"Don't worry about it. If I wasn't nervous before a race, I'd be a moron and probably not sharp enough to avoid trouble. But when you're driving, you have a lot to do. You have to focus on the race, or you won't make it. It's very step-by-step."

Alex had heard more than one person say that about military battles, and she'd experienced it herself in hand-to-hand combat and firefights.

"The same in my business," she said. "If you think too much about what could go wrong when you're taking apart a Morbidelli eight-fifty, you'd never be able to change the spark plugs, let alone open up the engine case."

He laughed. "See, we're practically in the same business." He fell quiet before adding, "Every driver crashes once and a while. At least anybody who's any good. You have twenty cars in a tight space going blazing fast around turns. Even if you don't take chances, you can still get clipped by someone who's less careful. Thankfully, the cars are well designed and most of the time you walk away with no more than bumps and bruises."

"Most of the time?" she said.

"Almost always. Do you know the last time a driver was killed in a Formula One race?"

Alex had to admit she didn't.

"Five years ago. In the old days, they could lose ten percent of their drivers in a single season. Nowadays a single death is rare. Everybody on the Renard team knows what they are doing. The chief has been doing this twice as long as I've been alive. And Alonzo has more hours on the track than almost any other driver. Sometimes it pays to be the junior partner. He's taught me a lot."

"Believe me, I know all about that," Alex said.

"Really?" said Terry. "I thought you worked for yourself."

Alex cursed herself for slipping. "I'm the youngest person I know in my business," she said. "And Lily is... well, Lily."

"You don't have anything to worry about," he said.

"Have you *seen* her?" Alex said.

"I have, but to be honest, she's not my type," he said.

"What *is* your type?" Alex asked.

Terry stopped her from walking and put his hands on her shoulders. "I don't have one. But I know it when I see it," he said and kissed her.

They finished the rest of their walk in silence and a few minutes later were back at the garage. By then, more people were milling around, and they mobbed Terry as soon as soon as he was back. He pulled himself away from the group and stepped over to Alex. "Thanks again for coming," he said.

"Thanks for the tour of the track," she said. Then she gave him a quick kiss and added, "Good luck today."

Terry disappeared into the mob of his teammates. Alex checked her phone and saw that it was almost time for her to meet up with Lily and raced back to the hotel.

* * * *

Bloch woke up at 9:00. She hadn't gotten much actual sleep, but it was the latest she'd been in bed since... Well, she couldn't actually remember the last time she saw 9:00 from her bed.

She was vaguely surprised that there hadn't been any emergencies that woke her earlier. Of course, the major threat was over, but there were still two new players out there.

One was ruthless and dangerous. The other was perhaps less overtly dangerous, but was skillfully organized, extremely capable, and highly unpredictable. And now they had a frightening supply of weapons-grade plutonium.

Of course, much of what she was thinking could be a mirage. Zeta had seen a few false alarms lately. Though perhaps *false alarm* was not the right term. It was more like *intentional misdirection.* That had almost certainly been the case in Malaysia.

Was everything that happened in Monte Carlo misdirection, too? Was Ares even real? Bloch found herself thinking about them as if they were. If Ares was out there, Bloch understood what would drive them to test Zeta and the other major intelligence services. For one, Ares—Bloch found herself using Shepard's name for them more and more—was able to test Zeta and everyone else's threat-detection systems.

But the intelligence person in her didn't think that was enough. Setting up a terrorist attack only to shut it down at the last minute was still costly in terms of resources. Even if you had unlimited funds, there was still a time and opportunity cost. In a cohesive organization you could only do so many things at one time.

Making Zeta chase its tail might be satisfying, but they'd still want to get something tangible for their trouble.

And then there was Monte Carlo. Was everything up until now a distraction to make it easier to pull off a nuclear detonation in that city?

If global chaos was their goal, that operation would have been a home run. There wouldn't be much point in setting up an elaborate hoax to suggest the existence of another player who had stopped the explosion at the last minute.

Besides pissing off Bloch, what would be the point of such an operation be? It just didn't feel right. Bloch sincerely believed that Ares had been foiled in Monte Carlo—and not by Zeta. Did Ares know that?

Bloch didn't think so. Even if someone else hadn't intervened, Zeta was minutes away from stopping the detonation. Bloch knew that if she were running Ares, she would be hopping mad right now. She'd want to hurt the organization that had foiled them. You would certainly want to reduce their capabilities as much as you could to protect your future operations.

If you wanted to do that, you'd eliminate as many of their resources as you could. Bloch was no Dan Morgan or even Lincoln Shepard. She was much more like Karen O'Neal. Her approach to the job was methodical and deductive. She didn't play hunches and she didn't lead from her gut.

Yet she was certain that something was very wrong. Suddenly it was no longer a feeling, she just knew. Someone was about to hurt Zeta—and hurt them badly. The only question left was whether or not she could stop it in time.

* * * *

"Conley here," Peter Conley said into his phone.

"This is Bloch. Where are you now?" her voice said.

"At a café across from our hotel," Conley replied.

"Is Guo with you?" Bloch asked.

"Yes."

"Ear comms, both of you," Bloch said.

Then Dani was on the line. "Guo here."

"You're a target—get out of Kuala Lumpur," Bloch said.

"Understood," Conley said. "Time frame?"

"Immediate," she replied. "Don't go back to the hotel. Get out of the city, using different ground transportation than you used to get in. If you left anything essential at the hotel, we'll send a team later to pick it up."

"Nothing that can't be replaced. We have our passports with us," he said.

"Don't use them. We'll figure out how to get you clean ones," Bloch said.

That was serious. *Clean* meant new, with names that hadn't been used before.

"Avoid CCTV cameras and put as much distance as you can between yourselves and the hotel. Standard evacuation protocols."

In this case, standard evacuation protocols meant avoiding any people or places they had interacted with before. They would also have to avoid any routines or routes they had used in their time in the city.

He and Dani were already ahead on that score. They had spent a little extra time in their room this morning—quite a bit of extra time, as it turned out. So they were diverging from any loose schedule they had maintained so far.

Conley paid the bill, leaving a generous but not unusual tip, and he and Dani started walking. They had gotten maybe five blocks from the hotel when they heard and felt the blast.

"What was that?" Bloch asked.

Conley turned and saw a burning hole in the place where their fifth-floor room had just been.

"The hotel. The good news is that you don't have to worry about picking up our things from the room. The bad news is that I don't think we'll be getting our security deposit back."

He heard strong language coming from Bloch's side of the call.

"Put some distance between yourselves and the capital, then let me know where you are," she said. "We'll arrange pickup."

Chapter 21

Let them chew on that, Bloch thought as she put down the phone. It was official: The US State Department would announce the death of two Americans in a Kuala Lumpur hotel.

That story would dominate the news since there were no other casualties, except minor smoke inhalation for two of the housekeeping staff.

In a couple of weeks, the Malaysian authorities would announce that their investigation was complete, and the deaths were connected to terrorist activity—specifically a dispute between a faction of ISIS and the local Al-Ma'unah terrorist group.

Bloch thought of the British, who had used strategic misinformation campaigns to fight the Nazis. They broadcasted false reports of the location of V-2 bomb strikes so Nazi engineers would mis-calibrate their rockets' guidance systems. England had also started a massive public health campaign to encourage its people to eat carrots to improve their eyesight. Carrots were said to fight night blindness and improve low-light vision.

Because carrots were plentiful in England during the war, they were a perfect cover for the massive advances in radar technology that allowed the British to see German bombers while Luftwaffe planes were still on the French side of the English Channel.

Carrots *were* good for eyesight, but the British had managed to convince the world—and most importantly the Nazis—that they could actually improve vision. Thus, the Nazis believed that it was the English spotters with carrot-enhanced vision who were able to "see" the bombers from a great distance. And the new radar technology remained secret.

The program was so successful that the Germans began feeding their own pilots massive amounts of carrots to get the same benefits. In addition, decades later in the US, when she was growing up, Bloch was still told by adults that carrots would help her eyes.

Up until now, Ares had been able to reduce the effectiveness of Zeta's threat-assessment system by creating or funding real threats, and then simply eliminating them before they happened. Kuala Lumpur and the murder of the terrorists there was the first time Zeta had been able to confirm the tactic, but Bloch was sure that there were others.

As a matter of resource management, if a threat didn't materialize, Zeta (or any other agency) just moved on. There was no point investigating things that hadn't happened.

But Zeta had gotten lucky in Kuala Lumpur and had seen the truth. Now that Bloch knew what was happening, she thought there might be a way to make some changes to Karen O'Neal's system to identify those false flag operations.

Perhaps more importantly, the hotel bombing told Bloch something about her opponent: They were pissed off that they had been foiled in Monte Carlo.

As a result, they had acted hastily and emotionally against Conley and Guo. Now that Bloch knew Ares could be rattled, she had some more ideas about how to really tick them off.

For too long, Zeta had just been reacting to their new foe. Part of that was the nature of intelligence work. Much of what you did was responding to threats or events, but you couldn't do that until those things became real. But now that Bloch knew the other side would react emotionally to failure, she had a few tricks to draw them out.

But first, Bloch had other, more pressing business to attend to.

As she approached the War Room, Bloch could hear voices. That wasn't a surprise, since all agents in and around Boston were assembled for what was about to happen.

The conference table had been moved to the back of the room and was now full of pizza and various snacks. The chairs were arranged in a rough semicircle around the situation monitor, the twelve-foot screen that usually provided real-time satellite imagery or secure teleconferencing with the Pentagon. It was now tuned to the pre-race coverage at Monte Carlo.

It was not the first time the screen was used for entertainment purposes. In the past, Bloch knew that the room had been commandeered by Dan Morgan, Peter Conley, Lincoln Shepard, and various other agents for movies. Most of those films were about war, or they involved cowboys, robots, space, large monsters—or unlikely combinations of those elements. The film showings were harmless and usually happened fairly late in the day.

Today's get-together made a lot of sense. The Formula 1 race was the culmination of a concerted effort of many of the people in this room. Even if Alex and Lily hadn't been on a mission at the Monte Carlo Grand Prix, Scott Renard was an important part of Zeta Division. Quite a few of Bloch's people owed Renard the success of their missions, if not their lives.

The least they could do was cheer on his racing team.

"Status?" Bloch said as she entered.

Spartan turned away from what appeared to be a serious conversation with Karen O'Neal to say, "The race will begin in fifteen minutes, Director. Just a few hours behind schedule."

Bloch was glad. It had taken time to sweep the city to make sure there wasn't another explosive device in the vicinity. It was all done under the guise of repairing a gas leak under the Monte Carlo Casino. The ruse was a good one, considering that the racing circuit took the race cars a hair's breadth away from the front of the casino.

Of course it had to be done. There was always the possibility that whatever had happened in the casino vault was a ruse, and the real bomb was elsewhere.

But after a massive international and interagency effort that the public would never know about, everyone involved was satisfied that the city was safe. It hadn't been easy to delay the race to complete that work. In the US it would have taken an executive order or an act of Congress, but in the case of Monaco, all it took was an act of royalty.

* * * *

As she watched the cars get into position, Alex realized she was nervous. It wasn't like the dull, cold fear she felt when she and Lily thought they were a few feet away from a nuclear bomb. The fear wasn't for herself, her partner, and the thousands of people around them who might be incinerated in a blast.

This was a more intense and immediate worry—a specific concern for a single person on the track. Of course, Alex wanted the Renard team to do well, but she was mostly thinking about Terry Fuller, and about the dangers he so casually dismissed.

She had seen video of some of the dramatic crashes of Formula 1 cars. Terry was right. Even in high-speed collisions, most of the drivers walked away.

The key word for Alex was *most.*

Some walked away injured. Some had to be carried out on stretchers. Some didn't make it to the ambulance, let alone a hospital.

Alex was used to worrying about other agents, but that worry was concern for a colleague, one for whom risk was a calculation and a part of the job.

She supposed Terry measured risk the same way, but that didn't lessen Alex's worry. She didn't care for the feeling, yet it occurred to her that she didn't want to be anywhere else.

As the cars took their positions, she found it easy to identify the distinctive red- and-black colors of the Renard vehicles. Terry's car was easy to spot in the fifth position.

Arranged in two rows, the cars started their engines and once again Alex could feel, as well as hear, their roar. Time passed so slowly as the clock inched closer to the start.

There were four red lights ahead of the starting line. Her heart jumped when the first light flashed on, then the second. When all five were lit up, they held for less than a second and then all flashed off.

The cars leaped forward and the race began. Alex could track the entire lap from the large outdoor monitors. It was just over a minute before the lead car came back around in front of the Renard garage. A few seconds later she spotted Alonzo's and then Terry's cars. The cars roared past them, and Alex found herself holding her breath until the last one raced below her.

Okay, she thought, *just seventy-seven more laps to go.*

* * * *

Bloch watched Karen O'Neal watch the race. The young woman sat still while her partner Lincoln Shepard responded verbally as well as physically, with jumps and gestures to the ebbs and flows of the contest. Bloch herself watched the race with interest, but was distracted by an idea that kept cutting into her concentration. The interruptions were frustrating because, though she was confident the idea might work, she had nowhere near the skills to develop it.

Even if it did work, it might take weeks or months to show results. Still, it wouldn't hurt to take the first step. She didn't think O'Neal would mind missing a few laps. Bloch approached her agent and said, "Karen, could I speak with you?"

Instantly, O'Neal was alert. Shepard turned around. "Is there a problem?"

"Not at all. I just wanted to run something by Karen," Bloch replied.

The two women headed to the back of the room and Bloch gestured to two chairs. As they sat, she said, "I've been thinking about your threat-assessment system. It's very effective at identifying threats, but we know Ares is gimmicking the system by supporting real threats and then eliminating them before they come to pass."

O'Neal appeared embarrassed and said, "I'm working on ways to filter out the false positives, but it's proved difficult."

"Oh, it's more than difficult," said Bloch, "because I suspect they are not really false positives. Rather, they are real threats that are eliminated by a third party. That means we are stuck in an endless game of trying to prevent threats that were real, but that no longer exist."

O'Neal looked stricken. "Director, I—"

"None of this is your fault," Bloch said. "I know that your system is nothing short of brilliant and has already saved countless lives by identifying real, traditional threats. But could you rework it to predict the kind of operations Ares has been executing?"

For a few seconds, O'Neal appeared to freeze. She didn't move; she didn't even blink. Then she snapped back into the conversation and said, "It would search for the sort of metadata patterns that accompany Ares's false flag operations, which are more like *real* flags."

"Exactly," Bloch said.

"I see a few complications," O'Neal said. "I have to assume that Ares is more careful in their communications and computer use than rogue nations and terrorist groups, so their operations undoubtedly have a smaller digital profile. And we have far fewer samples of actual, or even suspected, Ares operations. Whereas, with traditional threats we have years of data from hundreds of attacks."

"I didn't think it would be easy. You'd have to create a new system that got the same results with far less information," Bloch said.

"Let's assume we don't want to wait for more attacks to generate a larger sample of data," O'Neal said. "What if we could get access to the DARPA quantum computer or built something like it here? And what if you had help from an expert like"—O'Neal took a breath—"Maryam Nasiri."

For a moment, the young woman was as flustered as a ten-year-boy asking if he'd like to shoot hoops with Michael Jordan. "If she would do it, of course," O'Neal said.

"Ask her," Bloch said. "We've been playing whack-a-mole with these people long enough."

"I can start work on the modifications to the algorithm immediately," O'Neal said.

"I don't want to keep you from the race," Bloch said. There was little point to that. Bloch still had to sort out the hardware part of that equation.

"I can work while I watch," O'Neal said.

"Don't you need your computer?"

"No," said O'Neal.

Sometimes Bloch forgot who she was dealing with. When you worked with exceptional people every day, it was easy to forget exactly how different they were.

The agents in the room let out a gasp and a roar. Bloch saw one of the cars on the track trailing black smoke as it rolled into a pit area.

"Don't let me keep you," Bloch said.

"There may be a complication with Maryam Nasiri. She has made a request," O'Neal said.

"We offered her quite a bit when she assisted us with the Monte Carlo situation," Bloch said. "I also know the prince is personally grateful, so if there's any compensation—"

"It's not traditional...compensation. She thought you might be able to help her acquire something. Apparently, Ms. Nasiri is quite a fan of Christmas films."

"Christmas films?"

"Yes. In particular, she enjoys made-for-cable holiday films that involve romance, the death of a spouse or other loved one, children, and the—"

"I'm aware of those films. How can Zeta help Ms. Nasiri?"

"There are four films made about ten years ago that have never been rebroadcast because of a contract dispute with the actress. There are six other films that were cut to allow for more commercial time, but the shorter version was the only subsequent release."

"She is aware that we are an intelligence agency, and that our work is mainly in counterterrorism and the acquisition of state secrets?" Bloch asked.

"She is aware of that, but thought that with Zeta's resources it might be possible for us to help. Can we?"

"Obviously," Bloch said. "Just get me a list of the films she would like and I'll see what I can do."

O'Neal nodded and returned to her seat. Bloch watched Lincoln Shepard give her a questioning look, but O'Neal just smiled. Though the young woman's gaze was fixed on the oversized monitor, Bloch was certain that O'Neal's brain was no longer on the race.

Now it was Bloch's turn to deliver. Helping Nasiri would require a call to Mr. Smith. Though it might not be the most difficult call she had to make on this job, Bloch had no doubt it would be one of the most peculiar.

Of course, given what was at stake, it was a sacrifice Bloch was prepared to make.

Chapter 22

By the tenth lap it had required an act of will for Alex to stop holding her breath, and it only became harder as the cars approached the final lap.

For most of the race, Ferrari and Mercedes had battled each other for first and second place, but in the second-to-last lap, Mercedes had gotten a comfortable lead. The real surprise was that one of the Marussia cars—the one with Jenya at the wheel—was in third place. However, Alonzo from Renard was edging closer and closer to her.

At the same time, Terry surged in the last few minutes and edged through the middle of the pack. In the end, Mercedes crossed the finish line first, with Jenya taking third, Alonzo in fourth, and Terry in sixth.

Scott was beaming, and the rest of the team was very happy because both drivers had placed well and left the team in a good position with respect to the sport's complicated point system.

Terry made his way through the crowd to Alex but was quickly pulled away by the rest of the team, as well as a swarm of fans, sponsors, and journalists. Renard and the chief were in the center of the swarm with him. Alex leaned in to Lily and said, "They do all seem happy."

Lily smiled as she looked on. "He really loves this," she said.

Afterward, the prince and princess gave out the trophies to the first, second, and third place winners. After a brief ceremony, the team headed back to the paddock. The party was cheerful madness, with dozens of team members, as well as spouses, partners, and friends. Lily and Alex made their way upstairs to the top floor, where there was a quieter and more intimate celebration.

The chief had stuck by Terry's side for most of the post-race festivities and finally brought him over to Alex and said, "Sorry to monopolize him.

If it was up to me, I'd keep him up half the night talking about the race and preparing for Quebec, but tonight is a celebration."

People broke off into groups and pairings that were comfortable and mostly relaxed. Sometimes conversations were punctuated with loud laughter and good-natured arguments. It reminded Alex a bit of the few impromptu get-togethers she'd seen at Zeta, especially the ones they'd had after a successful mission.

These were people who spent more time together then they did with their own families. And this was their reward after almost two weeks of intense work—work that would start again tomorrow. As rewards went, Alex thought, it wasn't bad.

Terry found Alex outside on the deck, where she had spent a solid fifteen minutes looking out on the lights of Monte Carlo at night.

"I hope this wasn't too boring for you," he said.

"Anything but boring," she said.

Just then, Alonzo's two boys—who appeared to be between six and eight years old—ran onto the deck, with Alonzo and his wife trailing behind them.

"Terry, is there...anyone from home?" Alex asked.

"Anyone like a *girl*?"

Alex laughed at that. "After seeing the crowd around you today, that seems like the last thing you need."

"But it's like I always say: It's better to have an extra girl and not need one than need one and not have her," he said with a grin.

"My father says the same thing about guns," Alex replied.

"I'm not sure I want to meet your dad," he said.

"What I meant was, Is there any family?" she asked.

"My dad died about seven years ago and my mom has been sick. She may come up to Quebec for the next Grand Prix," he said.

"Well done today, Terry," said a female voice with a Russian accent.

Alex turned to see Jenya enter the patio, looking more like a runway model then someone who had just beaten seventeen other world-class drivers in an intense competition.

"Hello, Alex," Jenya said.

"Hi, Jenya," Alex replied.

"Thank you, but it really was more your day today, Jenya," Terry said.

"Of course—and you will continue to be in my rearview mirror—but as *I* move up I suspect *you* will as well," Jenya said. Then she turned to Alex and said, "How did you like your first Grand Prix?"

"It was intense and to be honest, it was exhausting to watch," Alex said.

"It is even more intense in the cockpit, as Terry can attest. We'll have to get you inside of one of our cars before you leave us. That is, if you are going to continue to Quebec. Or is it back to your motorcycles?"

"I'm going to stay at least through Quebec," Alex said.

"Excellent, then we shall see you there. Excuse me, I have to say hello to our host," Jenya said.

"Aren't they going to miss you back at Marussia?" Alex asked.

"Have you ever been to a Russian celebration?" Jenya asked.

"No," Alex said.

"By this point in the evening, it starts to get a bit morose," Jenya said. "They don't need me for that."

Then Jenya headed off to huddle with the chief, Scott, and Lily. Renard had really built something with his team—for people like Terry, certainly. But it was also something that people like Jenya—without family or a team like this one—wanted to be around the environment Renard had created.

As the evening wound down, people started to peel off, leaving a small cluster of die-hards around Scott, Lily, and the chief. Terry said his good-byes and then approached Alex on the way out.

"I'm going to head out," he said to her.

"Me too," Alex said. "I'll walk with you, if you don't mind some company."

Terry didn't just smile—he beamed.

* * * *

The protocols for emergency extractions were fairly routine. Bloch started by chartering a flight. Any charter booked less than twenty-four hours ahead would get noticed, so she made sure this one was booked less than twelve hours before takeoff.

It was enormously expensive and more than a little suspicious because there were only two passengers and no luggage, let alone cargo. And then there was the destination. From Malaysia, Bloch would have preferred an indirect route through countries that weren't obvious—like the Philippines or India—but this flight was straight to Australia.

The plane would cross most of Australia to Canberra airport near the Australian capital. It was also the closest major airport to the American embassy. The whole operation reeked of desperation, the kind of move a nervous intelligence agency would make to get its agents to safety.

Usually, Bloch avoided doing the obvious when she was genuinely worried. *Especially* when she was genuinely worried. But this situation was far from normal. Zeta had beaten Ares a few times now. A large part of that was due to the fact that her agents' work had been heroic and nothing short of brilliant. But Bloch didn't kid herself: Zeta had also been lucky.

If you were always playing defense, you couldn't afford to be right any less than 100 percent of the time. While Zeta had a better mission success rate than any other major intelligence agency, Bloch couldn't fool herself into thinking that they could maintain a 100 percent success rate for long, let alone forever.

It was time for their opponent to play some defense, and for that Bloch needed to set a trap. Of course, she had to walk a line. If her work appeared too obvious or too desperate, it would tip her hand.

Yet if Ares acted as she hoped, there was some real danger to civilians, so she worked with her contact at the State Department to make sure Malaysian security at the Sepang airport was beefed up, and was further supported by CIA and some local Zeta assets.

That was just insurance, however. With any luck, the confrontation would occur far from the airport, which was just thirty-seven miles out of Kuala Lumpur. Of course, normally she wouldn't use an airport so close to a security hot zone for an extraction from the Malaysian capital, but that was also part of the stagecraft.

The next step was to have her CIA contact file a notice with the Malaysian Special Branch that the US had two agents traveling from Kuala Lumpur to Sepang for extraction and would require a safe house for the night. The CIA further alerted Malaysian authorities to expedite passport control for agents matching Peter Conley and Dani Guo's descriptions.

The Malaysian Special Branch was a more-or-less honest partner in intelligence sharing with the West and was surprisingly free from corruption. Passport control was another story; there was a large problem with bribes for visas and numerous other abuses that allowed Malaysia's immigration system to facilitate human trafficking.

An alert through passport control that singled out Sepang airport was a good method of getting the word out to an organization like Ares. It would certainly kick up an alert on the Zeta system.

From there, it wouldn't be hard for Ares to identify a safe house on the way to the airport. The message came back from the CIA with the house's location surprisingly fast. There was also a warning from Malaysian authorities that the US agents would be on their own. If the CIA wasn't willing to provide operational details, the Special Branch would not offer any personnel. That was fine with Bloch, because this was likely to get messy and she didn't want any Malaysians to get hurt.

In the future, Bloch had high hopes that O'Neal, Shepard, and Nasiri's system would allow them to play the long game with Ares and not only anticipate their operations, but mount effective counterstrikes.

She was confident that the time would come for that, but she didn't need bleeding-edge technology to help read human nature. Ares had already reacted emotionally to a setback, and now Bloch was giving them a chance for payback.

That chance was in the form of a trap that would allow Ares to ambush two Zeta agents. The problem with a trap of this sort was that it required human bait. As a rule, Bloch didn't like to use people—let alone valued agents—for that purpose.

But desperate times...

Chapter 23

"When we get there, let me do the talking," Dani said.

"Fine with me. It's not like I'm fluent in the language," Conley replied.

"Keep your Glock holstered and out of sight," Dani said, as she removed her pistol from her handbag and slipped it in the waist of her Capri pants, making it not only visible but impossible to miss.

She read his expression and said, "Because I'm a woman, they will assume I am weak. This will help make sure they respect me enough to do business."

"Would it be bad if they respected both of us?" Conley asked.

"They will automatically respect you because you are tall and an American man. However, they will assume that also means you are stupid, and if they see you with a gun it will make them nervous."

"I think we should both be offended," Conley said

"I'm sure of it," Dani said. "But let's just get out of here with what we need and without drawing too much attention."

That he could support. This part of the mission required a low profile. When he worked with Dan Morgan, Conley would have handled the low-profile part. Dan could use stealth as well as any agent he'd ever seen, but he really excelled in the high-profile parts of his operations.

Dani, he had seen, could do both, and Conley suspected things were going to get high profile pretty soon, so he was eager to get this part done with.

The market they approached was closed, so the parking lot was empty, except for a few abandoned cars that Conley and Dani had already inspected. They leaned against their car and waited. They were driving an old, locally made Proton hatchback they had acquired in a trade for the motorcycle.

It was just a few minutes before a late-model Honda van entered the lot, drove around them once, and then parked about fifty yards away. "Now," Dani said, walking toward the van with Conley in tow.

As Dani had instructed him, Conley kept his hands visible and walked slowly. When they were just a few paces away, four rough-looking locals got out of the van. Each had a pistol visibly tucked into the waist of his pants.

Conley wasn't sure that made him respect the men more, but it definitely made him more alert. The leader of the group started speaking first and Dani replied. The exchange became more and more heated, with Conley only able to pick out stray words. Those words varied from the mundane, to the mildly insulting, to the *extremely* insulting.

Then Dani and the man seemed to reach a resolution. Once that happened, the man smiled pleasantly at her, said a few words, and turned back to speak with his partners.

"Do we have a deal?" Conley asked.

"Yes, we should wait by the car. They will bring the merchandise to us," Dani said.

Back at the Proton, Conley popped the hatchback, and they waited.

The arms dealers' van swung around and the vehicle's side door opened. There, they showed Dani and Conley the merchandise: two oddly-shaped, Austrian made Steyr assault rifles, two familiar Remington pump-action shotguns, and a single Milkor MGL military grenade launcher.

Conley had never seen one in person and he wasn't disappointed. It was a rifle with a circular magazine that made it look something like a tommy gun. Both the barrel and the magazine were very oversized since they were designed to accommodate 40-millimeter grenades, of which the magazine could hold six.

There were also a few boxes of ammo for each weapon and some extra rounds for each of their handguns. Once the deal was done, the four men actually became friendly and insisted on loading the Proton for them.

Once the Honda pulled away, Conley said, "It appears that we won them over."

Dani raised an eyebrow and said, "It's a complicated culture."

She drove to the safe house as Conley sat in the back to disassemble and clean each of the weapons. He was glad he did. None of them were new and given how things might very well go, they couldn't afford to have their weapons jam.

The grenade launcher was particularly interesting. The model had been used since the early 1980s, and he thought this actual weapon went back almost that far. When he was finished, he was satisfied that the grenade launcher would fire.

He was less confident about the grenades themselves, which were at least ten years old. With a regular round, if you had a misfire or—even worse—a delayed ignition hang fire, it *might* damage the weapon.

However, if the same thing happened with a 40-mm grenade, the results could be downright unpleasant. And yet it was a remarkable weapon that he would like to see in action and, more importantly, he knew that using it would probably become necessary.

They reached the safe house and there were no signs that anyone had been there. The fishing-line trip wire they had set up in the driveway was untouched. In addition, they had rigged the larger paths, which also hadn't been disturbed. However, there were still a number of ways the bad guys could reach the safe house on foot.

The safe house was not really a house; it was a four-story abandoned school. In many ways, it was an ideal safe house. It appeared empty but had electricity and water, and two apartments on the top floor with blacked-out windows. One of the apartments was in the front and one in the back.

Because the school was surrounded by a mostly empty and lightly wooded lot, the apartments had good sight lines in all directions. There were also additional lookout stations on either side of the school.

With a four-person security team, they would be able to see 360 degrees around them for at least five hundred yards. Of course, they didn't have a security team, so they would have to make do.

Had this been a Zeta facility, there would be electronic surveillance in all directions with infrared and night vision cameras. Of course, there would also be a decent coffee machine, but this was a cobbled-together operation.

Years ago, he and Dan Morgan had holed up in worse spots with only handguns. And while he would have liked to have Dan there, the fact was that Dani was very good, and her fluency in the local language had made the operation possible. Plus, he'd seen her in a fight and he knew she was good—very good, actually.

Both of their ear comms buzzed at the same time. Conley tapped his and said, "We have weapons and have checked the perimeter. Clear so far."

"I want you both to know that there is considerable risk here. And I can't stress this enough: If you continue, you will be bait," Bloch said.

"We're well aware of that, Director, and I know it makes you uncomfortable, but you also know that we volunteered. After what we've seen the last few months, I'm ready to hit back," Conley said.

"Guo, you're relatively new to Zeta. In your time with us you've made important contributions, but I want to be clear that you don't have to do this," Bloch said.

"Thank you, Director, but I know how important this operation is. Besides the tactical value, we are actually in a position to learn something useful about this enemy," Dani said.

"That may be a double-edged sword. In all of their operations so far, Ares has used proxies. We've never engaged with Ares personnel directly. But because of the short window that we have given them to act, there is an excellent chance they will take direct action against you. Also, any people they have in Malaysia have likely been there for months, so they may be very well resourced."

"We're ready for them," Dani said.

"I also think we may be able to give them a few surprises," Conley said.

"We've left plenty of bread crumbs, but there's always the chance that they won't take the bait. There's also a chance that we are chasing shadows and have made a number of assumptions about Ares that may not be accurate or true."

"Do you think there really is a chance that we're chasing shadows, Director?" Conley asked.

"Almost none. I think Ares is real, and I think you are going to meet them in the next few hours," Bloch said.

"Then we'll get to it," Conley said.

"Good luck. I'll wait for your report," Bloch said and cut the line.

They parked the car in a small garage that faced the front of the school. It was strewn with loose landscaping supplies. The Proton fit inside, taking up half the interior space.

Conley took half of the ammunition—except for the grenades—and carried them outside with Dani, while she carried her shotgun and assault rifle. In the back of the school, they had found a shed that was empty. Conley assumed it had been used for sports equipment. There were no windows, but the door faced the rear of the building, and they were able to knock out fire holes and viewing ports on the other three sides. It was relatively easy to do, but that was only because the walls of the shed were very thin. They wouldn't stop anything bigger than a BB or, perhaps, a .22-caliber round. Like Conley's garage, the best the shed would offer was concealment—and not even that if their enemies had infrared scopes.

On the plus side, the shed had convenient shelves that made for very good placement of ammo and weapons. Once again, Conley wished they had been able to go back to their hotel room to retrieve their body armor.

"Where is it?" Dani asked.

"Where is what?" he replied.

"The Milkor," she said flatly.

"I left it in the garage."

She raised an eyebrow and said, "Why do *you* get it?"

"I'm more familiar with it; I took it apart and cleaned it," he said.

She stared at him silently.

"Plus, the enemy is much more likely to make a frontal assault. That's why we put our decoys in the forward apartment," he said.

She didn't say a word and just kept looking at him expectantly.

Conley returned her stare and said evenly, "And I called it."

"You what?"

"I called it; therefore I get to use it," he said.

"What does that even mean?"

"It's an American custom," he said.

"A custom for American *adults*?" she replied.

"Just Americans."

Dani smiled. "Enjoy it, and make your shots count."

"Always," he said and then Dani melted in to him gave him one deep, quick kiss.

Pulling away, she was all business again. She tapped her ear comm and said, "Get your space ready. I'll be right here."

Jogging back to the garage, he noted that—like the shed—the walls were too thin to stop bullets. However, the car would provide limited cover on one side. He kept the assault weapon near the front window, but he decided to place the shotgun outside against a nearby tree.

If he had to abandon his position and his equipment in a hurry, he would at least have something waiting for him outside. When he came back to the garage he loaded up his fishing vest with spare clips for both his Glock and his assault weapon. The fishing vests were the closest things he and Dani could find to tactical vests, and they did the job.

It was dark and getting late, and it was quiet. Conley looked up at the apartment window. It was blacked-out and boarded up, so it appeared like all of the other windows in the building.

When they inspected it, they'd found the living space was actually comfortable and reasonably well appointed, certainly for a safe house. As a result, Conley suspected it was also used for more personal—and more intimate—purposes in addition to temporary storage for witnesses and agents.

For a solid hour, Conley scanned the front of the building and then made regular rounds to check the other windows to get a full view around him. The quarter moon provided minimal light, but it was enough to allow him to keep an eye on his surroundings. Regular comm checks with Dani kept him from losing focus, and he resolved to wait all night.

After all, given the way that Bloch had set the trap, it would still take some time for even a very well-resourced agency to track them here. Then Ares had to get a team equipped and transported to this location. That would be difficult for Zeta and could very well take most or even all of the night.

Before that thought was finished, Conley heard the faintest *snap* and a brief whooshing sound. An instant later, a ball of flame shot across his field of vision.

RPG, Conley thought an instant before the bedroom window of the safe house apartment exploded in orange flame. That told Conley two things. First, the team they were facing was very well equipped. And second, the space heaters they had rigged up in the apartment to show heat signatures had worked. There were Dani's idea, and she'd be pleased to know they had done the job.

The RPG also changed the game a bit. Conley had hoped they would be facing regular ammunition only. The RPG had a greater range and was even more powerful than Conley's own grenade launcher.

"Dani," Conley whispered into his comm. There was no reply. There had been no gunfire, so he assumed the Ares fire team had managed to jam comms. That meant they were very, very well resourced.

Conley and Dani would have to be careful. If their shelter was inadequate to stop high velocity rounds, it would do absolutely nothing against RPGs. Or course, his Milkor still packed a punch. He just needed a target.

He lifted it to his shoulder and kept it aimed at the front of the school. He needed to be sure he'd hit something because as soon as he finished firing, he'd have to leave this position.

It was just a few minutes later that he saw a quick flash of automatic gunfire from behind the windows in the hallway in the center of the building on the second floor.

Perfect, he thought. That meant that at least one of the gunmen had walked into the line he and Dani had stretched across the staircase. Most similar booby traps were at ankle height to trip enemies. Conley preferred to set them at throat height.

It was particularly effective in the dark when a fire team was hyperaware of the possibility of booby traps near the floor. If you got lucky, taking a taut line in the throat would incapacitate your enemy.

In this case, the gunman must have walked into a line and then accidentally discharged his weapon. That told Conley exactly where one of them was, and in less than a second he had taken aim at that position and fired the Milkor.

The launcher didn't disappoint. The grenade covered the three hundred yards to the structure easily. He'd have to adjust his aim a bit next time because it hit low. Still— just like horseshoes—with grenades *close* was still pretty good. The 40-mm shell detonated on contact and exploded pretty spectacularly.

The spring-loaded cylinder made one turn to put the next round into position. Conley didn't hesitate and took the shot. As the grenade flew, he heard automatic gunfire from up ahead, which told him Dani was engaging someone out there.

Conley's grenade flew into the second-floor window dead center. He adjusted upward to aim at the third-floor window and pulled the trigger... and then pulled it again.

Misfire, he thought and pulled it again.

When the shell didn't fly out of the barrel he realized that it wasn't a misfire; it was a hang fire. That meant the propellant in the round would probably ignite in the barrel and set off the grenade itself—and Conley didn't want to be anywhere near it when that happened. He needed to toss the grenade as far as he could and take cover behind the car.

"Stop," a voice said behind him. "Turn around and keep your hands in the air."

Chapter 24

"We've lost contact with Conley and Gou," Shepard said when Bloch answered the phone.

"Jamming?"

"More than that, there's a large service blackout in the area around the safe house," he said.

That was bad, she realized. If Ares could knock out cell service that meant that her agents were up against a very entrenched enemy. She had put Conley and Guo in the middle of that; and worse, she'd given the enemy a map right to them.

"Can you track them?" Bloch asked. If nothing else, the GPS chips in Zeta-issued phones would show their location—even if the phone was turned off.

There was an uncomfortable pause and then Shepard said, "I'm not getting a signal on either phone."

That was very bad, Bloch knew.

"Could Ares be jamming their GPS signal?"

"It's possible," Shepard said in a tone that told her that though it was possible it was very, very difficult.

"Keep monitoring," she said.

Had she done it? she wondered as she hung up. Had she gotten her agents hurt, captured, or worse—just to strike at an enemy who had been dogging Zeta for too long? For what purpose? Anger? Revenge? Pride? And if Conley and Guo were lost, what would she have accomplished? Nothing, besides showing their new enemy that Zeta could be lured into a sucker's play.

Bloch had imagined she could bait Ares into making a mistake, but there was a very real chance that she had been the only one baited, and that Conley and Guo would be paying the price.

* * * *

Conley ran through his options and none of them were good. On the plus side, there was virtually no scenario that would play out in which the enemy behind him would walk out of the garage.

Of course, the odds on that count weren't great for Conley either. As he turned around, the dim beginnings of an idea formed in his mind, and he lifted the grenade launcher above his head with both hands.

The man spoke English with an accent Conley couldn't quite place—possibly German, maybe Swiss. Conley could see that the man was in his late twenties and at about six-foot-two, he was almost as tall as Conley was himself. He was also clean-cut and wearing black jeans and a black sweatshirt.

"Drop the weapon," the man said in a flat tone.

"Not a good idea. This is a Milkor forty-millimeter grenade launcher in the middle of a hang fire. That means it's about to blow up in my hands. Throwing it will only hurry that along."

"You're lying," the man said, though he sounded far from sure. "But even if it's true, do you expect me to let you go?"

"No, I expect you to do the only sensible thing you can in this situation… and that's to catch it," Conley said, tossing the weapon up and over to the gunman in low arc.

The man was cool under fire and clearly well trained, but his finely honed reflexes worked against him. He reached out with his left hand to pluck the Milkor out of the air.

Conley didn't wait to see what happened next. The split-second of diverted attention was all he needed, and he was out the door and running at full tilt. A 40-mm grenade would have a kill radius of about five yards but would cause serious injuries at up to one hundred yards.

He needed cover and raced for the nearest tree that seemed big enough to give him decent protection. He'd almost reached it when he heard and then felt the explosion.

The fact that he was still on his feet told him that it was only a partial detonation—a fizzle. And it had been partly absorbed by the grenade launcher's barrel. A second later, as he threw himself behind the tree the second explosion blasted the area. This one was much more powerful, as were the third and fourth, which came in rapid succession.

He counted off one second, then two—

A single, giant explosion rocked the ground under his feet and shook the tree behind him.

That would be the extra grenades in the box, he thought.

He waited a few seconds and then spared a glance around the tree at the burning wreck of the car and the few smoldering scraps of the garage that were left. It was a shame about the car, he thought. And the weapons. And the ammo.

For a second he checked for the shotgun he'd stashed against a tree, but realized it wasn't behind this tree. As he drew his Glock from his shoulder holster, he realized he'd have to make do. At least he had plenty of extra clips in his vest.

There was more automatic gunfire from behind the building. That meant Dani was still out there and she might need his help. He didn't have time for anything elegant, so he just sprinted the couple of hundred yards to the northeast corner of the building. He was relieved not to take fire from inside.

With any luck, his first two grenades had taken out whoever was in there. In addition, the fact that no one shot him in the back as he ran told him that the gunman in the garage was the only one on this side. That left whoever Dani was dealing with. If she could hold out for another minute, he'd be able to get there.

He crept to the corner of the school, scanned the area, and stepped out when he saw it was clear. As soon as he took a few cautious steps, he saw a black-clad figure come barreling around the far corner and straight at him. Conley reacted instinctively. He raised his Glock, aimed, and fired in one smooth motion. He put two rounds into the running man, center mass, before the man stumbled forward to the ground. As he fell, Conley realized the gunman hadn't been running toward him—he'd been running away from something else.

Or rather, some*one* else. Then he saw another figure come around the same corner, leading with an assault rifle.

"Dani," he called out, just as she was raising the weapon toward him. "I got him," he said, pointing at the body of the man between them. "Any others?"

"Just him and his partner, who is also down," Dani said. "What about on your side?"

"There were four of them," he said.

"Four?" she asked as she approached him. She was close enough that he could see her raised eyebrow.

"Yes, four, but they are taken care of. What about inside? I saw movement and fired two grenades. I'm pretty sure I got someone."

"I don't see any signs of movement now. I think they are all neutralized," she said.

"Then we have to get out of here," he said. "By now we've attracted some local interest. Problem is that the car is a loss."

Dani leaned down to turn over the body of the black-clad man. She checked him quickly and said, "No ID, but we have these." She pulled out a set of keys and said, "There's a van."

Conley took a few quick pictures of his face. Like the one in the garage, he was also in his late twenties, but dark-skinned. Maybe facial recognition would kick up something. Conley wished they had time to examine the other bodies, but they had to move now to avoid the local authorities.

They would also have to ditch the van quickly. There was too much risk that the enemy could track it. But first things first: They had to get the hell out of there.

He could already hear sirens in the distance and could see flashing lights coming toward them.

Chapter 25

Alex woke up to banging on the door. It was loud and went on well past the point of politeness. That ruled out hotel staff.

There was a pause and then the banging started again. This time, Terry stirred.

"I'll get it," Alex whispered. She'd seen that Terry could sleep through anything and would have no trouble getting back to sleep. Alex, on the other hand, knew she was up and would likely stay that way.

Through the peephole, Alex could see Jenya standing outside, a serious expression on her face. "Alex," she called out.

Alex opened the door a few inches and said, "Hi Jenya."

The older woman pushed into the dark hallway of the suite and said, "Good morning, Alex."

She scanned Alex quickly, eyeing the T-shirt she was wearing and shook her head. "It's been two days, Alex. You have to give the boy some rest. He must prepare for his race. Now get dressed and come with me."

Still shaking off her cobwebs, Alex said, "Where are we going?"

"It's a secret and a surprise. A little bit of both, actually," Jenya said.

"What do I wear?" Alex asked.

"Whatever you have. Just be quick," Jenya said.

Ten minutes later, Alex scratched out a note and left it on the bedside next to the sound- asleep Terry. As Alex and Jenya walked through the lobby, Alex made a point of stopping by the concierge. "Bonjour, Edouard," Alex said. Like Paul in Monte Carlo, Edouard had golden keys embroidered on his lapel. As such, he was a friend of Pierre, and when Alex arrived he had made it clear that his local network had nothing to report. Alex was glad for that. Monte Carlo had been a bit *too* exciting. Of course, it *had* been successful as a mission. Though, to be fair, someone else had done the heavy lifting there and disarmed the nuclear bomb for them.

Of course, that same party had also taken the plutonium. Since they'd stolen a large amount of money as well, there was at least a possibility that they were driven by greed and intended to sell the nuclear material.

That boggled Alex's mind. Had the people who had taken the plutonium and prevented the death of hundreds of thousands—as well as the decimation of a large part of Europe—just for money?

What would stop the same person or group from selling the plutonium on the black market? It was refined, enriched, and ready to drop into a bomb casing. Merchandise like that would be almost priceless.

"Bonjour, Ms. Morgan, have a good day," Edouard said. He didn't hand her a message, which told Alex there was nothing to report. That was fine with her. Montreal was a beautiful city and she hadn't gotten to see much of it yet. She'd been too busy to take her bike out in Monaco, and she hoped for a nice, long ride while she was here.

Then the concierge smiled at Jenya and said, "Mademoiselle Orlov, nice to have you at L'Hotel."

"Bonjour," Jenya said as they headed out.

"Have you stayed here before?" Alex asked.

"No, he must know *of* me," Jenya said.

"Of course, I forget you are a celebrity."

"There are only twenty Formula One drivers in the world, and there haven't been many women," Jenya said.

"I'm sure you can get a table at any restaurant," Alex said.

"That's not so much, nothing your concierge friend can't do for you," Jenya said, an uncharacteristic cloud passing over her face. It lifted quickly. Jenya smiled and said, "Of course, men find it irresistible."

That was true. Alex had seen the way men stared at Jenya. Some of that was the mystique of driving; certainly it affected the way women looked at Terry. And for Jenya, there was also her appearance in various ad campaigns and on at least two posters that Alex had seen. But for all of that attention, Alex realized that she had never seen Jenya with a man.

Jenya flirted somewhat shamelessly, but harmlessly, with Scott and Terry—though that had seemed to stop now. But Alex had never seen her *with* anyone. Of course, that might have been a by-product of her work. Between her training, her driving, and her endorsements, Jenya most likely didn't have time for a relationship.

Alex understood that very well. She had only met Terry because his appearance in her life had coincided with a mission. Eventually, the mission would end, though Alex didn't want to think about that.

"Can I ask where we are going?" Alex said.

"Of course Alex, you can *ask*," Jenya replied as they got into the limo.

The oversized vehicle seemed like an absurd way to travel, but Jenya, like Scott, had an image to maintain. That was something Alex also understood. An image was like a cover: Sometimes it was necessary for the job.

The limo took them through the old city in which the Renard team's hotel was located. It really was beautiful and Alex made a note to herself to see more of Quebec while Terry was preparing for the race.

The car crossed the St. Lawrence River to Notre Dame Island, a man-made island that had been built for Canada's centennial celebration in the 1960s and had subsequently been modified to be a Formula 1 track.

Alex knew the track was one of Terry's favorites because of the high speeds and the heavy braking required—which apparently made for an excellent challenge for the drivers. It was also a dedicated track and didn't borrow from the city's streets. That meant it could be optimized for safety, unlike Monaco, which was notoriously dangerous.

Terry's job had built-in risks, but Alex was grateful for the small favor of the slightly safer course. Of course, given what she did—and what she and Lily had risked in Monte Carlo—it was absurd for Alex to be bothered by the risks inherent in *his* job. But Alex was too honest with herself to pretend otherwise.

The car dropped the women off at the Marussia garage. There was a steady hum of activity and plenty of people around, but Alex was struck by how quiet it was. The team seemed to be mostly Russian but, like all Formula 1 teams, had a number of people from different countries.

The team all acknowledged Jenya but didn't greet her, and they showed no interest in Alex. Suddenly, Alex understood why Jenya spent so much time in the Renard garage and paddock.

"I'd love a tour of the garage," Alex said.

"I don't think so. You've seen the Renard garage. How would you like to take a car out?"

"Really?" Alex asked.

"Of course. You can drive a stick, no?"

"Yes, but..." Alex had learned a bit about Formula 1 cars. They had eight forward gears and one reverse, and they didn't have a stick. Instead, there were two paddles behind the steering wheel.

"Same principal," Jenya said. "You will pick it up in no time."

Jenya brought Alex to her dressing room and helped her get into one of her racing jumpsuits. Since Jenya was a little taller than Alex, the suit was a bit big, but that only meant it was less tight on Alex's frame.

There were multiple layers of fire-resistant Nomex clothing, topped by a snug hood that covered her neck and head, leaving only her eyes free. Surprisingly, it wasn't uncomfortable.

"I should have asked you this earlier, but are you claustrophobic at all?" Jenya asked.

"Not so far," Alex replied.

"Good, it's tight in the cockpit, and with the helmet it can be a bit much if you are," Jenya said, then she walked her outside where a car was waiting in the pit area. She helped Alex climb inside.

It was tight in the cockpit and the steering wheel was more like an oversized video game controller than a traditional steering wheel. It was covered in buttons for everything from starting the car to traction control.

"You can ignore most of the buttons. It's still got a gas pedal and a brake pedal," Jenya said. Then she gave Alex a quick primer on shifting and said, "I'll talk you through the rest as you go."

Alex put on her helmet and lowered her visor. As soon as she did, Jenya's voice was in her ears. "Don't worry. I'll talk you through it and I won't let anything happen to you. That is, unless you run straight into a barrier. There's not much I can do about that," Jenya said.

"I'll keep it in mind," Alex said.

She hit the *start* button and the engine roared to life.

Alex thought she could feel the sound in her chest when she was in the stands. *Fair enough*, she thought, *it's idling at 6,000 RPM.*

The whole car seemed to vibrate with power. It occurred to Alex that she probably should have logged some time on a simulator before she took a machine like this out on the track. On the other hand, if Jenya thought she could do it, Alex wasn't going to pass up an opportunity like this.

She pulled out in low gear and could feel the power of the engine behind her. It was intoxicating. Jenya took her through the just-under three-mile circuit at no higher than normal highway speed. This gave Alex a feel for the brakes and the shifting, which felt natural to her—a lot like changing gears on her motorcycle. She learned to hold the throttle on full when she was upshifting and release it when she was downshifting.

On the second lap, Alex inched up the speed, getting faster and faster on the shifts, which were necessary as she braked for the turns, particularly the track's S-turn and its nearly 180-degree hairpin turn.

As she edged to an average speed of over 100 miles per hour, she could feel the strong g-forces of the acceleration on the straightaway and the even stronger forces on the turns.

"How are you doing, Alex?" Jenya asked, a note of concern in her voice. "Are you comfortable with your speed?"

"Actually, it feels a little slow," she said as she throttled up even more. This was where she understood how punishing racing was physically. Fighting the g-forces was tough and even keeping her head straight up on the turns took a tremendous effort.

Alex could hear other voices on the line. There was some shouting and more than one Russian curse. "You're doing great, Alex, but watch your speed," Jenya said calmly.

As Alex ran the next few laps she brought the car to maybe two-thirds racing speed, hitting almost 150 miles per hour on the straightaway.

The cursing on the other side increased in volume and Alex could hear Jenya shouting at the men around her. "You're making an impression here, Alex," she said, humor in her voice.

"Just a couple more, then it will be time to take it in," Jenya added.

Alex did just that and used the last lap to push the car as far as she could tolerate. It was exhilarating and she regretted it when she had to pull the car back into the Marussia pit.

Alex was greeted by a smiling Jenya and a scowling pit crew.

"How do you feel, Alex?"

"Incredible—sore as hell, but incredible," Alex said.

Then Alex saw something she had never seen on Jenya's face before: The Russian woman was impressed.

Jenya leaned in to the cockpit and said, "You may have aged the crew five years."

Alex shrugged. "Tell them the steering was getting a bit sluggish at the end, and they should check the hydraulics," she replied.

* * * *

To Conley's surprise, Bloch was waiting for him and Dani when they arrived at Zeta headquarters. That was new. Usually, when she wanted to see him on arrival she just instructed Conley to head to her office.

"Good work in Kuala Lumpur," Bloch said.

She'd met them at the door and led with praise. *What is happening?* Conley wondered.

"Thank you, Director," Dani said.

"Facial recognition hasn't turned up anything on the man you photographed. However, we were able to pick up the Ares van you stashed. I'm having it sent directly here."

Conley was glad to hear that. With the authorities bearing down on them, they hadn't had a lot of good options for ditching the Ares van they had used to escape the scene, and they'd had to abandon it in a parking lot. They hadn't even been able to search it properly.

"It was clearly a local rental," Dani said.

"Yes, but I'm hopeful that it will turn up some DNA, if nothing else," Bloch said.

"Good luck to Ares on getting their deposit back," he said.

The three of them entered Bloch's office and the director sat them down on the small couch. Then she sat in a nearby chair and faced them across the coffee table.

"I look forward to your tactical report," Bloch said.

"Clearly, they have strong operational capabilities," Conley said.

"They put together the fire team and the equipment in a matter of hours," Dani said. "And they were very well trained."

"But not as well trained as you," Bloch said.

"They were maybe a bit overprepared and over-resourced. I suspect it made them arrogant, but even with all of that we got lucky," Conley said.

It was true and he wouldn't deny it. The agent he'd faced in the garage had gotten the drop on him in the middle of a firefight, when his own senses were at their peak. If his Milkor hadn't jammed, he wouldn't be here to make his report.

"I agree. You did exceptionally well, but there was too much luck involved for my taste, and I wanted to…apologize to you both. I put you into a dangerous situation with inadequate planning and resources."

"We did volunteer," Conley said. "It was risky, but it gave us our first operational intelligence about the organization."

"And perhaps some physical evidence from the van," Dani added.

"All true. Those things are very valuable, and we've also put Ares on notice that Zeta is no longer just reacting to their actions. And most importantly, we won. Even if there was luck involved, all Ares leadership will know is that two Zeta agents took out a team that outnumbered them and had a significant advantage in firepower. I just want *you* to know that I appreciate the risk you both took to accomplish that."

Then the meeting was over. Conley left Bloch's office shaking his head. Bloch seemed troubled by the fact that she had sent them in to that fight, and she'd actually *apologized* to them.

Conley had very rarely seen this human side of Diana Bloch.

It was unsettling.

Chapter 26

Alex saw Terry as soon as she stepped into the lobby. She called out to him just as he was grabbing his phone. He saw her, smiled, and rushed over.

"Hey," she said, leaning over to kiss him.

"Hey," he replied. "Saw your note. Everything okay?"

"Yes, sorry to be mysterious, but Jenya didn't tell me what we were doing. She took me to the Marussia pit and let me drive a car."

"*What?*" he said, unable to hide his surprise.

"I'm sorry—is that something you wanted to do?" she asked. She didn't know what the rules were when you were dating a Formula 1 driver. Actually, given how much of her life had been work for the last few years, she didn't know much about the rules for dating anyone.

"It's not that. I would have loved to, but I'd never get away with it. I can't believe they let her. I'm sure you're a good driver, but it's a fifteen-million-dollar car," he said.

"From what I heard over the radio, some of the guys in the garage weren't too happy about it," she said.

"She did put that team back on the map," he said with a shrug. "Your friend is something. It looks like you two are trouble when you're together," he said.

That made Alex smile. He wasn't wrong. She had told him a *very* modified version of their night out at the Monte Carlo Casino.

"I'm only sorry I missed it," he said. "How do you feel?"

"Sore as hell. I had no idea what you went through," Alex replied.

"I'd like to say you get used to it, but I'd rather you think I suffer for my work," he said. "I've got to get over to the pit for some prep. Will you be around later?"

"Sure, I just have to check in with Lily," she said.

He kissed her one more time and she headed across the lobby. Before she got three steps she heard a familiar voice call out, "Mademoiselle Alex."

She headed over to the concierge desk where Edouard greeted her with a smile.

"Most of the better hotels in the city are reporting an unusually high number of very wealthy first-time guests," he said.

"Could that be related to the race?"

"They have no interest in the race and as far as we can tell, they have no interest in each other. No meetings in hotel facilities. No dinners together. They seem to have nothing in common, but they all arrived in the city yesterday and are checking out the evening *before* the race."

"Thank you, Edouard, that's very helpful," she said.

She caught Lily in her and Scott's suite and relayed what Edouard had reported.

"What do you think is going on?" Lily asked her.

"That many people fitting that same profile, all of them showing up and leaving at the same time, with no connection between them—I'd say that someone is up to no good. And either they don't know each other or are taking pains not to be seen together. Again, suspicious. I think we'll know more once Zeta creates a list of these people and does a workup."

"Agreed," Lily said. "The question is whether or not this is something new or something related to the other problems we've seen on the Formula One circuit so far."

Problems was one way to put it, Alex thought.

"The simplest thing is to track the movements of a couple of them and see where that leads us," Alex said.

"My thoughts exactly," Lily replied.

* * * *

Diana Bloch studied the list in front of her and said, "Any clear connection?"

"None, besides the fact that they are all very wealthy and all seem to have ties to either terrorist groups, illegal arms sales, or rogue regimes," Shepard said. "The only ones that don't have those ties are the ones who appear to be operating under aliases. We're working on fully identifying those parties now."

That was tricky. The Canadian government would not want to start rounding up very rich and very powerful people in Montreal without proof—particularly on the eve of a major event that involved hundreds of thousands of tourists. They would need proof of their accusations before they could expect any help.

"Keep digging and see what you can find. In the meantime, would you care to speculate?"

"If I had to guess, I'd say it was an auction, possibly for technology but almost certainly for weapons. Most of the people in this group appear to have never even met; they have never before shown the slightest interest in Formula One, and they aren't staying for the race. The simplest thing to do is to keep an eye on them and see if they ever all go out at the same time," Shepard said.

"That will only work if they attend this auction, or event, in person," Bloch said.

Shepard nodded. "It's possible that only the winner or the winners of the auction would need to be there in person to make a cash transfer or take delivery. We've seen that before."

So far, this year's Formula 1 season had seen acts of terrorism, major thefts, and then both at the same time. Maybe now was their chance to be one step ahead, instead of three steps behind.

In Monte Carlo they had been in a desperate race to find a nuclear bomb and had come in second. Maybe they could turn that around here.

Or maybe this was another mirage, another illusion created by Ares to waste their time and resources so they missed the real attack somewhere else.

It was exhausting, which was the point. Zeta only had to miss the ball once and thousands, or millions, could pay the price.

Maybe Karen O'Neal's new project would bear fruit. Though that would be weeks or months away, at least. For now, they would have to do things the old-fashioned way, and that had worked in Kuala Lumpur.

* * * *

Terry would wonder where Alex was, and she'd have to figure out what to tell him later. Lily had it easier, since Scott not only knew what she did, but also helped out on a regular basis.

Of course, Alex and Terry had been dating for a week and that was definitely a week-two conversation.

On the plus side, Alex was able to get out on her motorcycle. She'd been happy to retrieve the red-and-silver Ducati from the hotel garage. It had been too long since she had taken it on a proper ride.

And she had planned to explore Montreal. Though she had seen a fair bit of the world since she started at Zeta, she had somehow never been to Canada. Of course, she'd planned to see it with Terry, who had been there as a driver but had never really seen the city. She'd likely have to lie to him about where she had been today. Certainly, she wouldn't be able to tell him that she had been tracking potential international criminals and terrorists.

Another week-two conversation.

The bike roared to life and then the engine purred. She put on her helmet and pulled out of the hotel parking lot. The Old City in Montreal did not disappoint her. The eighteenth- and nineteenth-century architecture was remarkable, and the winding streets were made for her bike.

Alex's target was a Syrian businessman who didn't have any overt criminal or terrorism ties, but his identity had been flagged by Zeta as likely false. Alex parked on the street outside his hotel. Through his network, Edouard had been able to confirm that the Syrian businessman had not left his hotel today.

That would make it easy. Alex had spent enough time in five-star hotels that she knew how to blend in. She checked in with the concierge—also a friend of Pierre—and then made the rounds to the café and the hotel bar, ultimately settling down in the lobby. She checked in with Lily, who said that her target had just finished lunch at the hotel restaurant and had gone back to his room.

Alex resigned herself to the fact that she might not see her target until dinner and settled in for a long wait. She'd have to make apologies to Terry when she caught him at the Renard paddock later—assuming her stakeout had ended by then. She had just finished that thought when the concierge called to tell her that Mr. Antar had summoned his limousine and would be departing shortly.

Alert, Alex put on her motorcycle jacket and got ready to move. She had parked right on the street out front so once Antar appeared, she would have plenty of time to get to her bike and trail the limo.

Less than a minute later, the elevator doors opened and five men stepped out. They were wearing Western business suits and two of them were visibly bandaged.

Alex realized that she knew these two men. Next she saw Yousef Antar, who she knew under another name: Sheik Nazer.

Alex was reasonably certainly that the sheik hadn't seen her, but to be sure she put on her motorcycle helmet and walked outside to wait by her bike. She watched the entrance closely and got on the bike as soon as the men exited the hotel. When the limousine pulled out, Alex was right behind it.

Chapter 27

Alex followed the car for about ten minutes as it headed south, away from the city. The car pulled into a warehouse in a suburban industrial area. The sign outside said *Électroniques*.

Alex strongly suspected there were very few electronics warehoused in the building. Though the façade and grass were well kept, there were no trucks at the loading dock.

She pulled her bike into the parking lot of the building next door. This one was empty and clearly not in use. Alex was willing to bet that the building on the other side of the electronics warehouse was also empty. That meant that whatever business was going on inside the warehouse was profitable enough that the owner could afford to carry the empty commercial real estate just to buy themselves some privacy.

Alex left her bike and made her way through the overgrown lot between the two buildings. It was an easy matter to find a break in the chain-link fence that separated the two buildings.

She knew she had to be careful now and didn't move forward until she could identify the external security cameras. They provided good coverage of this side of the building, but one was visibly broken, giving her a solid hundred-yard corridor in which she could approach the warehouse.

Alex didn't want to take any chances and drew her 9mm.

She approached the building and flattened herself against it. There were windows at eye level but they were blacked out from the inside. Alex slowly crept toward the front of the building.

As long as she kept herself against the warehouse, she would be out of the field of vision of the working cameras. With luck, she'd be able to see inside from the windows in the front.

If Sheik Nazer's bodyguards were the only human security on the premises, Alex was confident that she could safely enter the building itself and deal with them. She knew for a fact that one of them was still nursing the badly broken right arm she had given him, and the other wouldn't be 100 percent after the blow Jenya had given him to the windpipe—to say nothing of his bandaged, broken nose. That left only two men who were not injured. At the casino, she and Jenya had taken two of them out unarmed, while wearing evening dresses and heels.

As tempting as it would be to finish this herself, she'd call Lily for backup before she moved in. When she was less than twenty feet from the front of the building, two men who hadn't been with the sheik stepped out from in front of her with guns drawn and pointed at her.

They shouted at her in Russian to put her gun down. The calculation was simple. If there was a single armed man, she might fire first and take her chances. But with two at this close range, one of them would probably hit her before she could get both of them.

Alex pointed her gun to the sky and then started to slowly lower her arm. But before she finished the motion, an arm that felt like steel wrapped around her throat from behind as another hand grabbed her Smith & Wesson.

She only had a few seconds to pull against the arm that had tightened around her throat before she felt a pinch at the back of her neck. The world wavered in front of her as she struggled to keep her eyes open. Very quickly that became too much of an effort.

She felt consciousness slipping away from her and fought to stay awake, but like keeping her eyes open, that was simply impossible.

* * * *

Alex woke up suddenly. She felt a shock of cold and then she felt wet. She was trying to shake herself awake when she felt a second splash of cold water on her face and upper body.

As she opened her eyes, she tried to lift her arms, which she realized were tied to the chair she was sitting in. Even with her eyes open, the world swam in front of her and when she tested her legs, she found they were also tied to the chair.

Whoever had immobilized her had known what they were doing. No handcuffs, no ropes. She could feel the bite of zip ties against her wrists and presumed that her ankles were bound the same way.

She would try, of course, but she didn't think she'd be able to free herself soon. *This isn't going to be pleasant*, she thought as she felt the sting of a slap across her face. That completed her journey to consciousness and the world snapped into focus. Her head reeled back as she felt another slap on the other side of the face.

She shook it off and saw Nazer looking down at her.

"Alex Morgan," he said, holding her open wallet.

The sound of her name startled her, and then she remembered that she was undercover as herself. Next, the man held her phone in front of her face. He tapped the screen to activate the facial recognition software. The phone flashed open and Nazer scanned it for a full two minutes.

Alex was knew he wouldn't find anything sensitive. Though the phone appeared to be a normal consumer phone, opening it required both facial recognition and a thumbprint.

In the event the phone was activated with only one method, the screens that opened were dummies—designed so that undercover agents and sensitive Zeta information wouldn't be compromised in a situation exactly like the one Alex was in now.

"We will have time to examine this more closely. I don't need you conscious—or even alive—to open it again," he said.

Good luck with that, Alex thought. A month in a CIA lab *might* get a team of experts into the data on that phone.

"Tell me, where is your friend? The Russian, the driver?"

"I came by myself. She doesn't know I'm here," Alex said. She regretted that Jenya might now suffer because she knew Alex. Nazer clearly knew who Jenya was and might be laying in wait for her at any time.

This organization, whatever it was, wasn't staffed by morons—at least not entirely. One of their men had been able to get the drop on her. They'd had drugs ready and the man she'd faced with the gun was cool under pressure. If these people wanted to get their hands on Jenya, sooner or later they would.

The thought made Alex angry and she pulled against her restraints.

"You will not be going anywhere, Ms. Morgan, not under your own power. And you will not leave this room alive," he said calmly, with an unpleasant leer on his face.

He turned and walked to the door, leaving the men she and Jenya had beaten up at the casino to glare at her.

She heard voices in the hallway. There was an angry exchange in English and then some shouting in Russian. She could make out only a few words in each language and realized that something else was going on here.

It seemed to her that the sheik wasn't in charge and whoever was, wasn't happy with him. That explained why the men outside were more capable than Nazer's guards.

She didn't know how she might be able to exploit the dynamic between Nazer and whoever was in charge, but she'd try if she got the chance. Nazer stepped back inside and Alex knew that whatever she was going to do, she needed to do it fast.

"I'm afraid that we don't have much time. Now you will tell me why you are here," he said.

"I followed you," Alex replied. She needed to keep him talking, but she knew this would go nowhere fast.

His hand swept across her face again and he said, "This is pointless. Tell me why you are here."

"I followed you because I recognized you from Monte Carlo, and I wanted to see where you were going. I was hoping to find you doing something I could report to the police," Alex said.

"Now you are lying to me," he said and pulled her 9mm out of his jacket pocket. "You think I will believe that you came here with this to report me to the police? Who are you working for?"

"No one," Alex said. "I just wanted to see you on your ass again. Maybe rough up your guards one more time."

Nazer's hand lashed out and clocked her with a closed fist. She was grateful that he was holding the gun in his left hand. If he'd been holding it in his right, Alex was sure he would have struck her with the weapon. Nevertheless, his fist caught her on the cheek and the blow rocked her head back.

Then he pulled out her phone and dropped it on the ground, lifted his foot, and brought it down hard on the device. He stomped on it two more times to make sure it was destroyed. Clearly, he'd changed his mind about trying to break into the phone. Or the people who were really in charge here had insisted he destroy it.

There was some more shouting from outside. Nazer pointed the 9mm at her chest and said, "I'm afraid we are out of time."

Alex felt a sudden rush of anger. Anger at being threatened by this little man. Anger at having her own gun pointed at her. And anger at the fact that Nazer was doing it with the *safety on*. It was downright insulting to be threatened by such morons.

He held the gun on her for a few seconds and then handed it to one of his guards. "Kill her. Be quick," he said. Then he spared her one last unpleasant look and said, "But not *too* quick."

* * * *

If there was one thing Lily had learned in Mexico City it was how to spot cartel, and her target was definitely cartel. There was something about the combination of their body language and their treatment of subordinates; every movement and inflection screamed arrogance. For members of criminal syndicates, cartel leaders seemed to take pride in calling attention to themselves.

Perhaps it was because in their own country, they often functioned as local warlords, but they seemed to enjoy flaunting the fact that the law couldn't touch them. Every public appearance was a dare to the authorities to challenge them.

They moved about with large entourages of physically big bodyguards and seemed to make a point of barking at them and generally treating them poorly. Yet they also made a point of being excessively generous tippers to service personnel—all to keep up the appearance of a powerful man of the people.

Lily always thought it must be exhausting to maintain that image.

She watched as her target, Joséf Guzman, left the hotel. He was over six feet tall, though his four bodyguards were all at least two inches taller. Guzman made an extravagant gesture of handing the doorman a handful of what Lily had no doubt were fairly large bills.

To Lily's amusement, the French Canadian doorman took the money with a very understated and polite thank-you, and the baffled cartel boss continued to his over-the-top Hummer limousine surrounded by his four bodyguards. He shouted at one of the bodyguards and the man rushed to open the door for him.

Small men, Lily thought.

Of course, the fact that a man like that thought and acted small didn't mean he wasn't dangerous. In fact, it usually meant the opposite.

She followed the limo to the outskirts of the Old City, to a well-appointed, four-story nineteenth-century building that tickled something in Lily's memory. A quick check in the Zeta database told her that Guzman had just entered one of the oldest brothels in Montreal.

You are just determined to be a cliché, Lily thought.

About ten minutes later she saw a man leave from the side door in a hoodie and jeans. He had ditched his expensive suit, but Lily recognized the arrogant walk.

However, his men didn't notice him and Guzman walked away from the brothel in a bit of a rush. Lily followed him on foot for four blocks until he entered another, similar building that had a sign outside that said *Danse de Salon.*

Ballroom dancing, Lily thought.

This was getting interesting. Here was a cartel boss who had something to hide from his own men, something that went on under the cover of what appeared to be a reputable dance academy.

Perhaps there was more to Senor Guzman than Lily had first suspected. A quick walk around the building told Lily nothing. If she wanted to know more she'd have to go inside, and the simplest way was through the front door.

She was greeted by a polite receptionist who smiled and to Lily's surprise offered her a tour. The receptionist called for one of the instructors, a pleasant, middle-aged woman who asked Lily what she was interested in. When Lily explained that she and her fiancé wanted to learn some dances for their upcoming wedding, the woman seemed genuinely pleased and offered to take Lily to the second-floor studios.

Lily marveled at the place. It was either the worst cover for an international criminal enterprise, or the best. She saw two classes of four couples each and then a series of smaller studios where people were engaged in individual lessons.

What she saw in the fourth room stopped her cold. Joséf Guzman was dancing with a pleasant, attractive middle-aged woman who was teaching him to waltz. They were clearly early in the process, but Lily could see that Guzman had already mastered the box step and open right turns, though he was struggling with his reverse turns.

Lily thanked her guide and promised to return with her fiancé. Before she reached the outside, the first alert sounded on her phone. Someone had tried to access Alex Morgan's phone. That was bad. It could mean that the phone had been stolen, but in Lily's experience it was never that simple.

Less than ten seconds later, her ear comm buzzed. It was Bloch. "You received the alert?"

"Yes and I tried Alex's phone. No answer," she said. "I'm on my way."

"Do you want me to send a local asset to stay with your target?" Bloch asked.

"Not necessary. He's not an immediate threat," Lily said.

"I can send a team from Renard security to back you up at Alex's location," Bloch said.

That was tempting. Lily had picked that team herself and added to it after the explosion at Logan Airport, but she doubted it would do any good. Lily was closer and there just wasn't time for the team to get there. "If I need it, I'll call for backup when I arrive," Lily said.

Dance lessons didn't mean that her target wasn't in Montreal to buy illicit arms, but Lily felt confident that he would stay out of trouble for the rest of the afternoon.

She had to fight traffic and was still a few minutes out when the second alert came. That one told her that Alex's phone had been destroyed. This was a new feature, the result of a recent mission. When someone tried to smash or crush the phone, it sent out a final distress call and a GPS signal.

This signal told Lily that Alex was in serious trouble. Lily wanted to floor the gas, but instead she could only curse the traffic.

Chapter 28

Alex heard some commotion out front. There were shouts. Then curses. Then a series of gunshots. Nazer rushed back into the room. He barked something at his men in Arabic and the one with the broken nose stepped into the hallway.

There was a single gunshot and then Alex heard the man fall to the floor. The second bodyguard had Alex's gun in his hand, but she saw two problems with that. First, because Alex had broken his right arm, he was holding the gun in his left hand, which was clearly not his dominant hand. And second, he still had not turned off the gun's safety.

He raised the gun very unsteadily and was pointing it at the open door when Lily stepped into the doorway and fired her own weapon, hitting him once in the center of his chest. As the man fell, Lily scanned the room quickly, looking past Alex and settling on Nazer, who had his hands up.

"He's not a threat," Alex said.

At that point Lily studied Alex and asked, "Are you okay?"

Alex nodded and said, "Yeah."

Then Lily spotted the small table that held the interrogation tools they had intended to use on Alex. She picked up small wire cutters and used one hand to free Alex while keeping an eye and her gun on Nazer.

Alex got up slowly and rubbed her wrists to bring back the circulation. She was still a little woozy from the drug they had given her, but she felt better once she was on her feet.

She picked up her 9mm and felt better still.

Lily kept her gun leveled on Nazer and said, "Your call, Alex."

"Please," the sheik muttered. "I will tell you...anything you wish."

Alex raised a hand to shush him and said, "I think we need him alive." Then she pointed her own gun at Nazer and said, "Give me your phone."

With shaking hands he pulled out his phone and tried to hand it over, but quickly dropped it. He picked it up and then gave it to Alex.

"We can take his absurd limo. I parked my car by your bike. We can come back for them later," Lily said.

"I won't give you any trouble," Nazer said.

"I'm sure that's true," Alex said. Before she finished speaking, she could hear distant sirens.

"That's a complication," Lily said. "You—lie down on the floor."

"No, please," Nazer said.

"She's not going to kill you," Alex said. "Just lie facedown. The police will have to deal with you."

Nazer hurried to comply as Lily approached him. Nazer whimpered and said, "She said you wouldn't kill me."

"We won't, but I didn't say I wouldn't hurt you," Lily said. She quickly lifted her foot and brought it down very hard on his ankle. As Alex looked on in shock, Nazer screamed and then Lily repeated the action with his other ankle.

"Lily…" Alex said.

"We need to move and we can't have him running off," Lily said.

"Fair enough," Alex replied, closing the door to the room behind her, which muffled the man's cries.

"I saw a side door by the fence," Alex said.

Lily and Alex headed down the hallway at a run.

Chapter 29

Once they were back in Alex's room, Lily said, "What did they do to you?"

"I'm okay, really. They didn't have me long and I'm sure it looks worse than it is," Alex said.

It didn't *feel* great. And when she saw herself in the mirror, she realized it didn't look great. She had swelling over her left eye and a clear bruise on her right cheek, with swelling under there as well.

The concierge was able to find a reliable and discreet doctor who made a shockingly fast house call, examined her, and took some blood.

After an hour of Lily's fussing, Alex said, "I'm okay. Just let me get some sleep."

She did need the sleep. It had been a long day. She had been sore after her drive in the Formula 1 car with Jenya this morning. Of course, that was before she'd been drugged and tied to a chair.

"If that's true, Bloch will clear you as soon as your blood checks out. You're on your feet and lucid, so it was probably a garden-variety knockout drug," Lily said.

Alex found herself getting annoyed. Having Lily fuss over her was like having her mother or an older sister hovering. "If I had to, I could go to work right now."

"Really, you are physically and mentally mission-ready?" Lily asked.

"Yes," said Alex firmly.

"Okay, why don't you call Terry and tell him you'll meet him at the paddock," Lily said.

Alex had no response for that.

"Exactly," Lily said. "You're right about the fact that you need some sleep. I'm sure Bloch will clear you tomorrow. In the meantime, I'll tell

Terry you're not feeling well, and you can think about what to tell your boyfriend in the morning."

That stopped Alex cold. Her cover on this mission was that she was a friend of billionaire Scott Renard's girlfriend—not someone who regularly got into bar fights. This would be tricky. And her effectiveness on this— or on any covert mission—was dependent on not calling unnecessary attention to herself.

Alex felt the weight of the day pushing down on her. "Okay," she said.

Lily gave her one last glance and then left.

Once Lily was gone, Alex realized that what she felt most now was embarrassment.

Embarrassment that she had let herself get taken by the sheik's associates.

Embarrassment that she'd had to be rescued by Lily, who marched into the same facility, got Alex out, and still looked like Scott Renard's glamorous girlfriend.

Once again, Alex felt like Lily's junior partner. To be fair, Lily was several years older than Alex, and she'd already had a substantial career at both MI6 and at Zeta. Alex was hopeful that would be as good an agent eventually, provided she didn't get herself killed first.

* * * *

Alex snapped awake at just after 8:00. She inspected herself in the mirror and saw that the swelling had gone down in both places, though there was no question that she now had a bruise on one cheek and a black eye. The good news was that the soreness from her driving and being tied to a chair was mostly gone, and she figured that by tomorrow she'd feel completely human again.

A shower made her feel even better, but as soon as she got out, there was an aggressive banging on the door. Alex checked the peephole and saw an impatient Jenya standing outside.

"Alex, you look terrible," Jenya said, pushing into the room.

"It looks worse than it is," Alex said.

"I certainly hope so. What happened to you?" she asked.

Alex had thought about this. She had two options. Until now, she was leaning toward a mugging. But she realized that it would raise too many questions with Jenya—who had seen Alex fight.

"I was riding in the city and someone opened a car door. I had to drop my bike," she said. This was one of the most common motorcycle-crash scenarios and something that had actually happened to her.

"Good thing you were wearing your helmet."

"I always do," Alex said.

"Very smart, my young Alex. Like driving Formula One, a motorcycle is already a dangerous business. There's no sense in courting more trouble." Then Jenya was smiling her usual smile. "Maybe you should drive one of your father's muscle cars."

"I do sometimes, but I like my bike," Alex said.

"We all think we're immortal," Jenya said. "I just wanted to check on you. I have a date tonight, so I will have to see you tomorrow."

"A date?" Alex said, unable to keep the surprise out of her voice.

"Does that seem so impossible?" Jenya asked.

"No, I didn't mean it like that. It's just that I've never seen you with—"

"The curse of the Formula One driver is that we're irresistible, but our work leaves little time for love. You should be flattered that Terry has made you a priority."

Alex hadn't thought of that and now that Jenya had said it, the notion pleased her.

When Jenya left, Alex thought the woman's concern was a pleasant surprise, but one thing left her wondering. She knew for an absolute fact that she'd told Jenya that her father dealt in *classic* cars, not *muscle* cars. Yet Jenya had known that Dan Morgan's interest was in muscle cars. Alex wondered if the woman had looked her up online and had caught something about her father. She couldn't decide if it was a touching show of interest in a new friend, or an invasion of privacy.

She decided to take it as a compliment that—like with Terry—someone like Jenya would take an interest in her. As far as both of them knew, she was just a girl from Boston who fixed motorcycles.

Alex started on her face; she wanted to appear presentable when she met with Lily. She had to get back to work and she couldn't afford any doubts about her readiness.

* * * *

When Alex walked into Lily's suite, the other agent studied her and said, "You look well."

"I feel better. I feel fine, actually," she said.

"Good," Lily said and handed Alex a phone. "Courtesy of Shepard."

Alex turned it on and saw her home screen come up. "Same number, same everything—except for a longer battery life," Lily said. "You know Shepard."

They sat in front of Lily's laptop and Diana Bloch appeared on the screen. There were no preliminaries. "How are you feeling, Alex?"

"Fine," she said.

"Good, I'll send you the lab report, but what they injected you with is not particularly dangerous. It was already showing only trace amounts when the doctor took your blood," Bloch said. "If you're ready, you can get back to it."

"I am and I'd like to," Alex replied.

"Good, because there have been some developments. First, you should both know that Sheik Nazer was murdered last night in police custody, while he was awaiting transfer to Canadian Security Intelligence Service."

"What?" Alex said, not even trying to keep the surprise out of her voice.

"Through our CIA contacts we informed Canadian intelligence about an ongoing investigation. They were arranging to take custody of him this morning to interrogate him about his presence in Montreal."

"Do they have the killer?" Lily asked.

"No, and no leads. Whoever did it was very careful and we presume very experienced," Bloch said.

"We can assume his confederates didn't want him to talk to authorities," Alex said.

"That is our working assumption, but there were some irregularities in his death," Bloch said.

"Irregularities?" Lily asked.

"This wasn't a simple assassination, it seemed...personal, and it wasn't quick," Bloch said.

"A warning to other buyers in that circle?" Alex asked.

"Maybe, but this seemed *very* personal," Bloch said.

"He's no loss to the world, but his death is a setback for our investigation," Lily said.

"Not entirely. We did get a break. Alex, the phone you recovered turned up some useful information. Shepard and O'Neal were able to find messages from the party that we now think is the seller. They were using a messaging application. By tracing other users in that area and cross-referencing with our list of our potential buyers, we're confident we can tap their communications. If the sale is still on, we'll know about it. And since other people on our list are set to leave Montreal in three days, please be ready. It could happen any time."

"We will," Lily said

"We've been tracking the trouble on the racing circuit for months now, and this is the first real advance lead we've gotten. Good work, Alex," Bloch said.

* * * *

Alex met Terry in the lobby. As soon as he saw her, the concern was written on his face.

"Alex, what happened?"

He reached up and gently touched her face. "And is that a black eye?" he asked. "Lily said you weren't feeling well, but I didn't expect this. What happened to you?"

"I was out on my bike and someone opened their car door in front of me. If you think this is bad, you should see the door," Alex said, trying to put a little humor in her voice.

Terry didn't smile. Instead, he took both of her hands. "What about the rest of you?"

"Nothing, I'm really okay. I was going very slow and I had my gloves and leather jacket on when I went down. I just knocked my helmet into the ground and smashed my face into the front of the helmet."

"You should really see a doctor, then," he said.

"I already did. Lily had the hotel send a doctor up to my room," Alex said. She was relieved to be able to say something that was actually true.

"You have to be careful on your motorcycle. Those things are dangerous," Terry said.

"Really?" Alex said. "*You* are saying that to *me*."

For a full two seconds, Terry seemed genuinely and sweetly confused. Then he smiled sheepishly and said, "That's completely different."

"Is it?" she asked.

"Completely. This is my work. You ride the motorcycle for fun," he said.

"And you don't enjoy—"

"Okay, I can't defend it, but can you agree to be more careful on your bike?" he said.

"Yes, I can do that," Alex replied.

"It's not just about you. Think about the people who care about you," he said.

"People?" she asked.

"Yeah, people. The chief really likes you. I mean, he doesn't show it on the outside, but his feelings run deep. Then there's the pit crew," Terry said. For a few seconds Alex thought Terry might blush again.

"Okay, I'll be more careful for the chief," she said.

"All I'm asking," Terry replied.

Alex was relieved when the conversation shifted to a discussion of the course, the day's practice, and how Terry thought he would do in the race on Sunday.

It was safe territory and Alex was relieved that she didn't have to lie during the conversation. She realized it bothered her to lie to Terry, not because deceiving him was difficult for her, but because it was remarkably easy.

* * * *

"Tell me we have something," Bloch said as she entered Shepard and O'Neal's workstation. She'd been down here so many times in the last few days that she barely got second glances from the rest of the staff.

"There is something strange," O'Neal said.

"Strange unusual? Or strange like we're chasing another atomic bomb?"

"Both, I think," Shepard said. "We've gotten some odd readings on the radiation sensors in Montreal."

"Are we going to have to interview more cancer patients?" Bloch asked.

"No, these are short spikes in specific locations. They give very strong readings and then they disappear. Much higher levels of radiation than we were getting from the people in Monte Carlo."

"Can you track them?" Bloch asked.

"No. We can pinpoint the places where they happened, but then they are gone without a trace," Shepard said.

"That sounds impossible," Bloch said.

"It is, unless you are transporting the material in a series of shielded, lead containers and occasionally have to transfer it from one to another. Just handling something like plutonium would give us a reading, but then it would disappear. And it wouldn't leave much, if any, trace in the surrounding area."

"Can we assume that means that Ares has gotten better at moving the material around undetected?" Bloch asked.

"If it's Ares, or whoever it was that imported all of the cancer patients into Monte Carlo, then, yes—it might mean they have changed their transportation strategy. But it's also consistent with our theory that the material changed hands in the casino vault, and the new party who we are calling the sellers are just using a different strategy," Shepard said.

Once again Bloch had the feeling that they might be chasing shadows. Unfortunately, these shadows set up complex terrorist operations and then murdered the terrorists. In addition, they might have enough plutonium for a good-sized atomic bomb.

For the hundredth time this week, Bloch wished she'd stayed in the navy. Even in naval intelligence she virtually always knew the enemy's identity and objectives. But in Zeta's brand of international counterterrorism, she almost never had that information.

Bloch sighed heavily and asked, "Do we have any progress on the phone?"

"Yes," O'Neal answered. "We broke the encryption on the messaging app and have already tied it to a series of small-time illegal-arms auctions. We are in the process of confirming that Nazer was in the vicinity of each sale, but we think it's a safe bet that he took part in most or all of them."

"Good work. What about the next auction?" Bloch asked. She didn't have to add that the next auction was almost certainly for plutonium.

"Nothing yet, but we're watching the app network," Shepard said. "And if they switch to another app we'll be watching for a sudden spike of downloads of any other messaging apps in the Montreal area."

Was it possible? Were they really getting close?

The phone from one of the buyers had given them their first real break since this mission started. They weren't actually ahead, but they were right on the heels of the enemy—rather than a mile behind.

It was all because Alex Morgan had thrown herself into something and then gotten kidnapped and nearly killed by a vicious arms dealer. When Alex had started at Zeta, Bloch had hoped she would be different from her father—less prone to exactly that sort of action.

For the moment, however, Bloch was glad Alex was a Morgan.

Chapter 30

On the monitor, Alex watched Terry's last laps. She had seen enough in the last few days to know that he was doing well, maybe *very well*. Even without checking, she knew his lap times were getting better. More to the point, he was having very nearly-perfect laps. Precise shifting, good speed coming into and out of the turns, and great acceleration on the straightaways.

She could tell that both Renard and the chief were impressed—and so was she. Every day she worked with people who were at the top of their various games. From Shepard in engineering, to O'Neal in unfathomable math, to Bloch as a leader, and to the other agents at Zeta in everything from marksmanship to physical combat.

She was surrounded by excellence, so much so that she had begun to think she just wouldn't find it often in the civilian world. But Terry was very good and she suspected he was on the verge of being great.

When he pulled into the pit area, he conferred with the team and sought her out. "Are you impressed?"

"Yes," she said. "You were right. When we first met you told me that you drove very fast."

"I thought it was important to be up-front with you," he said. "I'm going to be here for a while, and I have to socialize at the paddock tonight. If you come early we can have dinner and we can hang out while I work."

"Sure. I wouldn't miss it. Plus, they always have those little hot dogs. I'd hate to miss those," she said.

"I agree. They are half the reason I joined the team," he said. Then he just smiled broadly and kissed her. "I missed you last night."

There was something endearing about how open he was about how he was feeling. And he didn't seem to care that he was in the middle of the garage, surrounded by dozens of his teammates.

Alex didn't need a mirror to know that the same expression was on her face; she was surprised to find that she didn't care that he saw it either.

She kissed him and said, "I'll see you tonight."

* * * *

Alex was ready for dinner when Lily knocked on her door. When Alex saw that Lily was still dressed for the garage, she knew something was up.

"What is it?" Alex asked.

"Zeta has intel on the auction. It's tonight and Shepard and O'Neal have reason to believe that there will only be one item: plutonium."

Alex's first thought was that she had plans with Terry tonight and she was instantly embarrassed. She and Lily were on a mission, and they had a chance to track down enough weapons-grade plutonium to worry about what might happen if that material fell into the wrong hands. It was in the wrong hands right now and it had nearly destroyed Monte Carlo a few days ago.

"You're worried about what you're going to say to Terry," Lily said. By her tone she made it clear that it was a statement, not a question.

The best Alex could muster was a sheepish grin.

"Don't kid yourself—it's important. One, because he's important to you. And two, because your cover is important. My advice is to keep it simple. Scott can make apologies for both of us and can tell Terry that I needed you for something.

"Give Terry some credit. He likes you—a lot—but he's a grown-up. He's also a world-class athlete who is part of a team that needs him to play a specific role tonight."

"I guess it's a bit easier for you since Scott knows everything," Alex said.

Lily gave her a thin smile. "It's not just easier, it's possible. When I was with MI Six, I couldn't get involved, not really, not even like you and Terry."

"What changed?"

"I left MI Six," Lily said. "When I did, I thought I was leaving the life. It was a change I was willing to make."

"What happened?" Alex asked.

"Zeta happened. Diana Bloch happened. A lot of things are possible there that aren't possible anywhere else. What happened is that I got lucky."

"Yes, please have Scott make our excuses. I'll figure out something to say tomorrow, and I guess it won't hurt that the news will be coming from his boss."

"Good, now let's get ready. We'll stop the international auction for fissile material, break up the ring of buyers, and see if we can get you back to your young man," Lily said.

All at once Alex's worry slipped away and she was back to the mission.

Her thoughts did occasionally drift back to Terry, but those thoughts were pleasant. She realized they weren't a problem; they weren't a worrying distraction. Instead, they helped her focus and gave her something to fight for.

Lily had made it work and her father had too. After years of trying, Dan Morgan had realized that his work with the CIA wasn't compatible with a family life. Given a choice between the CIA and his wife and daughter, Dan Morgan had chosen family.

Alex wouldn't kid herself. She'd known Terry for less than two weeks. He was a young, world-class driver in one of the most competitive sports in the world, and he traveled for most of the year.

In addition, Alex was an international security consultant, who traveled quite a bit herself. It was early for them and a future together was far from inevitable, but Alex realized that it might be possible.

"Grab what you need and meet me in my suite," Lily said. "The call could come any time and we need to be ready to move."

* * * *

Bloch approached Shepard and O'Neal's workstation and said, "Are you sure it's going to be tonight?"

"Reasonably," Shepard said. "Nazer's phone gave us some interesting intel. We found messages about two previous auctions. Each time there was an initial message that established the time, and then later there was a second message that gave GPS coordinates for the place."

That meant that even though Zeta would know the time and the place, there would be little time to coordinate a response. Of course, Bloch wasn't sure a coordinated response was even a good idea, given the thinness of what they had.

She could involve Canadian intelligence, who would likely bring in local police. However, if the intel was wrong or part of another misdirection campaign, an overwhelming response could be a disaster.

If the messages were another ruse, the response would show the arms dealer that someone was tracking their organization. Once they knew their security was compromised, they would disappear—and do it with a good-sized bomb's worth of plutonium.

And all of this would happen on North American soil.

This might be their only chance to take that plutonium off the table. It had to be done quietly and it had to be done right. That meant it would have to be done by Lily and Alex.

"Can we make a guess about the number of buyers that might be there?" Bloch said.

"All of the messages were direct communications. A group message would be helpful—even if it just showed us the number of buyers and not their identities—but no such luck."

If Nazer ever communicated with the other buyers, he didn't use his phone. That made sense. In her experience, rogue nations and terrorist groups were not friendly with one another. At best, they were competitors and most often they were bitter rivals or outright enemies. That was true even of groups who were ideologically aligned. Even when revolutionaries shared a belief system, they never seemed to agree about who should be in charge of the revolution.

Despite all of the good reasons to go forward with this mission, there was another possibility that Bloch was forced to consider: She might be ordering two of her people to walk into a trap.

Up until now, Zeta had been playing catch-up with their foe or foes. Certainly that had been the case in Monte Carlo. Though Zeta had come close, they had been hours behind whoever had snatched the plutonium from the casino vault.

That was at least a day *after* another party had smuggled a plutonium-based bomb into the vault. At this point, Bloch's operating theory was that there were two different parties operating on the Formula 1 circuit.

One group was committing or supporting acts of terrorism and—like her staff— Bloch had fallen into the habit of calling them Ares. The other group was engaged in a series of extremely high-value thefts and had been very successful, including the casino vault job. Zeta was calling this person or person the Sellers.

However you sliced it, Zeta had consistently come in third in a deadly race. And more to the point, Alex Morgan had already nearly died at the hands of a low-level figure in that contest. Now Bloch was sending two agents into a situation where those two enemies might very well meet.

"We've got a message," Shepard announced.

A few seconds later, O'Neal said, "Decryption complete."

Three numbers that Bloch recognized as map coordinates flashed on the big screen in front of them.

"Sending location now," Shepard said.

That was it. The clock was ticking and the next phase of this mission would begin in less than thirty minutes.

* * * *

"You seem disappointed," Lily said.

"More like surprised," Alex replied.

"What were you expecting as the location for an international auction for enough plutonium to level a city?" Lily asked.

"I don't know. A construction site. Empty high-rise. Seedy waterfront warehouse."

Lily grinned and said, "This makes sense. It's a large, abandoned space that attracts zero interest but has good highway access."

That was all true, but it seemed like an unworthy spot for the ending of this mission, which had begun in the glamorous Monte Carlo. Alex and Lily grabbed their duffels and headed for the door.

"Come on, Morgan, let's go to the mall," Lily said.

Chapter 31

Alex was glad to be back on her Ducati again. With the sun going down it was actually a beautiful ride. Geographically, Montreal was a lot like Manhattan. It was an island that sat between two rivers, the St. Lawrence River to the south and the Rivière des Prairies to the north.

In some ways, it was also a good place to contain a small, hostile force carrying illicit nuclear material, since the only way off the island overland were a few bridges or a boat.

Of course, shutting down those escape routes would only work if this were an official and sanctioned mission where Alex and Lily were working with the local authorities. But the women were operating alone, so whatever they did, they would have to do on their own.

On the plus side, it didn't appear that closing off the island would be an immediate necessity, since the sale was taking place near the almost exact center of the island of Montreal. *Le centre commercial d'argent* was a big, empty suburban mall that had been closed for years. Whoever was running this auction was apparently very confident, and they didn't feel the need to plan for a hasty exit.

That made sense. If the point of the auction was to sell plutonium, the Sellers wouldn't be leaving with anything more dangerous than money. The location was also a smart choice because it helped encourage everyone to keep a cool head.

If someone started shooting and succeeding in taking out everyone else there, they couldn't make a quick escape via a bridge or on a ship. First, they would have to race through miles of city with over a hundred pounds of fissile material in their possession.

Thus, the mall encouraged all participants to assemble quietly and have a friendly auction (or whatever passed for friendly in an auction attended by terrorist groups, criminals, and representatives of rogue nations).

Alex had to admit a grudging respect for the group Zeta was now calling the Sellers. In Monte Carlo, the arms dealers and Zeta hadn't been on the same side, but they had both been working against Ares. Here, the same party was trying to sell dangerous nuclear material to a group of some of the worst people on the planet. Zeta and Alex couldn't allow that sale to go through—especially so close to the United States.

When they approached the location, Alex switched on the night vision built into her helmet, turning the world into shades of green. "I'm dark," Alex said.

"Me, too," Lily said over the comm. Alex watched as Lily turned out the lights on the SUV that was just ahead of her.

"Shepard, I'm releasing your drones now, but have them keep their distance," Lily added.

"Will do," Shepard said.

The drones had been a compromise. They would give Zeta an overview of the situation, but if Sellers spotted the drones, they would know that someone else was in the game—or think that one of the other players was breaking the rules. Either way, that development would dramatically increase the chance that the sale would turn into a bloodbath.

Alex and Lily's plan required stealth and surprise. Both were essential in an operation like this where they would be significantly outnumbered. Chaos would not be their friend, and it would dramatically increase the chance that one of the bad guys would get away with the plutonium.

Recovering the nuclear material was the only objective here. Taking out the Sellers and their customers would be a bonus, but was far from essential.

They approached the south entrance and Alex could see lights inside the building. Since the mall had no power, she assumed they were temporary lights running off of a generator.

That was another smart move by the Sellers. Lights would give the auction the veneer of safety, making the buyers feel secure and less on edge. The lights also told Alex that the auction was taking place inside and that the Sellers had prepared the environment.

The heads-up display popped on inside the helmet just above Alex's sight line. The video feed from the drones made two side-by-side images of the mall. She could see that all four major entrances were lit up.

"Alex, I'll take the east side," Lily said.

"Then I'm on the west," Alex replied and headed to the left on the road that circled the parking lot.

The mall was T-shaped, with wings that jutted out from a glass-domed atrium on the roof. There was no movement that Alex could see, but the two drones were fairly high up, so if there were any people or vehicles with their lights off on the ground, Alex wouldn't be able to see them. That was the trade-off they had made for stealth. Their drones would stay out of sight, but the distance limited their view.

Alex took a position at the outer edge of the parking lot and stowed her bike in a smattering of trees that gave her reasonably good cover. It also placed her just outside of the ring created by the road that circled the mall. Now she had a good vantage point and would be very hard to see.

"I'm in position," Alex said.

"I am, too," Lily said.

"They are coming your way," Shepard said.

Alex checked the video feed on her heads-up display. There were two cars coming from the north and two from the south. No trucks, no escort cars. That meant there would be a limited number of people at this event. Even if the cars held four people each, that was a maximum of twelve—plus however many the Sellers had inside.

It wasn't ideal, but it was manageable if Alex and Lily could maintain the element of surprise. They didn't have to take all of them out: just the winner of the auction.

On her display, the four cars separated and each one parked in front of one of the four main entrances.

"I'm reading three people getting out of each car and heading inside," Shepard said.

That matched with what Alex saw in front of her. The SUV at her exit had turned off its lights, and she could see three people getting out. She was pleased that none of them were carrying rifles. That meant the Sellers had probably set down a handgun-only rule. It would allow each buyer to feel reasonably secure. And yet no one would be heavily armed enough to try to take out all of the others.

"Are you seeing all this? Looks civilized," Lily said.

It was normal that international criminals who operated at this level liked to keep their business calm and professional. The irony of that was that their objectives were almost always anything but civilized.

Of course, if they conducted their business the way they wanted to engage with the world, they would end up incurring quite a bit of personal risk—and to people like these, that *personal* risk would be completely unacceptable.

Well, there are some risks they can't manage, Alex thought, and that made her smile.

"I'm heading to the northeast corner on foot," Lily said.

"I'll head to the southeast on my bike," Alex said. That was the reason she had brought the Ducati. With no lights on, it was barely more visible then she would be on foot and it would give her more options if there were any surprises.

"Settle in, Alex," Lily said.

Alex took off her helmet and hung it from her handlebars.

"Anything on your Geiger counters?" Shepard said through their comms.

"Nothing," Lily said.

"No," Alex added.

"That doesn't necessarily mean anything. You'd have to be pretty close to get a reading," Shepard said.

They were also operating under the assumption that the buyer would insist on seeing and testing the merchandise before money changed hands. That would give them plenty of time to develop a plan.

Alex scanned the area and found what she was looking for—a ladder that went to the roof. "I've got a ladder here. I might be able to put eyes on the auction through the skylight if it takes place in the center."

"Do it, but be careful," Lily said.

"Copy that," Alex replied as she peered over the ladder. It was surrounded by a circular cage that was locked at the bottom. She reached for her kit to open the lock and it took her less than a minute to pick it. The door opened down and Alex started climbing up the ladder.

The mall was a tall two stories, so the ladder was maybe thirty feet at the top. Even though she wasn't afraid of heights, she noted that thirty feet seemed higher when you were looking down then when you were looking up.

"Alex, Lily, are you seeing this?" Shepard asked.

Turning her head up, Alex could only see a small circle of night sky at the top of the ladder's cage.

"No," Alex said.

"What is it?" Lily asked.

"Alex, you should probably climb down," Shepard said.

* * * *

Whatever this was, it didn't appear to be part of anyone's plan. The helicopter on the wall monitor in Bloch's office was too far away to identify.

It *could* be the Sellers delivering the plutonium to the auction, but that didn't seem likely. It called too much attention to the proceedings.

It could also be one of the buyers bringing in muscle to insure they left with the plutonium, but that would put the buyer himself in jeopardy. Clearly, the Sellers were savvy enough to insist that the buyers didn't use low-level proxies. The smart move was to make sure that each of the four representatives were high enough up in their respective organizations that they thought twice about starting trouble. That left one possibility that Bloch didn't like at all: Ares was raiding the game.

Bloch had Shepard patch her in. Whatever happened next, she wanted to give her people a choice.

* * * *

"I'll be able to make a positive ID on the incoming helicopter in a few seconds," Shepard said.

Hanging on to the ladder, Alex kept her eyes on her phone. The drones were looking down on the chopper, and at this angle and distance it was a dark blur. Shepard would have to get the drones closer to make an ID.

There was a brief flash of light on one of the feeds, and then half of the split screen went blank. A few seconds later, the same thing happened on the other side.

"They made our drones and used some sort our countermeasures," Shepard said.

"I lost direct visual," Lily said.

Alex knew why the helicopter was out of Lily's line of sight, because it was now landing on the roof. Though remarkably quiet, to Alex it sounded like it was right above her head.

"Bloch here," the director's voice said through the comm. "Apparently someone is raiding the game. This was supposed to be a simple operation; the two of you against a small group of lightly armed people. The smart thing to do is abort, and I want you to know that you have that option."

Alex noted that Bloch didn't order them to abort. That meant that though the danger for them just went up exponentially, so did the risk of someone getting away with the prize.

"Alex, what do you think?" Lily asked.

"Let me get a look at that chopper," Alex said and slowly crept up the ladder. At the top, she peeked her head up just high enough to see the helicopter coming in for a landing. She closed her eyes and quickly pulled her head down to avoid the sand and dirt the rotor was kicking up.

Alex recognized the chopper. "It's a Russian Kazan Ansat light utility helicopter," she said.

She didn't have to see everyone's faces to know that each person on that call knew what that meant. It was the same model of helicopter that took part on the assault in Tehran. That meant it was almost certainly Ares.

"I don't know if that makes it better or worse," Alex said.

"I do. It's worse," Lily replied.

Chapter 32

"The smart thing to do is get out of there," Bloch said.

Bloch was sure Ares wasn't sending people into the middle of an auction with very dangerous people with only hand weapons. Instead, they no doubt sent a fire team in an armored helicopter, and that meant that Ares had advanced intel on the auction and had had time to assemble resources and formulate an attack plan.

"I'm in a secure spot and out of sight," Alex said.

"As am I," Lily said.

"I say we wait it out. If we're lucky, the bad guys will wipe each other out, and we can just pick up the plutonium and be back in time for a late dinner," Alex said.

That gave Bloch chills. It was exactly the kind of thing that Alex's father would say. And every time Dan Morgan had told her that he would simply observe and report, the mission had ended with high casualties, extensive property damage, and general mayhem.

"Proceed with caution," Bloch said. Even as the words left her lips, she felt she was tempting fate and the Morgan gene pool. However, Bloch—like her agents—knew this was still their best chance to recover the plutonium.

And the fact was that it was on North American soil, just three hundred miles from New York and six hundred from Washington D.C.

* * * *

When the helicopter set down on roof, the pilot shut off the rotors. That told Alex something important: It meant that the team was confident and they didn't expect to be taking off in a hurry. It also meant that they were conscious of the fact that while the rotors were spinning—even with whatever noise-dampening technology they were using—they were more likely to be noticed by civilian authorities.

As far as Alex could tell, the Sellers and the buyers did not know about the helicopter yet. It had landed far enough away from the glass dome that sat over the center of the mall that the sound must not have carried down inside. Alex watched as a six-man fire team leaped out of the chopper, dressed all in black. They were each carrying an assault rifle and even at this distance, Alex could see that they were wearing tactical vests loaded down with what she presumed were ammo and grenades.

Alex was mildly disappointed when she saw one of the men—who she presumed was the pilot—step back into the helicopter. That told her that while they were confident, they weren't arrogant enough to send the pilot for their only means of escape into a firefight.

Fair enough. Overconfidence was one thing, but stupidity was too much to ask.

Alex whispered a quick report to Lily. Shepard and Bloch were quiet. Alex knew they were listening but wouldn't say anything unless asked a question. Since they had no surveillance to report on, any distraction could be fatal in the active phase of the operation.

The six-man fire team approached the glass dome quickly but carefully. Circling the dome, each man used hand tools to remove a large pane of glass in front of him. That done, they fixed ropes to six points around the dome and attached the other ends of the ropes to the harnesses on their vests.

"They're using single lines?" Lily asked.

"Yes," Alex said.

"That means they are going to drop in quickly using a tactical winch," Lily said.

That was new for Alex. She'd done her share of rappelling. The process required two ropes and was generally a one-way trip, especially if you were in a rush.

An electric winch would get you down as quickly, but it would also get you back up. That meant the gunmen intended to escape in the helicopter while it was on the roof.

Alex thought she might have something to say about that. "Lily, I think I can disable the helicopter without making a ruckus. Stand by."

Careful not to make any noise, she slipped onto the roof. It was a flat, tar roof with occasional cover provided by vents that were almost as tall as she was. With the chopper facing the dome, she was counting on the pilot focusing his attention forward.

She slipped behind the first vent and watched the fire team. One of the men made a hand signal and then at once, six people jumped into the openings where the panes of glass had been.

Alex didn't wait for what she knew would follow. She raced toward the rear of the chopper to where she thought she'd seen a fire hose. She had only taken five steps before she heard automatic weapons fire erupt from inside the mall with single-shot return fire. Alex ignored the noise and raced ahead.

The hose was long, more than long enough for what she had in mind. She tied one end of the heavy canvas and rubber hose around the rear of one of the chopper's landing skids. Then she traced the hose to its other end. She guessed it was at least seventy-five feet in length. Perfect.

She heard the sound of two flash-bang grenades and then at least one incendiary. The gunfire was less intense and now only came in short bursts, punctuated by single shots. Then there were at least almost a dozen shotgun blasts.

Alex wasn't sure, but she thought the fight was the sound of someone's carefully thought-out plan going to hell. In this battle, Alex didn't have anyone to root for. If Zeta, she, and Lily were lucky, both sides would lose badly.

But just in case that didn't happen, she threw the end of the hose down to Lily. "Have you got something solid to tie it off to?" Alex said.

"Yes, I've got a standpipe here," Lily said. "Now get out of there—it sounds bad inside."

Alex headed back to her ladder. She was glad she'd given the rear of the helicopter a wife berth, because as she approached, the top and back rotors came to life.

She scrambled onto her ladder and started making her way down. As she climbed, Lily's voice was in her ear. "Alex, do you want me to come around?"

"Negative. If the guys in the helicopter come out on top, they won't get very far. For people on the ground, we need to cover both sides. But you should get some distance from that standpipe," Alex said.

Seconds later, she had her helmet on and was starting her bike. She kept the lights off and switched on the helmet's night vision. She rode to her initial hiding spot across the parking lot and turned around.

She didn't have to wait long. Two figures came racing out of the eastern mall entrance. One was slight and one was very tall and broad. The big one was limping but still keeping up an impressive pace as they ran to a black SUV.

As the figure ran, Alex saw the helicopter rise above the mall. It turned toward the fleeing people on the ground. The flight lasted less than three seconds before the chopper used up all the slack in the fire hose.

Because the hose was at a nearly right angle to the helicopter's direction, the hose redirected the vehicle into an almost perfect arc downward.

The helicopter was heading to the ground when it disappeared behind the mall. Less than a second later, there was a large *boom* and a fireball that lit up the night sky.

"Lily, are you clear?" Alex said.

"Yes, I'm clear, but I've got no one on the ground out here."

"I've got two on foot who just got into a vehicle. I'm in pursuit. If nobody shows up on your end, you can join me."

Alex started her motorcycle, but kept her lights off. She switched on her helmet's night vision again and she was off.

Her Ducati maxed out at almost two hundred miles an hour, but where it really shone was in its acceleration. She leaped across the parking lot, rapidly closing the distance between herself and the black SUV, even though the vehicle in front of her was going full-out.

However, Alex was reasonably certain that the people in the SUV didn't know they were being followed. They had probably seen the explosion and would soon realize that the helicopter was out of the picture.

Once Alex was directly behind the SUV, the Geiger counter on her phone started to go off. The crackling wasn't strong, but it got stronger as she got closer to the vehicle. Soon, she was about two-tenths of a mile behind them and closing fast.

Alex needed to stop them before they reached the highway, or before they called for any backup they had in the area. As soon as she got within fifty yards she was confident she could hit the rear tires. If she stayed on the passenger side and swung out just a few feet, she would give herself a bigger target. That maneuver would also reduce the chance the people in the car might see her.

They would find out she was there soon enough, but Alex wanted to delay that until she could be sure she could disable their vehicle. Once that was done, the smart thing for her to do was to wait for Lily.

Still, she couldn't afford to underestimate these two. If they were the Sellers (which seemed likely, since they were carrying the plutonium in the car), they were formidable.

They had walked out of a firefight with a heavily armed six-person fire team who'd had the element of surprise. And they had done it in the middle of what must have been a complete free-for-all between the Sellers, the buyers, and the attackers.

Walking away from that required much more than luck, and Alex didn't want to face them alone. Ultimately, however, she didn't need to defeat them, just to separate them from the plutonium. If they fled the vehicle once it had been disabled, Alex would call that a win.

There was less than a tenth of a mile between them as the SUV approached the turnoff for the highway. Alex poured on the speed. She didn't want to start shooting with other cars around. Nor did she want an SUV full of plutonium to spin out of control on a highway.

But the road that ringed the mall was empty, as was the entryway to the highway. She'd have to take them here.

Then the vehicle put on more speed, and Alex saw they would make the turnoff before she could get to them. However, there was still time to get them on the off-ramp, which was a solid quarter-mile long.

Then the SUV veered away from the ramp and pulled to the right. That was Alex's first sign that something was wrong. The second wasn't far behind.

The rear window of the vehicle popped up, and someone started shooting at her. The first two bullets missed her entirely, while the second hit the bike's front body panel.

Alex and Lincoln Shepard had worked hard to make sure the body panels on the bike were armored but not so heavy that they slowed the bike down or significantly changed its center of gravity.

The armor performed well and the bullet ricocheted off the panel in front of her left leg. Of course, the finish would be shot and she'd have to repaint the whole panel, which pissed her off.

Alex swerved back and forth to present the gunman with a moving target. She also kept her head down, knowing that her reinforced helmet would give her excellent ballistic protection.

Even so, another bullet ricocheted off the small bulletproof windshield of her bike. Whoever was shooting at her was good and Alex decided that she'd have to end this quickly.

She added more speed, which was tricky given her side-to-side motion, and brought herself closer to the SUV. She'd given up on the tires; she'd have to take out the gunman and then go for the gas tank.

She had just started reaching for her holstered 9mm when she felt something hit the front of her bike. Alex was barely able to get her right hand back on the grip in time to struggle for control. She realized that her bike had taken a round to the front tire.

On any ordinary bike that would mean an immediate wipeout—and it almost did for Alex. She reduced her speed to get control of the wobbling bike. The run-flat tires that she and Shepard had developed for the motorcycle had saved her. Though common enough on cars, run-flats weren't practical on motorcycles. The rubber cores added too much weight and the stiffness of the sidewalls made angled turns nearly impossible.

However, they had hit on the right mix of materials and created probably the only set of run-flats on a high-performance motorcycle in the world. Unfortunately, with a compromised front tire she had to significantly reduce her speed from eighty to less than fifty.

Before she had time to regret that the SUV would get away, the vehicle spat out a quick series of shots and then pulled a hard right that put the vehicle into a skid and left it perpendicular to her.

Now Alex's problem was that she had too much speed. There was less than fifty yards between her and the SUV, and she'd need half that again to stop her bike before she ran into the vehicle.

Crashing a bike well took more skill that riding it—especially at any speed over twenty miles an hour—and she was going nearly fifty. There was no time to think; Alex had to react automatically and hope for the best. She slowed the bike as much as she could and then pulled it hard to her right as she leaned in the same direction.

It was the same movement she would make if she were making a tight right turn, except this time she leaned even further down. At first the tires skidded and then the side of the bike scraped the pavement.

This was the most sensitive part of the crash. If she stayed under the bike, her right leg would be trapped under the Ducati while both she and the bike were sliding and twisting to a stop.

As soon as the bike made contact with the road, she threw herself backwards, pulling her leg to her and then curling herself into a ball as she started rolling.

This is going to hurt, Alex thought as she executed the maneuver.

Chapter 33

Alex was surprised by two things. One, that she was still conscious. And two, that she was still—as far as she could tell—in one piece.

When she had rolled to a stop she was on her back. She also realized that she was completely vulnerable. While she was cataloging her injuries and trying to figure out what parts of her body still worked, the Sellers she'd been chasing could just shoot her. Or—if they were in a rush—drive over her in their SUV.

Her leather and Kevlar riding jacket and pants would give her some protection from bullets but zero from the three-ton vehicle.

Still, she had to try something and tested her right hand. If her gun was still in its shoulder holster, she would have to draw it quickly if it was going to do any good.

Alex was still testing her fingers when he heard noise above her. It was a voice, or maybe more than one. Then someone was pulling on her helmet.

The noise resolved into her name. "Alex," someone said.

No, not someone. It was Lily. That was good news. Better Lily than the people who had just been shooting at her.

"Alex, can you move?" Lily asked.

Alex took a deep breath and tried to figure out how to answer that.

"What hurts?" Lily said.

"Everything," Alex replied.

"Can you be more specific?" Lily said.

"Most of the outside of my body," Alex said, as she struggled to sit up. "And a good portion of the insides."

"Be careful," Lily said and Alex could hear relief in her partner's voice.

"I think I'm okay; I'm pretty sure I can move," Alex said. With Lily's hands under her arms, she was in a sitting position. "I also don't think anything is broken."

Slowly and with Lily's help, Alex got to her feet. She tried each of her limbs and they all worked. Her riding gear had spared her an awful full-body road rash, though on her right hip and both arms, the leather had been scraped away, revealing the Kevlar beneath.

"Any double vision?" Lily said.

"My head is about the only thing that isn't hurting," Alex said, saying a silent thanks to Shepard for the many improvements he'd made to the helmet. "Really, I'm okay. Nothing broken and I don't think anything is sprained. I think it's mostly bruises."

"So it will be no trouble for you to walk to the SUV," Lily said.

Alex grunted, got up, and started walking. "I don't suppose the bad guys waited around."

"No such luck. But it's not a total loss. The plutonium didn't fly away on the helicopter. That means it's still on the ground and still in Montreal. That also means we still have a chance."

"I got hits on the Geiger counter when I was following them," Alex said.

"Me, too," Lily added.

"Clearly, we have them right where we want them," Alex said.

Alex didn't like the way Lily was looking at her, so she straightened up and tried not to limp. Unfortunately, that effort was complicated by the fact that both of her knees were screaming at her to stop.

Still, Alex considered herself lucky. She'd seen people lose a leg under their bikes in lower-speed crashes than the one was walking away from. A week of bruises and some soreness was a small price to pay.

"We could have the concierge rustle you up a discreet doctor," Lily said.

"Unnecessary. I just need two aspirin and a good night's sleep," Alex said.

She'd almost made a liar of herself when she struggled to climb onto the running board and into the SUV, but she made it and sat heavily in the passenger seat.

As she sat, she saw sirens in the distance and then she remembered what she'd forgotten. "My bike!"

"It's on the side of the road. I don't think it'll run and I'm sorry, but we don't have time to load it up," Lily said.

Alex cursed under her breath.

"If no one notices it for a few hours, Zeta can send a local asset to pick it up," Lily said.

"How bad was it?"

Lily's tight smile told her everything she needed to know. "Nothing you can't fix," Lily said.

As they approached the hotel, Alex was struck by how both normal and alien it appeared after the night they'd had.

As they got out of the SUV, Alex got a glimpse of the soreness she'd have in store for her tomorrow. When the elevator dropped them off on their floor, Lily said, "I'll make our report to Bloch, and then I'm going to head over to the paddock and catch Scott. You just get some sleep. You did great tonight; you deserve it."

Then Lily disappeared into her suite and Alex continued on to her room. She was already dreading taking off her riding jacket and pants, but it had to be done. She'd likely only stiffen up more in the morning.

She groaned as she pulled her wallet out of her back pocket, and just had the key card in her hand when she heard a voice behind her.

"Alex!"

She turned to see Terry practically running up the hallway. He was smiling broadly, but his expression ran through a range of extremes as he got closer to her. His features finally settled on a baffled concern.

"Alex—Oh my God. What happened to you?" He reached for her instinctively, and she just as instinctively pulled away to avoid having him touching any of the patchwork of bruises on her body.

"Sorry," he said. "What happened to you?"

"I'm okay, really," she said.

"I'm pretty sure that's not true. Please tell me what's going on," he said. He was still concerned, but there was an edge in his voice now.

When she didn't reply, he said, "Let me guess: A problem on your motorcycle?"

That was the truth, but at this point she didn't think it would help. "It was. Please, Terry, could we talk about this tomorrow?"

"Don't do that. Don't make me feel like the guy grilling you about your night out with your friends. Something is going on with you. Why don't you just tell me what it is? And please don't tell me that you are just *really bad* at riding your bike."

"Terry, please," she said.

"Please what? Stop asking you questions about whatever it is you are keeping from me? What are you doing? Are you part of the underground Canadian street-racing circuit? A motorcycle fight club?"

"It's nothing like that," she said.

"Okay, so tell me what it is. I can't help you if I don't know what's going on. Let's go inside and figure this out," he said.

Alex wanted to do that, but she knew she couldn't. There was too much of a risk that she'd start talking—*really* talking—to him.

"I can't. Not tonight...tomorrow," she said. She needed time to figure this out.

"Right, because we've only known each other a couple of weeks, and I don't deserve an explanation. I'm not allowed to be worried about you, to want to help you."

"That's not it, you know it isn't," she said.

Terry didn't say anything for a solid few seconds. Somehow that was worse because in that time, his face shifted from angry to lost.

"But you can't tell me what it is," Terry said, sounding defeated.

She knew it was weak, but she said it anyway. "Tomorrow."

"Well, I have this thing tomorrow. I tell you what: You can come by tomorrow night. But do me a favor. Don't do it unless you want to really talk to me."

Alex met his eyes and said, "I'll see you tomorrow, Terry."

"Right, tomorrow," he said. Then he turned around and headed back to the elevators.

Alex was grateful that he hadn't stuck around and didn't see her struggling to pull to open the door. Her limbs were already starting to really stiffen up. She had hoped that she would feel better after a good night's sleep, but she didn't think that sleep would come easily now.

She and Terry couldn't continue unless she told him the truth, and yet that was completely impossible. The smart thing to do would be to let him go. Even if she managed to cobble together a story that he somehow believed, it wouldn't hold for long now that he suspected something was going on.

What would happen next time? The next time she was injured on the job. Or when she disappeared suddenly for a mission. Or got stuck overseas on important business—important *motorcycle repair business.*

It was impossible, but she didn't think it was pointless. And she wasn't ready to let him go, even if it was better for both of them. She had to do something. The problem was that she had absolutely no idea what that might be.

* * * *

It was bad when Alex woke up, but not worse then she had anticipated. She took more aspirin and went to survey the damage in the morning light.

Large bruises covered both of her upper arms, and she had a deep scrape on her left elbow where the road had eaten through her riding jacket.

Her left shoulder also had a bruise that covered most of her swollen tricep and the arm didn't want lift above 90 degrees. She was pleased that her right arm was in better shape. It had fewer bruises and almost a full range of motion, which meant she would be able to shoot.

Both hips were purple and her right thigh was bruised only in small spots. Her calves were also spotted, which told her she'd hit some gravel on the pavement. Her back and shoulders were the worst; they looked terrible and hurt when she moved in any direction.

The good news was that the bruises on her face had faded to yellow and would be easier to cover with makeup. Otherwise, she'd have to stick to slacks instead of a skirt or a dress, and she'd have to wear long sleeves, preferably something extremely soft.

The shower was no picnic and the twenty minutes of stretching was even worse. But by the time she was done, she no longer moved like she had just hit the pavement at nearly forty miles an hour.

Alex settled on soft cotton slacks, a T-shirt, and a hoodie. With makeup on she thought she looked almost human. As she was finishing up, her doorbell rang. When Alex opened the door, Lily was there. "How are you feeling?" she asked as she walked in.

"Okay," Alex said.

"Liar, but you look good, so that will have to do," she said.

"Any word on the Sellers?" Alex asked.

"No, they got away. However, they did kick up a few radiation sensors. The license plate number you provided was stolen, so no luck there. And we got a few hits on traffic cameras, but the SUV disappeared. Shepard has his staff scouring every camera in the city and surrounding area for the make and model."

"I had them, Lily, and then I got sloppy," Alex said.

"Sorry, Alex. You can't do that. You blew up the Ares helicopter and took out the survivors of their fire team. We stopped the sale and the Sellers had to go running. Sometimes the best you can do is disrupt the bad guys' plans. That's when *they* get sloppy and make mistakes. We just have to be ready," Lily said.

"They'll know someone is searching for the car. They'll have to transfer the plutonium and maybe we'll get a hit on the radiation sensors then," Alex said.

"Until then, are you ready to head to the garage? We're qualifying today," Lily said.

"About that. Terry stopped by after you left," Alex said.

"What did he make of you?" Lily asked.

"He was concerned, but I couldn't tell him anything, so he went away angry," Alex said.

"I'm sorry, Alex. This happens. It's hard on relationships, new ones especially. What are you going to tell him?"

"I'll have to figure that out while we watch today," Alex replied.

When they reached the lobby, Alex still had no idea what she would say. She decided she'd do what she did on a mission that went sideways: She'd improvise.

Chapter 34

Scott greeted them as they entered the garage. "How are you, Alex?" he said.

"Fine," she said, smiling. Though she was nowhere near 100 percent, she found that she felt significantly better than she had when she'd woken up. It would take her at least a week or two for the bruises to clear up and for her various muscle tears and pulls to heal, but she was grateful that she was functional.

It was a bonus that she could move around in public without getting stares. Certainly, that was essential to maintaining her cover.

"Fine. How do feel about today?" Alex asked.

"Great. Both Alonzo and Terry were strong in practice. The cars are performing well, and the new gearbox is better than we'd hoped for."

"Excellent. Good luck, then," Alex said.

As Renard walked away, Alex felt a pang of white-hot envy for Lily. Not only did he know about the nature of Lily's real work, but he clearly also knew about the latest developments. That meant that Lily was able to tell him everything and talk over issues as they came up.

Yet Alex knew that Renard was a special case. He had been assisting Zeta for years. And before that, he had gained high-level security clearance because of the software work he and Renard Tech had done for the US government.

Alex knew that her father had someone who knew the truth about him in the form of Alex's mother. That process of telling that truth had taken years, but it had to start somewhere. By the end of his time with the CIA, Alex's mother had known everything, and because she did, Alex's parents had decided together when it was time for him to leave the job.

Alex knew quite a bit about her father's career, and everything about how he started at Zeta—largely because she had witnessed many of those events herself. However, she didn't know how her father had begun the process of telling the truth to her mother.

Even if her parents had not been traveling the world, Alex doubted there was anything they could tell her that would help her fix things with Terry. Of course, Alex didn't have to solve that problem today. She merely had to enjoy the practice, while she waited for a break in the mission.

At any minute, she and Lily could get a call from Zeta HQ with a lead on the plutonium. It was better if she wasn't distracted when that call came; Terry had plenty to think about today.

She watched the cars run their laps and noted that while most of the drivers did pretty well, few really pushed themselves on each lap. Alex saw that Jenya was one of the drivers who gave her all on every lap. Given that she was one of the few women to ever compete at this level, that wasn't a surprise. Without that competitive streak, she would never have made it this far.

Alex was pleased to see that Terry was also pushing himself, just as he had done yesterday. He was taking every lap as a chance to improve some aspect of his driving. With the race just one day away, that spoke well of his chances.

Based on what she was seeing, Alex didn't think an outright win was impossible. Certainly, if he kept driving like this he would end up on the podium—either in this race or one or more of the others this season.

Alex hoped she was in his life when that happened. If not, perhaps she would look him up in the future. Maybe there would be a time when things would be possible for both of them.

"Terry is driving very well," Alex said.

"Scott has an excellent eye for talent and passion," Lily said.

"I was worried that after what happened last night..." Alex began.

"Don't worry about that," Lily said. "Alex, let me ask you: If you and I had to go to work right now—our real work—would you be able to do it?"

"Of course. Right now my limitations are purely physical, and even those you have to put aside during an operation."

"Exactly, and Terry is a world-class competitor. You don't get there if you can't put your personal life aside when you're on the track—even if you are a little lovesick. Give him some credit."

That actually made Alex feel better. She didn't want her work—and the trouble it was causing between them—to make his driving harder. It was too important to him and he was too good at it.

When it was time to break for lunch, Lily said, "Come on, we'll have lunch at the paddock. Scott and the crew will eat in the garage while they go over the plan for later."

Of course, Alex and Lily could join them, but there was no reason to remind Terry of the problems they were having and give him *more* feelings to put aside when he needed to be at his best.

Alex felt even better after more aspirin and lunch. The Zeta field kits included stronger painkillers, but anything more than aspirin would impair her slightly if she had to go into action. And since she was already not 100 percent, she didn't want to do anything else to potentially compromise her performance later.

That wasn't an idle thought. The fact was that for reasons she didn't yet understand, both terrorism and criminal activity were tied to the racing circuit. And now they were coming to the end of Formula 1 in Quebec— with trouble right on America's doorstep and possibly much worse to come.

She was relieved when the concierge called and gave her something else to focus on. She listened while he spoke and then said, "Thank you, Edouard."

Lily glanced up from her food. "Any news?"

"Just that my car arrived at the hotel. I asked Shepard to send it up last night," Alex said.

"Renard Tech security has vehicles, and the new detachment we've put on Scott has Zeta cars."

Alex knew what that meant. Zeta vehicles would have the standard Zeta armor and tactical package, which was nothing to sneeze at.

"I'd rather have my own ride," Alex said.

She felt a pang over her motorcycle. The Zeta pickup team hadn't been able to get to the bike before it was impounded by Canadian authorities.

Back at the garage, the air was electric. Everyone was enthusiastic, excited about the team's chances. Good starting positions could help put them over the top. Alex decided to stop in to see Terry and wish him luck, but he'd already left the garage to head for the pit area. She'd have to catch him later; certainly she'd make sure to see him before the race tomorrow.

The qualifying process was complicated and involved multiple sessions in which the drivers were eliminated in groups. After the first two sessions, the last ten cars competed for the first ten starting positions. Jenya, Alonzo, and Terry were all in that group, and the excitement in the garage was nearly palpable.

In the last session, two of the cars got too close and touched wheels. Both cars went into spins that took them off the track into the barricades. The drivers walked away and though both cars were mangled—with wheels shorn off and struts missing or bent—Alex knew repairs could be made in hours.

However, as a result, there were only eight cars now competing for the top spots. Terry was roughly in the middle of the pack when he passed the Renard garage and pit area.

Just ahead of Terry's car was one of the Red Bull racers. Alex saw an odd shimmy in its rear right tire, and then the tire flew off and the car was spinning. It was immediately struck by one of the Ferrari vehicles and that car flew into the air.

To avoid the mess, Terry turned to the inside and put himself into a sideways skid. It was a nearly perfect maneuver and Terry avoided what could have been a pileup. He ended up coming to rest near the inside barricade when the airborne Ferrari vehicle passed over Terry's car, spinning and turning into a twisted mess.

There were gasps from everyone in the garage, including Alex. Within seconds, there were people on the track spraying down the Ferrari and pulling the driver out of the vehicle.

As Terry had explained, the cockpit was the most solid part of the car and would protect drivers from even the most frightening-looking crashes. There was a rounded hump behind the driver that would further protect him or her if the car rolled.

This crash was no exception, and the Ferrari driver was on his feet and walking away from the wreck in well under a minute.

It was then that Alex noticed the chief calling Terry's name over and over again into his radio at the command center. For the first time since Alex had met the chief, she heard alarm in his voice. He shouted the last two times he called for Terry, and then he turned from the monitors to look out onto the track.

There were four people around Terry's car, but no one was pulling him out. Before Alex could say a word, Scott Renard ran past her, and then the chief was also sprinting out of the garage and onto the track.

Something was wrong and Alex was ashamed that it took her so long to react. Running toward trouble was what she had been trained to do. Instantly, she was on her feet. She needed to get to Terry.

And then two arms wrapped around her, stopping her.

"Alex, don't," Lily said, her arms feeling like iron.

"You can't help him. Let the people who can, do it," Lily said as Alex struggled in her arms. "You'll just be in the way."

That stopped Alex cold and she watched as the ambulance Formula 1 kept on hand drove onto the track. It only took seconds for the men with the stretcher to approach the car. Renard and the chief were there first, though. Staring into the cockpit.

It didn't make any sense. The car had no visible damage, but somehow Terry must have been hurt, and for some reason no one was pulling him out.

"Why aren't they moving? Why aren't they helping him? The ambulance is right there," she said. Alex tried to move forward, but Lily kept her arms on Alex's shoulders.

Then Lily turned them both so that Alex was looking into the garage and away from the track. There was shouting all around her and more than one scream. There were also voices on various radios, but Alex could only make out random words.

"Terry needs help," Alex said, unable to shake the feeling that everyone out there meant well but weren't doing enough.

"Alex, look at me. I need you to stay right here. Scott and the chief are there. Let them take care of him. I want you to just look at me," Lily said, keeping her eyes on Alex's.

A short time later—it could have been one minute or ten—Alex heard a siren. Only then did Lily relax the arms holding Alex's shoulders. Free, Alex turned around to see the ambulance pulling away, maddeningly slowly.

She also saw Renard and the chief walking back to the garage. They were also moving slowly and more than once she saw Renard grab the chief as if he were holding the older man up.

When they were close enough, Alex could see they both had blood on their team shirts, which didn't make any sense. The Ferrari driver didn't have a scratch on him and his car was a twisted heap. Terry's car had been barely touched.

When they were only a few paces away, Alex could see that both men were shattered. She saw the chief struggle to straighten his back as he walked past them into the garage. Renard stopped in front of them and said, "I'm sorry, Alex—he's gone."

"What?" was all Alex could say.

"He was badly hurt. There was nothing anyone could do," Renard said.

There were more words, but Alex didn't catch most of them. There were also audible cries from the garage and the pit.

She heard the chief's voice and then Alonzo's.

"One of the tires clipped his helmet," someone said.

There were more voices from various radios. Most of the words didn't make sense, except for someone who sounded like an announcer, or a reporter, who used the words "partial decapitation."

"Come on, Alex, let me get you back to the hotel," Lily said.

Then they were walking. Outside, there was a car waiting. As they climbed into the back, Alex noticed that the pain she'd felt since her tumble on her motorcycle had disappeared. No, it hadn't quite disappeared. Instead, it had shifted inward and had coalesced into a hot ball somewhere in the center of her chest.

Chapter 35

Lily brought Alex to her room and stayed with her. Alex wasn't sure how much time had passed, but it was turning to dusk outside. They didn't speak much, but Lily didn't leave her.

Lily checked in a couple of times with Zeta, but there were no leads on the plutonium, so the women were stuck in the hotel.

"Alex, why don't I get you something to eat?" Lily asked.

Alex said yes. She wasn't hungry and wasn't sure she would even be able to eat, but she knew that Lily wouldn't leave until she thought Alex was okay.

And she was okay, or she would be. This was not the first time she had lost a boy she had known for only a short time. She had survived that first loss and she would survive this one.

What she needed was to be alone, so she ate the soup and told Lily she was fine. "Why don't you find Scott?" Alex said. He would be upset. Alex knew that he and Terry were close.

"I wouldn't be helping. Scott has a lot to do now, and the whole team is looking to him," Lily said.

Terry had told her that it had been years since the last driver was killed on a Formula 1 track. Not anymore.

She thought of the signs she had seen in warehouses and factories: 54 DAYS WITHOUT AN INJURY. For Formula 1, that clock had just started ticking again. It might be years before someone else died. Or it could be in the next city.

When you had twenty cars crammed onto a narrow track, navigating twists and turns as they approached two hundred miles an hour, it could happen at any time. It was a risk that came with the job. That was something Alex understood.

She wouldn't dishonor Terry by pretending that his job wasn't important. It certainly was to him.

It was fully dark when there was a knock at the door. It was Jenya. She looked beautiful as always, but she didn't look well.

"Alex, I'm sorry about Terry. He was an excellent driver," she said. There was none of the usual irony or humor in the Russian woman's voice.

She sat at the small round table where Alex was sitting and said, "I'm sorry, Alex. I'm sorry about your young man."

"Thank you," she said automatically.

Then Jenya did something that genuinely surprised her. She took Alex's hand as they sat and said, "He really cared for you. You saw the way women looked at him—that is the way it is for drivers on the circuit. But you were the only one who turned his head, and I saw the way *he* looked at *you*."

That almost cost Alex her composure, but she kept her reaction to a thin smile.

"Lily, why don't you find Scott?" Jenya asked, then, before Lily could protest, said, "I'll stay with her."

"I'm sure Scott could use you," Alex added.

Lily agreed and left. Now, with luck, Jenya would wait only a few minutes before she followed her.

"I'm fine, really," Alex said, as evenly as she could.

"Obviously," Jenya said, reaching into her bag. She pulled out a bottle of vodka and said, "Let me show you how Russians mourn."

She poured out two glasses of the clear liquor and said, "To Terry."

Jenya raised her glass and Alex leaned in to clink the glasses, but Jenya pulled hers away. "No, we don't touch glasses, not for the dead." She raised her glass and Alex did the same. The vodka was smooth but still burned when it went down.

Jenya poured two more glasses, but before they drank, she said, "Alex, you're hurt."

"I had an accident on my motorcycle," she said.

"Dangerous machines," Jenya said. "You must be careful."

Alex didn't answer because anything she said would have been a lie or a half-truth, and she didn't want to do that now.

"We argued last night. He was angry with me," she said.

"Do you think that affected his driving? You saw what happened. It was nothing he did. And let me explain something to you. He was a Formula One driver. When we are in the car we put aside everything else we think and feel. We have to or we can't compete. Terry liked you, Alex. He liked you maybe more than was good for someone his age who did what he did, but when he was driving he wasn't thinking about you. And no thoughts he had or didn't have could have protected him from bad luck."

Jenya poured two more glasses and said, "*Vechnaya pamyat.*"

Alex raised her glass and said, "Memory eternal," and drank.

"You speak some Russian?" Jenya said, surprised.

"I have someone at work who has been teaching me. He's from St. Petersburg," Alex replied.

"Then let us drink to your Russian friend," Jenya said, pouring out two more glasses.

* * * *

Alex woke up in her bed, though she didn't remember getting into it. It was daylight, her head was pounding, and her mouth was dry. Then she remembered Terry, and the tight ball of grief in her chest returned.

She remembered that from the last time she'd felt this kind of grief. There were brief moments in the morning between the time she woke up and the time she remembered. Sometimes there was a full half-minute of feeling normal before it came rushing back to her.

That had happened for weeks the last time, and Alex wondered if it would be faster this time. Would she get better at putting it aside? How many times did it have to happen before she barely felt it at all?

The good news was that between her head and the hole in her chest, she barely felt the soreness in her body.

She showered and dressed, pulling the clothes over the dark purple mosaic that still covered a full quarter of her skin. When she was finished, Lily was at her door.

"I checked on you last night. When I got back you were asleep," Lily said.

"How is…" Alex started, knowing that it was an absurd question.

"Scott and the others are doing the best they can. The chief is having a hard time. You know they are racing today," Lily said.

"I assumed," Alex said. She understood. There was still a race and a season to finish. Those were things that Terry had worked for and been a part of. It was like a mission at Zeta. It didn't stop when you lost someone on it. In fact, it became more important when they were gone.

"Everyone will understand if you'd rather not go to the team breakfast."

"I'll be there. It's in an hour, right?"

Alex got ready quickly and made sure she was at Lily and Renard's door early. Scott answered and he didn't look good. There were dark rings under his eyes and it looked like he hadn't slept.

"How are you doing, Alex?" he asked.

"I'm okay, Scott, how are you?" she said. She tried to keep her voice solemn. She knew that was expected, and that Scott and Lily would worry if she didn't behave normally.

And she had work to do. She would be much less effective if people thought she had lost it. She couldn't help Terry now—Lily had been right about that—but there were people she could help, deaths she could prevent if she did her job well in the next forty-eight hours.

There was plenty to time for her to feel whatever she was going to feel when the mission was finished. For now, Terry would have to keep.

The three of them rode together to the garage where the mood was... well, like a funeral. People shuffled around trying not to make noise, talking in whispers. She gave them credit for carrying on. *Most civilians couldn't do it*, she thought and then caught herself. Most *people* couldn't do it.

There was something about this group that was like the people she'd known at Zeta, and the people she'd known who were in the military. There was a shared sense of purpose and a clear mission. Those things made people up their game and function when most others could not.

When Renard, Lily, and Alex walked in, things got quieter—if that were possible. Then Alex understood something else. These people were a lot like a military unit and their leader had just walked in. Scott acknowledged them with a nod, and then people went back to what they were doing.

Alonzo approached them with tears in his eyes as both Lily and Renard patted him on the back. Then they approached the chief, who was standing over one of the cars. No, not *one* of the cars: *Terry's* car—the car that he had died in the day before. It had been cleaned and repaired and was ready to race.

Alex had a moment of vertigo staring into the cockpit. She had to force herself to turn her head up and focus on the chief. "Alex, I'm so sorry," he said. Like Lily, he was British and thus composed, but control seemed to take some effort for him.

"Scott, we've been looking over—" the chief started, and then he simply stopped speaking, almost as if he'd forgotten how. He turned back to Alex and hugged her. Alex was too surprised to react, and then the large man started to sob. She returned the hug and felt how close she was herself to letting go.

It would be very easy to lose herself and feel what everyone else was feeling—what the chief was showing. It took a massive act of will to fight the impulse and, aside from a few stray tears, she was able to keep hold of herself.

Finally, he released her, though he still held her by the shoulders. "I'm so sorry. He really liked you, you know. He talked to me about you and he never talked about anything but cars or the race."

Another act of will kept that hot ball inside her chest so it didn't escape up her throat. "Thank you, Chief," she croaked, and then the man let her go and wiped his face.

"If I could have your attention," Renard said, and then everyone gathered around him. "I first met Terry when he approached me at the Indy 500…"

It must have been a good speech, Alex thought, at least judging by the frequent outbreaks of tears and occasional quiet laughter from the group. Alex missed most of it, focusing instead on whether or not she'd have time to complete everything she needed to do between this assembly and the race itself, which was now five hours away.

Afterward, there was food at tables set up for the race-day breakfast, which was now more of a memorial service. Alex realized that this might be the only memorial for Terry that most of these people could attend. They would begin packing up tomorrow and then there would be breakneck preparations and setup for the next stop on the circuit, which was Paris.

There would probably be a service in Indianapolis for his family, she supposed. Then she remembered that his father had passed, and the only immediate family was his mother, who was sick.

Another thought she had to push aside before it swallowed her.

Alex accepted the food that Lily gave her and was eating quietly when Jenya walked in. She was in her racing jumpsuit and walked over to Renard. "I'm sorry, Scott. I liked Terry very much." Then she turned to Alex and said, "How are you, Alex?"

"I'm okay," she said.

Jenya looked her over and seemed satisfied. She approached Alonzo and then the chief, who she talked to for a full ten minutes. Jenya made her good-byes and Alex waited a respectable few minutes before she said to Lily, "I'm going to go back to the hotel. I'll call in to Zeta, see if there's anything we can follow up on, and then just be alone for a while."

"Will you be back for the race?" Lily asked.

"Of course. I'll just take a little time," Alex said.

"My driver will meet you outside," Renard said.

"Thanks," Alex said and she headed for the exit. She found that she had to resist the urge to rush out of the garage. At the hotel, she went straight to the concierge. She noted that there were three duffel bags sitting just outside his counter.

"Miss Morgan," Edouard said.

"Edouard, I see you have the equipment we discussed," Alex said.

"Yes, they were delivered a few minutes ago. I will have them sent out as soon as possible," he said. Then he paused and asked, "Is this hotel or the city in any danger?"

"No immediate danger. Each of those kits contains what we discussed: a compact air compressor and a complete flat repair kit. Each of the hotels in your…network will find them very useful in their garages. Even if they have equipment, I guarantee these are better."

It was true. Most good hotels with their own garages had kits like these available to the valets. And Shepard had promised that the compressors and kits—which included plugs to fix flats and hand tools as well as replacement valves and valve caps—were excellent. Besides the digital readouts for precise inflation, the compressors had some special features that weren't found on any commercial units.

"Edouard, I can tell you that the units also contain radiological sensors. We have reason to believe that someone will shortly be moving radioactive material in the city. There is little danger that it has been weaponized or might be in the short term. On the other hand, we don't know what the parties we are searching for will do if they are given enough time."

"I see," Edouard said, as if he were acknowledging a request for theater tickets. Then he raised his hand, snapped his fingers, and two young men from the bell stand rushed over and took the duffels. Then he turned his attention back to Alex, gave her a polite smile, and said, "Let me know if there is anything else I can do to be of service."

Alex headed up to the room, glad to be doing something. Shepard was tracking the Montreal radiological sensor system, but they had seen that those systems could be fooled. It was pretty clear that the Sellers were carrying the plutonium in a shielded container.

The Sellers also knew that their car had been seen and would want to transfer the material to another vehicle. These new sensors would supplement the existing system. Of course, they would only work in the top hotels, the ones with concierges who were members of Edouard's elite circle. Of course, that included all of the best hotels in the city.

If the Sellers were part of the trouble that had followed the Formula 1 circuit and had arranged a sale that was attended by the likes of Sheik Nazer, Alex was willing to bet that they would be traveling first class.

In any case, the sensors wouldn't hurt, and at this point Alex was willing to take any small advantage she could. Up in the room, she made a report to Bloch and then called Shepard.

"The units arrived. Is there any chance we might get a false positive?" she asked.

"No, someone getting treated for cancer won't kick up an alert. I calibrated the rad sensitivity to the readings you got on your phone, based on your distance from the plutonium, when your phone unit started picking it up. The sensors are pretty dumb and won't be good for much else. The compressors, on the other hand, are state of the art. As long as the operator inputs the correct pressure, they won't overinflate the tire."

Alex knew from her own shop that these kits always came in handy, and the digital unit saved the back-and-forth you usually had to do to get the pressure just right. And the fact that these were high-quality compressors meant that the valets and garage attendants would keep them handy.

"Nothing on the SUV?" she said.

"We're tracking all black SUVs of that make and model. Nothing unusual and no hits on the sensors. I think you're right. It's in a garage somewhere."

"Anything on the rentals?" she asked.

"Since your incident, we've checked all car rentals for any irregularities. Nothing suspicious. I can't say for sure, but I suspect that if they are going to move the plutonium to a new vehicle, it's one they already have in the city. We're also watching boats, helicopters, and planes for any short-notice charters in the last forty-eight hours. Nothing yet."

Alex was satisfied. They had covered all the bases. If the Sellers popped their heads up with the plutonium, Zeta would see them. If they tried to drive it out of the city, there would be time to catch them. Of course, Shepard's team would be watching every other mode of transport. If and when they tried to move, Zeta would be there, and more to the point, *Alex* would be there.

According to Bloch, Karen O'Neal's threat-identification system hadn't gotten any hits for Montreal for the next week. However, Alex had a system of her own and her gut was telling her that something was going to happen before they left Montreal.

Her mission in the city wasn't finished and she had business with the Sellers. If nothing else, they had cost Alex her motorcycle. After Terry, she felt no grief for the loss of her bike, but she was plenty pissed off.

Chapter 36

The crowd cheered and roared as they usually did during a race. That seemed wrong to Alex. Not that the race would continue, but that the excitement around it would still be there.

It was fair enough, she supposed. The crowd didn't know Terry, except as an image on a poster, or a personality in a video. For the fans, he was an abstraction, and his death was temporarily sad, but wouldn't get in the way of their enjoyment of the race. Though she knew it wasn't fair to the strangers in the crowd, that thought made her angry.

The Renard garage and pit were a different story. On the outside, the activity during the race appeared the same. The pit crew did their jobs with amazing speed. The chief and Renard were in the command center in front of the various monitors as the chief barked instructions to the drivers.

Yet there was no conversation outside of what was necessary for the race. Renard had dedicated the race to Terry and everyone was doing their jobs, but the mood was more like an extension of yesterday's memorial than a Grand Prix.

The team wasn't just going through the motions. The reserve driver—a man named Gunther—was hovering around the middle of the pack. Alonzo, on the other hand, was doing well and fighting for third place. Alex thought that this race might end with his first trip to the podium.

The big surprise for Alex was Jenya's performance. She seemed to be stuck in the middle of the pack with Gunther. Occasionally, she would move up a place or two, only to fall back again.

She wasn't making mistakes per se, but she wasn't driving with her signature aggressive style. Normally, she was a risk-taker, someone who would come dangerously close to cars ahead of her to pass them on the inside. Now, she actually let most of those opportunities pass her by.

Perhaps she'd been more affected by Terry's death than she had appeared. Alonzo had been deeply affected, but his grief, if anything, had made him more focused.

Maybe it was easier to do that for people like him, who wore their emotions on their sleeves. But whatever was going on with Jenya, it looked like this just wouldn't be her race.

Alex made polite observations to Lily from time to time, but her mind often drifted from the race. She kept coming back to the feeling that the mission in Montreal wasn't over.

While she wanted Alonzo and the team to make a good showing for Terry, she understood that if he ended up placing, there would be more activity, more celebration, and more required of the team. All of that would make it harder for Alex to get away. And whatever happened in the race, she needed to leave the track as soon as she possibly could.

A good showing would make it harder for Lily as well. If the mission turned into an active operation tonight, Lily would take whatever action was necessary, but that wouldn't help her cover, which required her to be by Scott's side at times like this.

Alex didn't have any of the same responsibilities and for that she was glad. People already looked at her like the grieving girlfriend; they would accept it when she disappeared.

The roar of the crowd brought her back to the race and she saw that Alonzo was now in second place, with the third-place car a good distance behind him.

"Alex, I think he might do this," Lily said.

Alex saw that there were five laps to go, enough for Alonzo to make a move against the Ferrari car less than two lengths ahead of him. On the last lap, the cars were practically touching as they entered turn ten, where the drivers had to shed most of their speed to make the hairpin curve. Alex thought Alonzo might make a move there, but the Ferrari driver stayed too close to the inside for that to be possible.

The next two turns were relatively gentle, and then the cars came to turns thirteen and fourteen—the ironically named Wall of Champions, which was the site of most of the crashes on the Canadian circuit.

Turn thirteen was a nearly 90-degree right turn that was almost immediately followed by a nearly 90-degree left turn. Navigating it required a perfect combination of initial speed, braking, and shifting. As a result, it was one of the best places on the track to overtake an opponent.

Alex knew that the Wall of Champions had been Terry's specialty on this track.

Alonzo was in the outside position on the first turn, which put him on the inside for the second. For a terrible instant, Alex thought he had too much speed coming out of thirteen, but he kept to the road through fourteen and came out of it a full length ahead of Ferrari.

After that it was a straightaway until the finish line, and Alonzo had been able to put another length between them when he crossed the finish line first.

The crowd roared and Alex heard shouts from team Renard. She remembered to call out and applaud. Lily ran to Scott and hugged him and then the chief as the rest of the team rushed into the pit to greet Alonzo.

Alex approached Scott and said, "Congratulations—that was amazing."

He beamed and said "thank you" as he was swallowed up by the team. The chief sought her out, hugged her, and then joined the group.

Alonzo took the first-place position on the podium and gave a good speech in which he dedicated the win and the season to Terry. When there was a break, Alex told Renard and Lily that she was going to skip the after-race festivities in the paddock and head back to the hotel.

"Do you want company?" Lily asked.

"Not at all. Enjoy. I'll call in and see if I can get some work done," she said.

"I'll have a car waiting at all times, and I will meet you if anything comes up," Lily said.

When Alex walked outside, she felt nothing but relief. It was just too much work to keep her head clear in that environment.

At the hotel, she checked in with Zeta, picked up some of her equipment, and called down for her car. She considered wearing her riding jacket, which also served as body armor, but it was too torn up to offer any real protection.

Well, she decided, she'd just have to take extra care not to be get shot.

The car was waiting for her downstairs. It had been a gift from her parents, a hunter green 1968 Mustang GT Fastback. It was famous for appearing in a film from that era and it had been her birthday present last year.

Dan Morgan had personally supervised the restoration of the car, though *restoration* was not quite the right word. Though most of the body, engine, and the drive train were original, the car had spent a fair amount of time in Shepard's auto shop in Zeta's basement. It had the standard Zeta armor and the full tactical package—as well as a few tricks that had not yet made it to the rest of the Zeta fleet. Of course, on the outside, it was just a very good restoration of an iconic vehicle.

Though she liked the Mustang, she usually favored her bike, which gave her stealth, a bit more speed, and the ability to go places cars just couldn't go.

Of course, the Mustang offered armor and more firepower. Since she didn't have her bike, there was no choice, but she couldn't say that she regretted having the extra firepower.

She'd tried stealth two nights ago and it had cost her her bike. And the fact was that she hadn't been able to stop the Sellers when she'd had them in her sights. This time, if she had the chance, she would use every weapon at her disposal to put a stop to the Sellers' business once and for all.

Outside, she was surprised at how empty the streets were. She knew that Montreal practically shut down for the Grand Prix, and both the residents and the tourists would be watching the closing ceremonies and wrap-up of the race. The Renard win would be big news: An upstart team started by a tech billionaire wins its first Grand Prix.

Then there would be after-parties and celebrations long into the night. All of that would keep the police distracted, breaking up fights and hauling in those who did too much celebrating.

It would be the perfect time to, say, transport plutonium out of the city. But while the city might be distracted, Alex felt extremely focused. When she had chosen the code name Raven, it had been because it reminded her of a boy who had died on her first undercover mission.

She hadn't thought much about the meaning of the word. Now she did. Ravens were ill omens, harbingers of death and misfortune, and that suited Alex very well right now. She wanted some payback, not because the Sellers had anything to do with Terry's death, but because they were the nearest target and had plenty else to answer for.

The Sellers were about to find out that sometimes life wasn't fair, and sometimes luck was just bad. That was something that Alex now understood very well.

Shepard buzzed her and the call came through the car. "Alex, we have something. There was a hit on the sensor in the garage at the Sofitel Montreal."

"That means they probably have moved the plutonium; do we have any security camera video?" she asked.

"No, no video in the garage. In fact, someone shut down the hotel's whole system. And before you ask, all city traffic cameras are down for a ten-block radius. As far as I can tell, they got the surrounding private systems as well. I'll keep checking to see if they missed an ATM or a bodega system."

"Scratch that *probably*. They have definitely moved the plutonium," Alex said.

As she suspected, the Sellers were now in a rush to get the material out of the city. If they were in a hurry, there was a chance that a camera at a local business might have caught the vehicle on its way out of the hotel. The problem was that the Sellers could also be out of the city by the time Shepard's team had hacked every surrounding security system and examined its feed.

"Anything on late charters out of Montreal?" Alex asked.

"No such luck," he said. "The only activity was an attempted break-in at the docks earlier today. It's a storage facility for water taxis. The police chased them off and nothing was stolen."

Alex was instantly suspicious. The Sellers had used a "failed" break-in to a hotel vault in Monaco as a cover to get into the Casino de Monte-Carlo's vault. It had worked and had left Zeta two steps behind them.

Not this time.

There were only three ways out of Montreal: land, sea, and air. And Alex was willing to bet her winnings from the casino that it was going to be sea.

"No ships missing?" Alex asked.

"No, and we're monitoring all police and harbormaster activity," Shepard replied.

"Since we know that the Sellers can access security systems, can you set up alarms on the city's radiological and traffic camera systems? Something that will tell you if someone accesses them?"

"Sure, we can create alerts for any unauthorized access. Plus, now that we've seen some of their hacks at work, we have some examples of their digital fingerprints," Shepard said.

The Sellers were smart and given time, they or their organization would change-up their methods, but Alex and Lily had disrupted their plans and now they were leaving town in a hurry. Alex was counting on the fact that they would be relying on familiar methods, not reinventing the wheel as they tried to make a quick getaway.

"Keep an eye on the bridges, tunnels, and airports of course. I'm going to focus on the waterfront. The air taxi dock is part of the Old Port?"

"Yes, how did you know?"

"A hunch," Alex said.

"Also, have the system keep an eye out for more black SUVs of the same make and model as before. Look in particular for two or more identical vehicles together." Alex knew that intelligence agencies and criminal organizations tended to favor certain vehicles. Part of that tendency was practical, since they bought or upgraded vehicles for their fleets in groups.

Even if the Sellers transferred the plutonium to another vehicle, they would want an escort.

"I'll put the image-recognition system on it and make sure it's tied in to traffic cameras and any security systems I can find," Shepard said. "We'll track as many of those vehicles as we can."

"Meanwhile, I'll head to the Old Port area and look for likely candidates," she said.

Alex called Lily, who said she'd grab a team from her handpicked security detail for Renard and check out the Sofitel. Maybe something would turn up there. With luck, the Sellers had ditched the SUV from the mall. The car might help them determine the identity or identities of the Sellers, even if they did somehow manage to slip out of the city.

But Alex decided that path would be a failure. They had been playing catch-up since this mission started. Now Alex knew the Sellers were on the move, in a hurry, and most likely to make a mistake. If Alex was right about the Sellers using the river to get away, there was a real chance of stopping them.

Of course, it wasn't solely a hunch. The Sellers had used an abandoned mall for the auction. The Old Port area had the greatest number of abandoned places in the city—and the only ones that had available docks on the river.

* * * *

"What do you have for me, Lily?" Bloch asked.

"We found the SUV that had been carrying the plutonium. We're nearly certain that this was the one Alex faced on her motorcycle. It's definitely lighting up our Geiger counters."

"Anything inside we can use?" Bloch said.

"They didn't leave anything but radiation," Lily said.

"Okay, secure it and we'll have a team bring it back here," Bloch said. However, by the time that happened and any meaningful analysis was completed, the plutonium would likely either be recovered or lost.

Shepard and O'Neal's team had already run the vehicle identification number. It was owned by a company affiliated with the governing body of Formula 1, and that meant precisely nothing. With time, they could maybe track it down further, but Bloch doubted the enemy would give them that time before they acted.

"Where's Alex?" Bloch asked.

"She's staying by the waterfront in case the Sellers try to escape by the river," Lily said.

That made sense. With Lily on Notre-Dame Island and Alex at the port to the west, they could cover more ground. But it was a big city and Bloch only had two of her people there—aside from some local assets and the security people Lily had around Renard.

Bloch could push the panic button and call the State Department to let the Canadians know there was loose plutonium in hostile hands in their city. The normal response would be a limited or total lockdown. Of course, that would only happen if the Canadian government took the warning seriously. And even if they did, that sort of action required a complex decision-making process. Then implementation of a lockdown required the coordination of multiple agencies, and that would take time. And the Sellers needed only minutes or maybe an hour to leave the city and disappear.

The only advantage of warning the Canadian government was that it would absolve Zeta of responsibility for the nuclear material. However, it would also mean that a good supply of weapons-grade plutonium would be in North America, unacceptably close to the United States. In the end, it wasn't much of a choice at all.

Bloch decided to bet on her people.

* * * *

Alex headed south, past the sparkling, tourist-friendly sections of the Old Port and into the industrial section. If the Sellers were going to move the plutonium by water, this is where they would do it, most likely in an empty or abandoned section of the area that still had a functioning dock.

Shepard called her periodically just to check in. The Sellers were kicking up no alerts anywhere in the city. There was the possibility that they had already gotten out of Montreal, or gone to ground, but Alex didn't think so.

She couldn't shake the feeling that the Sellers were close. Of course, that might be wishful thinking, since it would mean that Alex hadn't failed in her mission and let them slip away with their deadly cargo. The operation was feeling more and more like a failure when she turned around to head north again. As it was shifting from dusk to evening, Alex felt her chance to put an end to this thing slipping away.

She scanned ahead of her in the waning light. To her right were a series of old and abandoned warehouses, and behind them was the river itself. The port road had little traffic and nothing that struck Alex as out of the ordinary.

Until Alex saw the black SUVs.

There were two of them, the second following the lead vehicle closely. It was the same model as the one she'd faced two nights ago, and Alex was suddenly certain that she had found the Sellers.

"Lily, I've got two black SUVs that look very familiar. I'll pursue and keep you posted," Alex said into her comm. "Sending you my position."

"Alex, I'm heading out there. We're getting nothing here anyway," Lily replied.

Alex swung her Mustang around and followed the SUVs, making no attempt to keep her distance. If it was the Sellers, she wanted them to know they had been made. Between her car and the SUVs was a red sports car. It was actually a vintage Alfa Romeo from the later 1960s. The car was a convertible but the top was closed.

That was another reason to let the SUVs know they were being followed. Once they started taking evasive action, it would take them away from the civilian with the fancy car.

Then Alex realized that something was off about the Alfa Romeo. It was a smallish sports car that already had a low center of gravity, which allowed it to corner well. This car was riding *very* low in the back, as if its shocks and springs were nearly shot.

However, that didn't seem likely on a car that appeared to have rolled off the lot yesterday. In fact, Alex realized it was sagging in exactly the way it would if it were overloaded and carrying a few hundred pounds of a lead enclosure full of plutonium.

"Lily, I think I've got them," Alex said, as the two SUVs turned sharply to the left into an empty lot in front of a warehouse. Alex ignored them and stayed with the Romeo, which put on speed.

The Italian sports car would never have matched her Ford for raw power, even if it wasn't hauling heavy cargo and Alex's car was stock. Under the current circumstances it wasn't even close.

Closing the distance easily, Alex considered her options. She could simply bump the car off the road. If she incapacitated the Romeo, the plutonium wouldn't be going anywhere for the time being—and with Lily and a team on the way, that was all Alex was worried about.

The sound of the bullets striking the side of her Mustang was loud, and Alex jumped in her seat as a matter of reflex. Of course, there was no danger of the bullets getting through, but there was a visible pit in the bulletproof glass of the passenger-side window.

Then she saw the one of the SUVs coming at her diagonally from the parking lot. She knew she couldn't afford to get into a game of bumper cars with the Sellers' thugs— while the plutonium disappeared.

Alex shot forward and pulled hard to the right, jumping a short curb to reach an overgrown parking lot. She leaped forward to put some distance between her and the other cars and pulled a fast 180.

She was now approaching one of the black vehicles head-on. She had no time to waste, so she just opened her window and drew her pistol with her right hand. She quickly switched it to her left and started firing.

She was a fair shot left-handed, though nowhere near as good as she was with her right. It didn't help that she still had to drive with one hand. However, her rule of thumb was that if she couldn't be accurate, she'd put as many bullets into the air as possible.

Her clip held seventeen rounds and she counted off eight of them. The first three went to the SUV's front tires, the next two to the radiator, and the last two to the windshield. Alex didn't have time to access how much damage she'd done to the car and driver before it veered sharply to her right. She did notice smoke coming from the front grille before she passed the car.

She saw the Alfa Romeo and the second escort car disappearing ahead of her. The Mustang leaped back onto the road and surged forward. The SUV was limited by the speed of the Romeo and Alex caught them easily.

When she was in firing range, she flipped the car into auto-drive and grabbed her pistol again. Shepard was particularly pleased with the auto-drive feature. It was the most advanced system on the market, but it would only work if she didn't ask it to do anything more than follow the car in front of her.

Evasive maneuvers were out, but if Alex worked fast she wouldn't need them.

She heard shots pinging off her car as the passenger in the SUV opened fire. However, he could only hit her passenger side and the rounds were nothing the car's armor couldn't handle.

The driver was just getting smart and pulling to the left to give the passenger riding shotgun a better line of fire, but before they got into position, Alex emptied the rest of the clip into the SUV's back tires and gas tank.

She was still shooting with her left hand, but she was able to brace her wrist with her right as the car drove itself. Armor must have protected the gas tank, but she hit the tires without a problem.

The SUV shuddered, but the driver didn't lose control. Clearly, they had run-flat tires, which would keep them on the road—even if the car was a little wobbly.

As it turned out, a little wobbly was all Alex needed.

The SUV was still tacking to the left when Alex clipped its right rear bumper as she accelerated. The rotational force she put into the SUV, combined with the compromised tires, caused the vehicle to veer sharply to the left and tilt forward.

By the time the SUV was rolling over, Alex could only see it in her rearview mirror. Now it was just Alex and the red sports car. Through the small rear window Alex could only see the driver. That was good and meant that there would be only one person to shoot at her.

It didn't take long to catch the Alfa Romeo and soon she had less then fifty yards between them. Since it was unlikely that the little car was armored, Alex put her Mustang back into auto and put in a fresh clip. Zeta could very easily pull the plutonium out of the wreck of the car.

Before Alex was able to take aim, the Romeo turned into a parking lot in front of a very large, abandoned building. It didn't appear to be a warehouse. It was too tall and oddly shaped. Alex guessed it was a factory of some kind.

The last time she had faced the Sellers, it had been at an old mall. Alex liked the idea that the mission would end in front of a seedy waterfront building, and this time she had both armor and firepower—more than enough to take care of a single person in a four-cylinder showpiece that was an underperforming thoroughbred prone to electrical problems and general reliability issues.

Nevertheless, the sports car was making for the waterline and then Alex saw why: A boat that was either a small ferry or a water taxi was at the dilapidated concrete dock. Alex didn't want to take any chances.

"Shepard, send Lily my position. I'm tracking a car that I'm positive is carrying the plutonium. I'll hold them here."

"Copy that. Lily and her team are just a few minutes away," Shepard said.

Alex felt every ounce of frustration and anger she'd had since this mission started come forward at once, joined by the grief she'd forced down when Terry had died. She wanted to take all of it out on whoever was left from the Sellers' team.

It might not have been fair to the person in that car, but neither was trafficking in materials that could kill millions. Whatever happened and whatever she needed to do, Alex was determined to make sure that the plutonium didn't get on that boat.

She put her thumb on a small pad on the dash and part of the instrument panel flipped over to give her a video screen and a targeting monitor. She touched the screen to target the boat, adjusted a few settings, and hit *track*. The car's targeting system would now keep the boat locked in as long as she kept the car pointed roughly in that direction.

The Alfa Romeo made that easy when it pulled to the waterline and stopped. Alex did the same thing thirty yards out. As soon as she stopped, she hit *fire* on the touch screen.

Nothing happened; at least, nothing visible.

Shepard had been very excited about the tactical laser system he'd added to the car. It was based on systems the navy and air force were experimenting with in their ships and fighter planes.

This one was a good system, powered by capacitors that her Mustang always kept charged. Because of the limited power of the system, Alex kept it on one of the lower settings. The invisible beam would steadily keep building up power and burning into the ship in the area that Alex thought was above or at least near the fuel tanks.

Alex was genuinely unsure what would happen to the boat, but she was willing to bet it would be interesting. She got out of her car slowly, keeping the door between her and the sports car.

"It's over," Alex said. "You can't get away, but you might survive. Either way, your cargo isn't going anywhere except with me."

Nothing happened for several long seconds, and then the Romeo's driver's-side door opened and someone got out with their hands up.

That's promising, Alex thought. *Even if it's a little disappointing.*

"Alex, don't shoot," a familiar voice said—a familiar voice with a light Russian accent.

Alex placed the voice before she could make any sense of the image in front of her.

"Jenya…" she said.

Chapter 37

"Alex, why don't you put the gun down," Jenya said.

It took Alex a few seconds to find her voice. "I'm not going to do that. Just step away from the car and we will sort this out."

"I don't want you to get hurt. I sincerely don't," Jenya said.

Alex struggled to make sense of what was happening while she was trying to shake off the roar of blood rushing through her ears.

"You don't want *me* to get hurt?" Alex said, taking aim at Jenya's chest.

"Typical American arrogance," Jenya said. Or had she said: typical *Morgan* arrogance?

Alex had to physically shake off the vertigo that was rising up in her head. "Jenya, I don't know what you are playing at or what you are mixed up in, but I will help you if I can."

Jenya surprised Alex by laughing out loud. "My dear young Alex, you are in no position to help me." Jenya put her arms down and took a step toward Alex and said, "But I think that I may be able to help you." Her tone was maddeningly casual, as if they were having a normal conversation. "I could have killed you when you interfered with my auction."

There it was, Alex thought. Jenya was the Seller, or one of them at least.

"You were driving the SUV," Alex said. "It figures—you tend to overwork your brakes on hard turns," Alex said.

Alex was pleased to see that the criticism irked Jenya, and for a second her placid expression faltered.

"Once you and your bike went down you were helpless. I let you live," Jenya said.

"Now I'm prepared to return the favor," Alex said.

Jenya laughed gently at that and took a step forward.

"Stop!" Alex said, and Jenya did, but there was a blur of movement and then Jenya was pointing a gun at her.

Alex cursed herself for allowing the woman to distract her.

"You are playing a very serious game with very serious people, people who tried to detonate a nuclear device in Monte Carlo. And they would have, too, if I hadn't—" Jenya said.

"Stolen their plutonium," Alex said. "Well done there. Of course, you turned around and tried to sell it on the black market."

"We all have to live in the real world. Now *you* put the gun down, Alex. I'm short on time," Jenya said.

"That's not going to happen. My partner is going to be here in a few minutes and we will have plenty of time to sort this out."

Jenya shook her head and said, "Of course, Alex. You think your *overseer* is your partner. You don't understand what you are involved in and who is pulling your strings."

Alex felt anger rising up inside her again. Jenya was trying to manipulate her and play for time. In this case, however, time was on Alex's side.

"Maybe, but nevertheless, I'm just a simple motorcycle repair-shop owner who's going to stop you from killing millions by selling that plutonium to one of your degenerate associates," Alex said.

"No, you are not. You're a child dressing up in your father's clothes, thinking you can get into his business," Jenya said.

How did Jenya know about Alex's father? There it was again. The anger. It helped her focus.

"My father runs a vintage car business. He's also the founder of the New England Classic Car Show. If you like, I can get you tickets for this fall."

"We both know that is not his real work," Jenya said, looking genuinely sad. "You can't lie well enough for this job, Alex. His business isn't what you think it is. And you father isn't who *you* think he is. Did he ever even give you a choice? Or is he just using you before he throws you away?"

"I'm doing what I want to do," Alex said.

"Then he is better than I thought. The illusion of choice is necessary if you are to be really useful to him and his masters."

"You don't know my father; you don't know anything about him," Alex said.

"I know enough. I know more than *you* want to know. I also know you well enough to know that you will never be cold enough to be like him. Don't let him destroy you. Imagine the worst things you are thinking of me, and know that Dan Morgan is worse by far."

"I'll be lucky if I can be anything like my dad," Alex said. "You'd prefer I be like you?"

"You do not wish to be like me. I am what my family made me, and I do not wish that for you."

Over Jenya's shoulder, Alex saw a flash of light on the boat, which was followed by a burst of flame that shot up from the deck.

"If I were you, I would be more concerned with your transportation," Alex said, watching the flames climb higher.

Jenya kept the gun on Alex, but turned her head to the boat. The deck was almost completely engulfed in flames for a few seconds, and then an explosion tore up through the deck and obliterated most of the ship.

Jenya swung her head back around to Alex and said, "What have you done?"

"My job," Alex said. "My real work. I stop people like you. It's the same work my father does."

Jenya seemed genuinely pained. "This isn't what I wanted. This isn't how I wanted things to end between us."

"I'm getting used to living with disappointment. You will, too," Alex said.

"I like you, Alex. I really do, but you are giving me no choice," Jenya said.

"You always have a choice. Who says you don't?"

"Ask Dan Morgan. Ask our father," Jenya said.

Alex wanted to dismiss it as a trick, but Jenya's face was twisted in pain. Alex didn't like that expression: It looked like the face of someone who was about to do something terrible, something they didn't want to do.

The gun in Jenya's hand roared and Alex felt something tear into her chest.

* * * *

A maddening beep invaded Alex's dream. She was back at home and in her room. Her alarm was going off, telling her it was time to get up for school. Alex tried to raise her arm to hit the snooze button but found it was too heavy.

She tried to ignore it, but the steady beeping was relentless. There was no point in fighting it. If it was time to get up, it was time to get up.

When she tried opening her eyes, she realized that was a mistake. It was much too bright and her arm hurt. Better to go back to sleep.

"Alex," a voice said to her.

She tried to ignore it, but the voice called out again, "Alex."

She knew this person. It was a young woman's voice. Was it a friend?

She braved the too-bright light and forced her eyes open to see Karen O'Neal's face staring down at her. "Alex, are you awake?"

"Is there an answer I can give that will make you go away?" Alex said.

"No," O'Neal said, without a trace of humor in her voice.

Alex blinked to clear her vision and saw that she was in the infirmary at Zeta. That realization was enough to make her remember why she was there.

Jenya shot me, she thought. When someone started to answer, she realized that she must have said that out loud.

"She's disappeared," Diana Bloch said. "We think she jumped in the water a few minutes before Lily arrived. There was no trace of her, and no one has heard from Jenya Orlov since." The director turned to Karen and said, "Give us the room."

O'Neal left and Alex said, "The plutonium?"

"Recovered from her car. You did good work, Alex. Of course, you could have saved yourself a lot of trouble if you had waited another few minutes."

Alex saw that her left arm was in a sling. The pain in her shoulder told her where she had been hit.

"It was small caliber, more blood loss than real damage," Bloch said.

"Have you reached my father?" Alex asked.

"We tried, but your parents are off the grid. We left messages, but you know your dad," Bloch said.

"Yeah," Alex said. "Orlov admitted to me that she took the plutonium from the vault in Monte Carlo."

"As we suspected," Bloch said. "I presume she was behind the auction at the mall."

"She was; it looks like she and Ares have been playing tag. I think we'll find that Ares was behind the terrorism on this year's Formula One circuit, and Orlov was behind the thefts," Alex said. "What do we know about her?"

"Nothing about her early life. Now she appears to be...*affiliated* with Russian intelligence," Bloch said.

That made sense. It explained how Jenya was able to transport the plutonium to Montreal and move it around in the city.

"It appears she is not Ares, which is still making trouble around the world. Conley and Guo actually faced Ares agents in Malaysia. And though Orlov was working against Ares, it doesn't appear she is on our side," Bloch said.

"I suspect she's on her own side. And she's dangerous. She's highly capable and was willing to sell weapons-grade nuclear material to the highest bidder," Alex said.

"Did she say anything to you that might help us track her down?" Bloch asked.

"No," Alex said. She was relieved that Bloch didn't ask her any more questions. She didn't want to lie to the director, but she wasn't going to tell Bloch the last thing Jenya had said to her—at least until she had spoken to her father.

Alex knew that Jenya was a trained operative. She could have been lying to get under her skin, to gain a momentary advantage. But Alex didn't think so.

"We'll talk more when you're feeling better," Bloch said. "And there's a line outside."

Lily came by a few minutes later, followed by Spartan, and then Shepard.

"Alex, the good news is that Bloch recovered your bike," Shepard said. "It's in the auto shop downstairs. We can get started or..."

"Just have it sent to my shop. I'll take care of it there," she said.

That, at least, was something she could do for herself. She could start the work whenever she had two good hands again.

Because of the gunshot, she knew she'd be off active duty for a few weeks. But her bike and the Morbidelli rebuild would keep her busy for a while.

At least until she could talk with her father.

Epilogue

This is long overdue, Bloch thought.

When she got off the elevator, she realized that the air smelled different and it took her a minute to place the scent. Bloch could see that the lights were low in the War Room, but the hum of voices told her that this week had a good turnout.

Most of her active agents were there—at least the ones who were in Boston at the time. Dan Morgan was incommunicado and was still on his trip, but Alex Morgan was there, her arm in a sling, sitting quietly with Lily Randall.

Bloch quickly identified the source of the new smell. In the corner, there was a commercial popcorn machine on wheels with a Renard Tech logo on top of it. That was new.

The staff had moved the conference table from the center of the room to the side, where it now held drinks and various snacks. The chairs had been moved into a semicircle in front of the main screen. It was the same basic configuration her people had used to set up their viewing of the Monte Carlo Grand Prix.

Bloch could see that they also had a guest. Maryam Nasiri was in an apparently deep discussion with O'Neal and Shepard. While Dan Morgan wasn't there, Peter Conley was, and he was in the middle of a very animated discussion with Spartan.

"I don't know how you missed it," Conley said.

An exasperated Spartan nearly shouted her reply. "I missed it? How could she believe in Christmas until she learned to believe in herself?"

"Wait," Dani Guo called out, and all heads turned to Bloch.

"Director," Shepard said.

Her entire staff froze like high school students caught having a house party by a parent.

"I thought I would join you," Bloch said. Silence hung in the air for several long seconds, and she added, "For the movie."

She approached Nasiri, Shepard, and O'Neal and said, "Could someone bring me up to speed?"

Maryam Nasiri turned to her and said, "In the first *Holiday Carousel*, Pamela Grant was a partner in a large law firm in a major city. But she had to return home when..."

As the mathematician spoke, Bloch's people started to relax and slowly resumed their various conversations. Someone handed Bloch a box of popcorn as someone else dimmed the lights.

Nasiri was still talking when they all took seats, finishing her account as a shot of a rural town appeared on the screen and pleasant music swelled.

Don't miss the next Alex Morgan thriller by Leo J. Maloney

HARD TARGET

Coming soon from Lyrical Underground, an imprint of Kensington Publishing Corp.
Keep reading to enjoy a sample excerpt…

Chapter 1

"You and your team will be there in a backup capacity only," Diana Bloch said.

"Backing up what, exactly? I presume there will be plenty of Secret Service, FBI, and local PD," Alex said. She wasn't pushing back—at least, not exactly—but there was something about this mission that didn't feel right.

"I understand your concerns. You don't even have to list them. This is coming from our contact at the NSA. They are in the middle of some kind of turf war with the FBI and don't think the feds are taking the threat seriously enough."

"Has our system identified a threat?" Alex asked. The Zeta threat-assessment system was proprietary, and in the past it had been extremely effective—almost spookily so. It had identified threats that no one else had seen and had saved countless lives.

"No," Bloch said, clearly frustrated. "As you know, we've gotten quite a few false positives lately, but on this we get nothing. The NSA is worried, however. And the feds and the locals can take care of traditional threats."

"Then what will we be there for?"

"Everything else," Bloch said. "As you know, that is what we do at Zeta. You'll have temporary NSA IDs, but you'll really be floaters. Your job will be on-the-ground real-time assessment and security. You and your tactical team will have full discretion to take whatever action you deem necessary."

"Floaters?" Alex asked. "It sounds like we'll be more like assets."

"Somewhere in between, I suspect," Bloch said, with a hint of humor in her voice. "Spartan is assembling the TACH team, I'd like you to take a look at the file and brief them this afternoon. Then I'll need you all on-site in five days."

That time frame suited Alex just fine. Whatever her doubts about the mission, she had very clear thoughts about how to spend the next few days.

* * * *

Alex had not been disappointed in the trip.

Three days on the road, two Great Lakes, and over eight hundred miles later, she could see Chicago looming ahead of her. In Boston, US Route 20 followed the path of the old Boston Post Road that was used to carry mail from Boston to New York as far back as the seventeenth century. Then the historic highway continued through the Finger Lakes and on to Lake Erie, Lake Michigan, and then Chicago.

It was the perfect ride for Alex's Ducati and the motorcycle had performed flawlessly. As she approached the city, traffic forced her to slow down. The pleasure part of the trip was over. It was time to get to work.

After she'd secured the bike, she checked in with Spartan by phone and went right to the location. Federal Plaza was an open space, the size of a city block and surrounded by office buildings on three sides.

On the ground, the only remarkable feature was a large, curved modern sculpture. Made of steel and standing on four legs, it was called *Flamingo*, but to Alex, it looked ominous—vaguely like a scorpion.

Alex thought the plaza was a reasonably nice, if generic, urban space. She was much more interested in visiting the spot that marked the beginning of Route 66, which was just a few blocks to the east. She made a note to do that when the speech was over.

Because the plaza was a large, open space and surrounded by various federal buildings, it was a favored spot for speeches and big public events. Of course, from a security standpoint, it was a nightmare. Too many windows on all sides where a sniper would have a clear shot at almost anyone down below.

And since the open plaza was essentially a box defined by buildings and busy streets, any sort of attack could mean a lot of casualties. Certainly, a bomb would be a disaster, and even a small-scale shooting or knife attack could lead to a stampede that would be devastating.

Alex called Diana Bloch and said, "I just don't like it. It has all of the problems of an enclosed indoor space with the easy access for bad actors that you get with outdoor events."

"Noted," Bloch said. "But we're leaving the final threat assessment to the feds. We have to trust that they know what they are doing."

"Director…" Alex began.

"You're right, and I know how that sounds, but in this case you're just there to help out."

"Or pick up the pieces," Alex said before she hung up.

Spartan approached from across the plaza. Like Alex, she was dressed in nondescript black trousers and a black jacket. Alex could see her frown from twenty paces away.

"I don't like it. It has all the vulnerabilities you get with an indoor arena, plus the uncontrolled access you get with a major outdoor venue," she said.

"On that we agree," Alex replied. "I've already voiced my concerns to Bloch, but it looks like we're stuck with it."

Spartan shook her head and grunted. She was probably the best TACH team leader at Zeta. Alex knew that her dad and Spartan had a lot of mutual respect—though Alex wasn't sure they liked each other very much.

Dan Morgan seemed to have a lot of those relationships.

Almost exactly twenty-four hours later, Alex stood in the plaza, with thousands of people around her. She wore the Zeta uniform of the day: black blazer and slacks—with an NSA ID around her neck.

About two-thirds of the people attending were supporters of the vice president and about a third were protestors who were screaming and waving angry signs.

That wasn't a surprise. Alex knew the vice president was there to announce a new civilian nuclear-power initiative. That was bound to stir some people up.

As she circulated through the crowd, she saw Spartan and the other three Zeta TACH people doing the same.

All things considered, the security was as good as could be expected. There were plenty of uniformed officers, as well as police and sharpshooters in key positions in the buildings around them. She also saw a number of local PD and federal agents in plainclothes.

There was a rustle of excitement and then the vice president took the podium, followed by applause and hoots, along with a number of angry shouts. The crowd settled down after a few minutes and he began his speech.

"As you know, I'm from the great state of Illinois, but that is not the only reason I am here today. It was over eighty years ago, on December 2, 1942, that the University of Chicago operated the first atomic reactor in the history of the world. Today, I'm here to announce the next major step the United States is going to take in clean energy—"

Alex stopped listening when her ear comm buzzed. She tapped it and Lincoln Shepard's voice was in her head.

"Alex, I may have something here," he said, sounding unsure.

"Something odd?" Alex replied.

"More like something *too normal*. The federal buildings and the post office around the square have standard alarms and security, including motion and sound sensors. However, I'm getting a reading from one of the underground walkways that doesn't seem right. There's a tunnel that connects the Dirksen Courthouse with the Kluczynski Building. It was used by IRS employees to get to the court until 9/11, and then it was closed off. It still appears on the security system and has active sensors. And that's the problem: I'm getting nothing on the sensors—no movement, which is normal, but no sound either."

"You said it was closed off," Alex said.

"Yeah, but underground there should be something— vibrations from traffic, the boilers, as well as air and water circulating pumps from the physical plants of all the nearby buildings. There should be a minimum amount of sound even in the empty spaces under there. It doesn't feel right."

That was it, Alex decided. The plaza was teaming with local and federal law enforcement. Her team would provide little in the way of additional security. Underground, they might actually do some good—especially if all of the various federal agencies had missed something.

She called Spartan on the comm and asked her to have the team meet up at the Kluczynski Building. It took a minute for Alex to weave her way through the crowd to get to the door.

Spartan and the team were waiting for her out front. Though the building was closed to foot traffic, their NSA IDs got them inside.

Building security escorted them to the freight elevator bank, when Alex explained that they were going to do a quick sweep underground. Alex shuffled through the security key cards for the plaza buildings and found the right one. The five of them assembled in the elevator and headed down to the concourse level.

The elevator doors opened to a short, empty hallway. Alex was the first out. She kept her hand on the butt of her Smith & Wesson 9mm, which was holstered under her blazer.

Up ahead were large steel doors that looked like they were put in well after the place was built.

"Those big doors ahead of you are the entrance to the walkway," Shepard said through her comm. "The smaller door to the right leads to the mailroom and maintenance areas."

Alex noted the dust on the floor and said, "Looks like this area doesn't get used much."

"Hardly at all. The walkway is closed and that's a side entrance to the mailroom that was only useful when the walkway was in service," Shepard said.

And then Alex saw what was wrong.

"The floor outside of the walkway doors is clean," she said.

"Clean as in clean? Or clean as in—"

"As in the doors have been opened, and recently," Alex said.

"Not according to the building logs," Shepard said. "Those are electronic locks that haven't been opened in years."

Alex motioned Spartan forward, and each woman put an ear to the doors.

"Can you get us in there?" Alex asked.

"Not without authorization," Shepard replied.

"Can you get us in there *now*?" Alex said. "We're sort of on the clock here." The vice president had less than fifteen minutes left in his speech. If someone was going to make a move, it would be soon.

"Those are secure electronic locks. They're not even online," Shepard said.

"Interesting information. Can you get us in?"

Alex could hear Shepard sigh. She also heard him tapping on a keyboard through her comm. "I can't do it from her, but I can send you a code. Hold the skeleton key against the back of your phone."

She took out her phone and the Zeta-issue skeleton key, which was actually a programmable security card. It came preprogrammed to open most private security card systems and quite a few state and local government ones.

"Give me a second on this," Shepard said. Before Alex could take a full breath, her phone beeped, telling her that the new code was now on the card.

"Thanks, Shep," she said, placing the phone against the electronic pad next to the door. It immediately flashed green as she heard the locks click.

Alex pulled on one of the double doors, while Spartan pulled on the other. Carefully, Alex peered into the hallway. It was over a hundred yards long and completely empty.

Motioning the team inside, Alex pushed her door against the magnet on the wall that held it open. Spartan did the same.

"What do you see?" Shepard asked.

"Empty," Alex said.

"Wait, something's going on. I've got chatter on the FBI lines," Shepard said.

Then Alex could hear movement behind them. There were voices and footsteps and then people were bursting in from the mailroom door.

Alex was drawing her gun when she heard someone shout "FBI!"

Then the hallway outside was filling up with armed men in black, wearing FBI IDs around their necks.

"Hold," Alex called to her team.

"Hands up!" the lead agent said.

Alex thought for a moment before giving the order. If these new players weren't really FBI, her team would be sitting ducks.

She did a quick count—eight agents on their side.

If it came to a fight they would be badly outnumbered. Either way was a risk, but only one way gave them a chance of avoiding a shooting match.

"Do it!" Alex said. She quickly holstered her gun and put her hands up as her team did the same.

"We're NSA," Alex called out.

"Okay, let's just take a minute to get to know one another," the lead agent said, taking one step forward.

As he moved, the elevator doors opened behind him.

She saw the lead agent twitch. He wasn't expecting that.

But before he could even turn around, half-a-dozen men poured out of the elevator, firing at the FBI team from behind.

The gunmen were dressed as building security. In fact, Alex recognized two of them from the lobby.

"Pull back," she shouted to her team as she drew her pistol. She backed up, looking for a shot at the men firing on the FBI agents.

The feds were in the way, however, and there was no clear shot.

Looking over her shoulder, Alex saw that there wasn't any cover in the hallway, just smooth walls ending in another set of double doors at the other end.

Meanwhile, the FBI agents were starting to fall, at least the ones who hadn't been killed instantly. It was awful, but it was giving her brief angles of fire on the gunmen. She saw the lead agent go down, providing the first clear shot she'd had since the shooting had started.

She squeezed the trigger and called out to her people, "Open fire!"

About the Author

Photo by Kippy Goldfarb, Carolle Photography

Leo J. Maloney is the author of the acclaimed Dan Morgan thriller series, which includes *Termination Orders, Silent Assassin, Black Skies, Twelve Hours, Arch Enemy, For Duty and Honor, Rogue Commander, Dark Territory, Threat Level Alpha,* and *The Morgan Files*. He was born in Massachusetts, where he spent his childhood, and graduated from Northeastern University. He spent over thirty years in black ops, accepting highly secretive missions that would put him in the most dangerous hot spots in the world. Since leaving that career, he has acted in independent films and television commercials. He has seven movies to his credit, both as an actor and behind the camera as a producer, technical advisor, and assistant director. He is an avid collector of classic and muscle cars and has won numerous prizes in tenpin bowling. He lives in Venice, Florida.

Visit him at www.leojmaloney.com or on Facebook or Twitter.

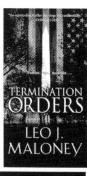

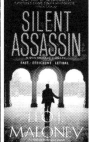

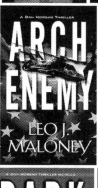

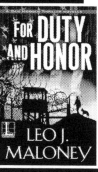

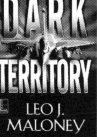

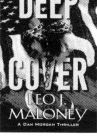

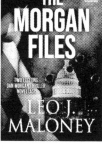

Printed in the United States
by Baker & Taylor Publisher Services